PINNED UP

THE PINNED UP TRILOGY, BOOK 1

PINNED UP

C. MICHELLE

Sugar Skull Design & Model Retouch by Michele Catalano
michelecatalanocreative.com

Book Cover Design by Sarah Hansen from Okay Creations
www.okaycreations.com

Author's photograph by Monroy Custom Photography
www.monroycustomphotography.com

Book Design by Maureen Cutajar from Go Published
www.gopublished.com

Copyrighted Material or Trademarked
Betty (Bettie) Page, Marilyn Monroe, Betty Boop, NLCS, Major League Baseball, UC Berkeley, San Francisco State University, Millennium Tower, Sergio Romo, (MLB) Giants, (MLB) Cardinals, (MLB) Tigers, Spotify, Pandora, Instagram, Words with Friends, Twilight Zone, Twister, Splenda, diet Coke, Slurpee, Snickers, Doritos, Takis, Tapatio Hot Sauce, Pop Rocks Candy, Patrón Tequila, DEA, iPhone, Google, Walk for Life, Cirque du Soleil, Exotics Racing, Wynn Hotel, Belagio Hotel, Dirty Dick's, Ben & Jerry's, Gary Danko's, Mitchell's, Roxie's Deli, Harley-Davidson, Armand de Brignac Champagne, Henry Cavill, William Levy, Range Rover, GMC, Bentley, Mustang, Porsche, Lamborghini, Ferrari, Ashton Martin, Nissan, Mercedes, McLaren, Audi, *Twilight, Fifty Shades of Grey, Friends, Jersey Shore, Mob Wives, The Real Housewives of New Jersey, True Blood, American Idol, Toddlers & Tiaras, Grease, She's the Man, Troop Beverly Hills, Interview with a Vampire, the Notebook, The Godfather, Scarface, Carlito's Way*

ISBN-13: 978-0615985329
ISBN-10: 0615985327

Acknowledgements

To my bratty sisters, Betsy Lopez and Quiana Moreno, for your feedback and eagerness on the completion of this book. You have been my confidants since the beginning of my writing journey and I thank you for your support. I can't tell you how much I enjoyed getting drunk with you and discussing Nina, Josh, and Kade. I love you dearly and cherish your opinions highly.

To Juliet Fowler, founder of the SMI Book Club, for encouraging me to write a book and for the continuous support throughout this process along with Magda Pereira, Stephanie Juarez, Pam Rivero-Chavez, and Myra De La Rosa (aka my twin). I appreciate you ladies cheering me on, listening to me rant, and for our raunchy conversations. You wenchoes rock y las quiero mucho!

To my mom, the best mother in the world! Gracias for coming over and cooking for us, watching my kids, and allowing me the opportunity to write. Thank you for believing in me and for your constant prayers. I love you! I hope your eyes don't come out of their sockets from reading this book. And dad, thank you for coming through for me.

To my daughter, Yasmin, a million thanks for your enthusiasm and believing in me. I'm sorry you can't read this book anytime soon due to its unsuitable content for a girl your age, but when you reach an appropriate age (like 65, for example) and choose to read this book, you'll no longer have to wonder what runs through my mind. You'll have it in writing. (Mom is a bit twisted.)

Last, but most definitely not least, I'd like to thank my best friend and hubs who also encouraged me in writing a book, has been extremely supportive of me, and didn't complain too much when I made the family "fend for themselves" due to my writing. Thank you for everything, babe...I love you.

Playlist of Songs

1) "Adorn" by Miguel
2) "Kryptonite" by 3 Doors Down
3) "Don't Let No One Get You Down" by War
4) "Siete Vidas" by El Gran Combo
5) "Superwoman" by Lil' Mo and Fabolous
6) "Be Without You" by Mary J. Blige
7) "I Need Your Lovin'" by Teena Marie
8) "Swimming Pools (Drank) by Kendrick Lamar
9) "Rehab" by Rihanna
10) "Black Betty" by Ram Jam
11) "Is This Love" by Bob Marley
12) "You're the Only One" by Eric Benet
13) "Heavy Cross" by the Gossip
14) "Suit and Tie" by Justin Timberlake

Dedication

To my hubs for once telling me, "We have a road ahead that is unknown, but as long as you're loving me, I'll be there every step of the way..." and holding true to your word. Thank you for making my journey with you such a crazy venture. I love you and look forward to a future of wonderful and exciting discoveries.

Table of Contents

Chapter 1 (Nina)

Sock Bun

Today was particularly exhausting. Out of all days, why did this photo shoot have to feel so tiresome? I need to remind myself I've been a nonstop force the past few weeks and exhaustion has finally taken over. I usually enjoy getting dolled up in retro clothing and making slight attempts to resemble iconic pin-up models, Betty (Bettie) Page and Marilyn Monroe. I'm a big admirer of the forties and fifties; I regularly turn to these eras for fashion inspiration. This afternoon, my heart just wasn't in the poses I took nor did I bask in the pleasure of getting prepped up to look like a sensual, yet sophisticated vixen. The shots were all about extraordinary prestige, I posed next to a 1947 Bentley Franay Mark VI Cabriolet. The black vintage collectible with white interior is considered one of the most desirable Rolls-Royce/Bentleys of all time. Standing next to this classic beauty earlier, I felt intimidated and prayed I did the shots justice. This masterpiece belongs to a billionaire tycoon who possesses a lavish compilation of elite cars. Dillon, the photographer whom I've worked with on several occasions and is responsible for this photo shoot, thought I would be the perfect model alongside such a coveted vehicle of this caliber.

Since the Bentley is a slick, shiny jet black color with a snow white immaculate interior, Dillon and the stylist on set felt red would be the best color for my attire. I'm wearing a satin form fitting, structured wiggle dress with black straps and belt that enriches my bust line. The pumps are red satin with a peep toe, a shiny black contrast heel, and a ruffle detail at the vamp. The cat eyeliner with exaggerated lashes and red lipstick on my porcelain face make the forties inspired look reach perfection. My long brown hair has pin curls that slightly drape the left side of my face making the overall look Hollywood glamorous.

I enjoy being a pin-up model as a side gig. I love to indulge myself in wearing kick ass wiggle dresses, bustiers, and some awesome "fuck me shoes." What can I say, sometimes I have over the top girly moments. I really should consider taking time off my regular job and modeling though, that is if I want to maintain what's left of my sanity.

"Cheesecake! Where are you, doll? I can't live without you!" Kade's loud voice interrupts my thoughts.

"Kade, I'm right behind you." I exit the restroom I had been using as a dressing room throughout the photo shoot. As I approach him, I'm putting my hair in a bun. "No need for you to yell. I swear, you can be so dramatic sometimes. I guess it's my fault for humoring you too much."

"Hey, I resent that! I'm hilarious, even if I do say so my-self." He feigns a hurt expression. "You need to rest ASAP, you're barely standing. That's what happens when you bite more than you can chew. Remember...you're not a spring chicken anymore." Kade smirks at me showing off a dimple on his right cheek. He puts both hands in his pockets and leans against the wall right across my dressing room. "Hurry up and get ready so we can leave."

Ugh! Sometimes, he can be so annoying! Who am I kidding? I love Kade. Despite his overzealous personality and blatant comments, he's my ride or die bestie. Kade is my rock and knows how to knock sense into me even when I supplicate him not to. He's too cute for his own good. He has dirty blonde Ivy League hair that is short at his crown and gets longer towards the front. He's average height for a man, slim, but toned. His overall look is very clean cut. He has sapphire eyes with long eyelashes and finely sculpted features. He's definitely pretty to look at and he knows it.

"Whatever. You could be more supportive, you know. The last thing I want to hear is that I'm working too much and can't handle the load." Since I hardly ate today, I'm agitated and feel like biting someone's head off. Kade is the closest nearby and will do as the perfect victim if he continues to run his mouth.

"Cheesecake, as your super fabulous and ridiculously good looking best friend, it is my obligation to speak the truth and not waste my breath telling you what you wanna hear. You're lucky to have me in your life. Who else would tell you the loose sock bun you're rocking looks like a dog's turd on a sidewalk? You're fortunate to have amazing chocolate eyes with full lips and a nicely defined nose to distract people from that hideous bun. Let's not forget that sweet rack, a person can do the motor boat on those bad boys for days, once again forgetting about that hair disaster of yours. I loved your pin curls, why did you have to ruin your hairstyle by putting it into that dreadful bun?" Kade questions me with repulsion in his features.

"Don't respond. Just get ready." Kade smacks my right butt cheek and directs me to the restroom.

I attempt to give him an evil sneer, but fail. "You're lucky I'm too tired to argue back or give you a piece of my mind.

I'm just glad I thought ahead and brought my pj bottoms and shirt. I'm definitely crashing the minute I get home." I sigh and push the swinging door open.

After I change into my comfy pjs in the dressing room of the warehouse we were shooting at all day, I decide to remove my makeup. I lather the thick green cleanser and begin scrubbing it onto my face. With my rear, I open the swinging door and walk out with my eyes closed still massaging the makeup remover on my cheeks.

"Kade, let's stop somewhere and grab a quick bite. I'm starving! Anything sinful and packed with calories sounds bomb right now, I'm tired of being good these past few weeks. Now that this calendar shoot is over, I can finally let loose. I need some grease and chocolate in my life, damn it! So, what? Are you game?" I ask as I fantasize of stuffing my face.

"Um, Cheesecake...Can you please wash your face? Dillon is here and wants to introduce you to his friend, *Joshua*." Kade emphasizes the name to discreetly inform me Dillon's friend is male.

Oh, great. Did I just sound like a porker? Please God, don't let him be cute. Let him be ugly or gay or an old geezer, anything...but cute.

"Sure, give me a sec." I turn, too embarrassed to open my eyes. I walk back into the restroom and wash off the green cleanser. After I pat my face dry, I scowl at myself for being so vain. I rarely wear makeup throughout the week, so who cares if a stranger just saw me looking less than glamorous and knows I'm a girl who actually likes to get her grub on? What's the big deal? Frankly, I'm too drained to give a rat's ass. I gather my belongings and head out.

Fuck me...hard.

Dillon's friend looks absolutely delicious...He stands over six feet tall with a cocky smirk on his striking face. He has a young look about him, but the stubble along his jawline reflects some ruggedness. Yum! He appears to be in his late twenties. His hair is light brown, the sides are trimmed, but the top is slightly tousled since it's longer. He's wearing a black pea coat with a plain white shirt underneath, loose fitted denim jeans, and some black work boots. His broad shoulders give a hint at an athletic build. The perfect toppings to this guy are his hypnotic hazel eyes beneath long, thick lashes and amazing full lips. I feel my eyes popping out of their sockets...*traitors.*

Focus, Nina!

I do my best to maintain composure and direct my attention towards Dillon. Why didn't he tell me about his hot friend? Would it have killed him to give me a heads up? Men! What does it matter anyway? The last thing I need is to get caught up in a relationship. I'm focused on my two careers right now. I don't feel like being another notch on this guy's belt. No thanks. Why are these ridiculous thoughts even crossing my mind? I'm absurd. Although, honestly speaking, my poor vagina probably has cobwebs by now from so much neglect. With that sultry mouth of his, I'm sure he could give both sets of my lips the attention they crave. Mmmm...

"Nina!" Kade yells and gives me an incredulous look.

"Huh? What?" Shit. Did I just zone out?

"Dillon was introducing you to his friend and you seemed kind of spaced out." Kade struggles to contain his laugh. Since he feels himself failing, he turns away to compose himself. *Jerk.*

Dillon intervenes as he's running his hand through his thick black hair. "Like I was saying, Nina, this is my good friend, Joshua Ryan. He heard about the Bentley I was photographing and wanted to see it up close and personal before it was taken away by security." Dillon smiles warmly at me. He's genuinely a nice person; I like him as a friend. He's in his mid-thirties and a bit on the serious side. He's not the type of guy who strikes you as deliciously handsome right away, but once you get to know him, his personality shines and you find him more attractive as time passes by.

"Hi, I just had to stop by and see this sexy machine for myself. It's truly a rare beauty with fine lines and amazing curves. It makes me want to take it for a long ride." Joshua maintains eye contact with me, but his glare makes me feel vulnerable, even naked. He smirks when he sees my discomfort.

I accidentally drop my keys and gain that moment to gather my thoughts as I pick up the keys from the floor. Is it just me, or does this Joshua guy appear to be amused by my disheveled appearance? Am I being paranoid?

"I like that bun you're wearing. It's...cute." Josh says as he's hovering over me.

Damn you, Kade! He was right about my bun looking like a piece of turd and now this guy is mocking me. Great. That's okay, though. No one makes me feel awkward, especially this pompous prick. I'm done with this conversation.

I stand in a dignified manner. "Thank you. I'm Valentina Moretti, but everyone calls me, Nina. I apologize for seeming dazed. I'm simply exhausted and ready to head home. It was nice meeting you, Joshua." I attempt to shake his hand quickly, but he grabs my hand with a double grip, the whole time keeping his eyes locked with mine. *Why is my breathing escalating?*

"Please...call me Josh. It was truly my pleasure, Nina. Take care." He says with a smoldering look.

I hastily remove my hand from his and look away towards Dillon, immediately I can sense Joshua's eyes burning through me.

"Dillon, I'll see you soon. Please let me know what the owner thinks of the shots and let him know I truly enjoyed being next to such a beautiful car. Good night." I give him a half hug, a small peck on his cheek, and walk away with Kade following me waving goodbye to both men.

As soon as we enter my car, Betty, a 1966 sky blue Mustang GT convertible, Kade gives me a disbelieving look.

"What, Kade?" I ask pretending to be annoyed.

"What's with you, Cheesecake? You didn't give me a chance to get to know my future baby daddy! Okay, Miss Rude and Miss I-don't-care-if-Kade-ever-gets-laid-again!" He says with an exasperated tone.

"Kade aka Mr. Drama-Queen-to-the-highest-degree, can you please calm down? I need to rest, remember? I just worked twelve hours straight on three hours of sleep; I'm physically and mentally drained. Why don't you talk to me while I drive so that I can stay awake?" If there's anything Kade finds irresistible, it's talking, he absolutely loves the sound of his voice.

"Sweet. Baby. Jesus! Did you see the bod on that beef cake? He looks absolutely sinful, but in a delicious kind of way. I don't care how many calories he's worth, I'd tear him up in a heartbeat! Let me tell you, the man was clearly into you, with all the eye fucking he was giving you, he's definitely interested." His smile is so big, it reaches his baby blues.

I'm shocked. "What? He wasn't eye fucking me, liar! Why must you exaggerate everything, Kade?" I try to remain serious, but start laughing hysterically. Kade has such a vivid imagination.

"He was to! I should know because I was busy eye fucking him. I know a good eye fuck when I see one and trust me, that hot piece of meat was thoroughly eye fucking you. Even in your raggedy pjs and ridiculous bun, you're absolutely beautiful. The man has amazing taste, you have to give him credit for that."

"Enough of this Joshua Ryan guy, I'm over his fine looking self." For some reason, I feel the urge to change the subject.

Why does the thought of Josh make me feel nervous? I push the notion aside. "Are you ready to get your grub on with some greasy, fattening take out that you'll regret eating to-morrow?" I ask.

"I knew I saw you drooling and also thought I heard your bottom lips smacking themselves at the mere sight of him." Kade laughs.

Great. He caught me checking out Josh.

"Yes, I'm ready to get my grub on and regret it tomorrow. How can I resist when you talk dirty to me?" He winks at me while giving me a devilish grin.

Chapter 2 (Nina)

Waitress

The weekend comes and goes, unlike the regular fog that glooms around the bay and refuses to dissipate on most days during this time of the year. San Francisco has my heart, a city full of life, diversity, and spontaneity. This weekend I close off the vibrancy of the city and autumn's chilling weather. I catch up on sleep, bum around the house in pjs, watch reality TV shows, and eat four different flavors of Ben & Jerry's frozen treats. I'm a hardcore ice cream lover and with the ice cream alone, I consume over four thousand calories. Go big or go home! I also make it a point to wear the bun on my head Kade seems to love so much.

I reside within the Haight District, right in the center between the upper and lower parts of the area. One section is geared more towards its shopping zone with its exclusive boutiques, vintage clothing shops, and cool restaurants. The other half of the neighborhood is more diverse with a grungier feel to it. It includes record shops, bars, clubs, and remnants of the flower power era still in effect. I love the mixture of ravers, tourists, and shoppers. Once Kade and I moved here, the Haight immediately became our home.

My house consists of two levels with outside stairs on the left side of the house and no front yard. The two car garage contains a laundry room and workout area while the main part is on the second story. When you enter, the living room with its cool, grey and white tones is to the right. It has pops of red, purple, and small touches of yellow that give it a refreshed and inviting feel. A glass dining table separates the newly remodeled kitchen and living room. The kitchen is a soft yellow with black lacquer cabinets and white counters that have silver specks. All the appliances are red with a retro flare that makes a perfect combination with the black and white checkerboard design on the tile floor. To the left of the entrance are two bedrooms, an office, and a bathroom down a hallway covered in vintage memorabilia and artistic pieces of Betty Page, Marilyn Monroe, and Betty Boop. It's a small house, but it's perfect for us.

"Cheesecake, that turd on your head...it's not cute. Quit trying to make such an ugly fashion statement." Kade teases me as he plunges himself on the couch opposite of me.

"You should talk! Mr. 'I'm going to put all kinds of homemade concoctions on my face, hair, and walk around like a stiff smelling mummy.' That egg mixture you had on last week was by far the worst. I'm home, relaxing. I don't need to look presentable for anyone." I pout my lips and roll my eyes at him.

"Valentina Moretti, I KNOW you're not hating on my homemade beauty remedies. I enjoy taking care of myself. If I don't do it, nobody else will. Life is too short to be ugly." Kade gives me the biggest, cheesiest smile he can conjure up.

"You're worse than the housewives, drag queens, and moms of *Toddlers & Tiaras* on television." I point out.

Kade chuckles faintly. "And if I were any different, life would be insanely boring. Being normal, reserved, and proper is monotonous. I have too much essence to be dull. Now, my dear Cheesecake, I'm off to the gym to find some spice that will compliment my flavor. Would you like to come with me and drool over the buffet of hot, sweaty bodies?"

"No, thanks. I already made Lucifer my bitch this morning, I ran six miles." I state proudly.

"When will you stop referring to the treadmill as Lucifer? If you have a pessimistic view of exercising, eating nutritiously, and living a healthy lifestyle, you'll get negative results." Kade sighs dramatically.

"Clearly, you weren't listening. Lucifer. My Bitch. Six miles. Enough said. By the way, I can't believe you're actually getting ready to go to the gym. Who does that? Well, I hope you have a great time looking for your next prey, boo."

"I'm going to some high end gym on Market Street. I'm looking for my next sugar daddy or sugar momma, I don't discriminate. I need to look casually sexy since I'm flirting my way in. I know people, who know people who want to get to know me. It's not my fault my sex appeal is so strong I can use it to my advantage. Don't wait up." Kade winks at me and gives me a devilish grin as he leaves our home shutting the door behind him.

"At least, you're modest!" I yell at the door and laugh uncontrollably.

God, how I love him. He's the brother I never had. When we first met over a decade ago, we were two lost and damaged souls. Ever since, we've been inseparable. My mom also considers him family, more like her loud, flamboyant son with no filter who she unconditionally adores.

During my last year at UC Berkeley while I was finishing up my Master's degree in social work, I decided to start looking for my own place. Without any contemplation, I knew Kade would be eager to be my roommate. Leaving my mother proved to be more difficult than expected. She owns a home near her bakery in Little Italy which is located in the North Beach district. Luckily, our house became available for purchase and was only a short distance drive to my mom's duplex. Now, I have the best of both worlds. I have my own place and I'm still in close proximity to my mother should an emergency arise.

My mom, Victoria Moretti is a New Jersey girl, born and raised. She moved to California in the mid-eighties. She became pregnant a year later and as a single parent, raised me. I've always been her priority and we've never been apart. My mom, Kade, and I are the only family we each have. Our small unity and the obstacles we've overcome have made each of us resilient.

Since the weekend has come to an end, it's time for me to prepare for a work week ahead. I lay out my clothes for tomorrow. I usually dress conservatively at work adding a dash of retro to maintain a hint of fashion. I work for the public sector, in a division of the district attorney's office. I enjoy my line of work and do it to the best of my ability, it's the least I can do.

It's Monday, as I'm preparing my morning diet Coke with extra ice, Kade walks into our kitchen half asleep wearing a t-shirt that reads, "I Shaved My Balls for This?" Even at the crack of dawn he manages to make me smile. He's fortunate not to have the standard eight to five job since his employer allows him to telecommute. Kade is a web and graphic designer. The company he works for is in the Silicon Valley, he's lucky to avoid commuting in the bay area, it can definitely be nerve wrecking at times.

As Kade is rubbing his eyes, he yells, "Cheesecake! You should've gone with me to the gym last night. You missed out! Guess who was there? Dang!" He pauses to observe my drink. "How can you have something so cold this early in the morning? And soda out of all things! It's so bad for you. Gross." Even though it's fairly early and he just woke up, Kade still looks well put together as he's making his coffee. How does he do that? When I wake up, I'm a hot mess.

"If I recall correctly, I wasn't offering you a sip of my drink. I suppose coffee and alcohol are healthier since you tend to drink those quite a bit." I can sense today will be a long day, it's going to be one of those Mondays that just sucks balls. It's too early for my patience to be running thin. "Keep your negativity to yourself. Kade, I don't have time for guessing games. I'm leaving for work in a few minutes. Who was there? Was it your next flavor of the week?"

"I wish! It was Josh, the dude who was eye fucking you after the Bentley photo shoot AND he looked good enough to eat!" As an afterthought, Kade states, "Hey! I eat healthy and take care of my body throughout the week so that I can party hard on the weekends. In a way, it balances things out." He beams at me crinkling his entire pretty face. "Back to that yummy piece of man, I literally had to wipe the drool off my chin...twice. Get this, he was with his mom! What the fuck?! Who the hell brings their mom to the gym? For your sake, I hope he's not a big momma's boy. That's a major turn off. Being close with one's mom is great; being a momma's boy who is still sucking on that titty is a whole other story."

"How do you know that was his mom? Did you talk to him? Why must you always be such a perv? There's nothing wrong with having a close relationship with a parent. You just love jumping to conclusions." I chastise Kade about his crude comments.

13

As always, he shuns them away. "Did I talk to him? Ummm...of course! Do you not know who you're speaking to? I went up to him and said hello. I told him to feel free and call me KD like the rest of my friends do. He introduced me to his mom, Celeste. She's a brunette with emerald eyes, very beautiful and elegant. He was giving her a tour. He asked about you." Kade does his best to contain his smile, but walks away grinning.

"Kade Daly, get your butt back here! I cannot believe you asked him to refer to you as KD! No one calls you Killer Dick! No matter how much you push for it, it's never going to happen! So, let it go!" I'm truly appalled with his audacity. But, there's a more important issue at hand to address. "What did he say exactly, when he asked about me?" I attempt to ask nonchalantly, but clearly fail.

"Don't be such a hater. Josh doesn't know what it implies, for all he knows, KD are simply my initials. He asked how you were and said he thought about you the last time he ate a strawberry cheesecake." Kade stands across from me with his arms crossed, a smirk on his face, and his eyebrow raised. "Now, don't you wish you would've gone?" Kade starts dancing around in the kitchen and pretends to rub against me from behind.

"Wait. He said what? Oh, my God...I'm dying!" I do my best to contain myself, but treacherous excitement takes over. *What the hell?*

"He said the strawberry cheesecake he was eating and slowly savoring in his mouth reminded him of your beautiful face with its light, silky skin and red lips. He said he hasn't been able to stop thinking about you. Yes, girl! The man clearly has the hots for you. I say you let him dust off the cobwebs you have down there and get yours!" By now, Kade is fully awake and highly amused by my shocked reaction.

14

"Are you serious? Did he really say that?" My heart is palpitating so fast, I feel it might combust any minute.

"No, but wouldn't it have been awesome if he had said that? It's obvious you wouldn't mind riding that stallion." Kade cackles loud at my expense.

I'm so livid, I can feel my blood boiling. "Kade, you asshole! You play too damn much! You're such a dick sometimes. Ugh...can't believe I fell for your lewd imagination! Thanks for wasting my time and making me late to work."

I gather my drink, purse, and begin to leave my home, but Kade continues to ramble. "Hey, Cheesecake...rumor has it that he's a major player, he's never been seen with the same girl twice, so watch out. He did ask about you though and wanted me to say hi on his behalf. Keep calling me a perv and see how I mess with you next time." Kade sneers at me, but in seconds, gives me a dimple filled smile. "Have a great day, my dear! Don't forget to eat some veggies. Love you!" Kade yells from the kitchen as I close the door behind me. *Jerk.*

My office is located in the SoMa district and the day turns out to be hectic. I work with crime victims. My position consists of a lot of paperwork, but I don't mind. I revel in fast paced environments. I'm more productive and efficient when I need to haul ass.

Lately, I've been gravely focused on my careers. My nonexistent love life has taken a back seat to both jobs. I'm not big on the lovey dovey stuff when it comes to dating. Sex is always on my terms; I just fuck when I'm in need and call it a day. Although recently, I've been feeling destitute in the orgasm department.

As I'm driving home, passing the energetic rush of the city, I decide to call my good friend, Emme. Yes, it's Monday, but I need a drink or six. The last time I checked, bars are always welcoming to fellow patrons in need of some feel good juice anytime of the week.

I met Emme who also majored in social work in college. We had several classes together. She's quiet for the most part, comes across as reserved, and has a short temper. She doesn't like dealing with bullshit. I love her, it took me some time to trust her, but throughout these few years, she has earned it.

Emme meets me at my house. She's Mexican, with olive skin tone, long black hair, and light brown eyes. She doesn't cover her fine features with makeup, she wears glasses, but is still a very pretty girl. She's five feet tall with a slim figure. Today, her facial expression lets me know she's upset and really needs a drink. I quickly get out of my work clothes. I change into some skinny jeans, knee length stiletto boots, and a low cut shiny tank top with a thin draped collar sweater. I put on mascara, red lipstick, and style my long hair into a pompadour ponytail with a rock flare to it. My rockabilly look takes me less than ten minutes to achieve. As we're leaving, Kade walks in.

"Where are you headed looking like a street walker?" Kade raises his eyebrows and demands an answer. "I see you have on some 'fuck me boots' and a shirt you clearly bought two sizes too small. Except for you Em, you always manage to look nice and homely."

"You're such a prick. Keep running your mouth and I'll be sure to fry your balls for breakfast and eat them as my huevos rancheros." Emme's look is so fierce as she threatens to have Kade's balls for breakfast that his jaw drops.

Nice.

"We're headed over to a bar downtown. I called you, but realized you left your phone here. Are you going to the gym tonight or do you want to get shit faced drunk with us?" I ask impatiently, I'm still pissed from this morning.

"Since you put it that way, how can I resist? Let me wash up real quick, just in case I get lucky. Hey, why don't you call that photographer friend of yours? He's a bit on the serious side, but definitely fun to look at." Kade asks as if he did nothing to crawl under my skin this morning.

Is he serious? "After the stunt you pulled earlier today? I don't think so, brat."

"You called me a perv! I may be horny 24 hours a day, only prefer to discuss sexual topics, and a complete whore at times, but that really doesn't make me a perv. It makes me fun and sexually generous. A perv is an old dirty man who tries to lure kids into a van. I'm not a perv." He states in a decorous manner.

"Yes, you are a perv even though you don't try to kidnap kids. If you shut up, I'll call Dillon to see if he's available to meet us. I'll do anything to stop you from rambling." How is it that Kade finds ways of being so cute, yet so obnoxious at the same time? It's definitely a talent he's mastered.

"Sounds good. By the way, Em...I called dibs on Dillon." Kade winks at her and heads to his room to get ready.

Emme rolls her eyes at Kade's back and chooses to ignore him. Something is definitely wrong with her if she's holding back her threats. She's like a tomb, completely sealed off. Only she knows what's going on with her life. She discusses school, work, and on a rare occasion, guys she dates. Other than that, she's a mystery. She never converses about her family, past, or future aspirations. I guess some people just prefer to keep to themselves. I would inquire about her foul mood, but she always turns psycho when she's questioned. I decide to treat her to a few shots tonight. Maybe, that will get her spirit up.

We agree to take a taxi instead of driving downtown. A lot of alcohol will be consumed and no one is willing to be the unlucky bastard to remain sober and be the designated driver. As the three of us enter the sports bar, we immediately spot some people leaving a booth located in the center of the right wall. The bar has wood paneling throughout its walls and looks a bit run down. On a positive side, it has about fifteen plasma TVs. The walls are covered with sports memorabilia and the atmosphere is buzzing with excitement. I feel slightly overdressed. We were supposed to go to a more upscale lounge, but since we were indecisive, we ended up at the nearest hole in the wall bar. Dehydration will make you do that; pick a crappy bar out of pure desperation for alcohol. Normally, I wouldn't mind, but for some reason, I feel restless.

The bar is ridiculously packed for a Monday. Slowly, it hits me, the Giants vs. Cardinals game is tonight. How could I forget? They need to win game seven to head to the World Series. It's destiny, I was meant to be here and watch the game. Immediately, my mood lightens. As the waitress approaches our table, we instantaneously blurt out our orders. Screw the menu. Talk about desperate.

I remember to text Dillon of our change of plans and give him our current location. The service is slow and the waitress seems irritated. She's a pretty girl with burgundy hair and fake boobs, but has a look of disappointment written all over her face. Eventually, we get our beers. After Emme finishes her first drink, she finally relaxes. Kade and Emme begin with their usual banter. Talk about night and day. Kade is blunt, obnoxious, charismatic, and completely lovable. Emme is serious, uptight, focused, and intense. Sometimes, I wonder how the three of us are so inseparable. Among our small circle, I'm more like the referee, always trying to keep Kade and Emme from killing each other. With their focus on the game, the tension within us is relaxed. I love it.

"Oh. My. God. Don't turn around, but Josh and his fine self just entered the bar. Honey child, he looks mighty tasty. Yum!

And he's with Dillon. Fuck yeah! Our night just got interesting." Kade smirks and waves them over to our booth. I freeze.

What the hell is Josh doing here? Why do I care? Why am I acting like a stupid teenage girl with butterflies in her stomach? I'm a bad ass bitch, I've got this! So, why are my knees getting weak? Thank God I'm sitting down. What the hell? Get yourself together, Nina!

Dillon and Josh approach our booth. Before they have a seat, guys who are sitting at the bar recognize Josh and call out his name. He smiles and gives a lazy nod to acknowledge them, but doesn't approach them. Dillon and Josh focus their attention on us; Kade introduces the guys to Emme and scoots her to the end of the booth. She positions herself to lean against the wall. Kade sits in the middle and pats the seat next to him so that Dillon can sit. I'm across the table from the trio and realize I need to move over. As I'm relocating as close to the wall as possible, Josh sits next to me and grabs my left arm in an attempt to have me be right next to him. His touch sends an electric piercing throughout my body. Immediately, I want more of his physical contact. *Behave, Nina!*

I feel my heart skip a beat. The whole weekend I did my best to keep him out of my mind and now, there's no escaping him. It doesn't help any that he has such a strong presence. As we sit side by side, I can't help but inhale his clean, fresh, delicious scent. I wouldn't mind getting high on him for hours.

Josh directs his interest solely to me. "Hey, lovely lady...I hope you don't mind me tagging along with Dillon. He knows I'm a baseball fan and thought I would enjoy getting out for a while."

Wow. His honey colored eyes with specks of green are mesmerizing. *Fuckin' shit, Nina...stop drooling!*

"Are you kidding me?" Kade interrupts. "The more the merrier!"

Josh maintains a lazy smile that barely reaches his left eye. It's absolutely adorable. "Thanks." He doesn't lose his focus on me. "It's nice seeing you again. I had a chance to look at the proofs from Friday's photo shoot. They look amazing." Is that admiration I hear behind his words?

"Thank you. I can't wait to see them." I glare at Dillon who immediately looks away.

"Hey, do you always go to the gym I saw you at yesterday? It's really nice, very upscale. It's pretty cool of you to hang out with your mom." Kade's eagerness to find information about Josh is shameless, but I'm thankful.

"Actually, that gym is included in my mom's home owner's association. She's never stepped foot inside until yesterday. Since she recently retired, I want her to get out of her condo and become more active, maybe even meet new people. I was giving her a tour." Josh replies unperturbed to the insinuation that he might be a momma's boy.

"Your mom is retired? Wow! She looks amazing and definitely too young to be retired. So, what about you? Do you live around here? If you do, we should all get together the next few days to watch the final games. After the Giants win tonight, it's a given, they'll be headed to the World Series again." Kade smiles and winks at me as Josh places an order of Patrón double shots and a second round of beers for all of us. Is it just me or did the waitress's boobs get bigger and her shirt get lower?

Josh truly is sexy. I love how he just took charge and ordered the drinks without asking. Some might think it's rude, but I find it refreshing for someone to take the lead, usually that's my role. The disappointment on the waitress has vanished and a predatory look with raw lust has replaced her expression. The waitress is now batting her eyes and pouting her lips as her tits keep getting closer to Josh. He ignores her desperate moves. He looks at me and asks if I'd like a chaser to go with the Patrón. I shake my head. No chaser for me.

I should chase her ass away from Josh. The nerve of her! She doesn't know if I'm with him and is blatantly giving her rotten goodies out with a double coupon. What the fuck? How rude. I don't know why her messy actions are bothering me, they just are. I don't know anything about him. Get a grip, Nina! You're just horny, that's all. These over the top feelings will soon go away.

I take a moment to observe him as he's speaking to the waitress and taking off his coat.

My, my, my...his chest and arms are muscular. An athletic build, not too bulky, built just right. His skin is lightly tanned, complimenting his spellbinding hazel eyes. He has a vein that pops out from his forearm to his right hand. His hands look rugged, but clean cut...very manly. I wonder what line of work he's in. He has a straight nose and a masculine jaw structure that has the sexy five o'clock shadow. I notice him clench his jaw as the waitress leaves. God, I can't stop craving him! His luscious lips are begging to be sucked on. My mouth begins to go dry as my lips fiend to caress the stubble on his face back and forth. I wonder how he would taste if I worked my tongue from his neck down to his—

"Nina! Snap out of it, girl! Are you listening? Josh said he's down to hang out. Are you? How's your work schedule this week?" Kade questions me in a serious manner as if he's not dying to put me on blast for drooling over Josh.

I keep cool. "No overtime for me this week. So, I'm good, count me in. I'm glad everyone is so sure the Giants are winning tonight. With such enthusiasm, of course I'm down to keep the party going." As if on cue, the waitress shows up with our tequila shots. Since when is she trying to be employee of the month? She's smiling and focusing completely on Josh. Wow. This girl is determined to catch his attention.

We each grab our shot glass and lime wedge. Josh thanks the waitress and dismisses her politely. Before leaving, she makes it a point to let him know her name is Nicole, and that if he needs anything, she'll only be too glad to oblige.

Whore.

Nicole walks away, swaying her hips as if she has an itch in her butt crack.

As soon as whore number one leaves, whore number two walks by our booth and says, "Hey, Josh! Long time no see. I've missed you. Don't be such a stranger, kay?" She winks at him and then slides her hand from his shoulder to his arm as she leaves our area. *What the fuck?* I can sense Josh's discomfort, but since he chooses to ignore her, we do too.

The trio across from Josh and I lick the webbed part of their hand between the thumb and index finger and add salt. I turn to my left to find Josh staring at me. I hear Kade doing a countdown to take the double shot of Patrón. At the count of three, while still keeping my eyes locked with Josh's, we take our shots. It goes down smooth. No need for the lime with salt or a chaser. I slowly lick my lips; I'm ready for another one. I can't help but smile. Josh is staring at my mouth with a look of...hunger.

Chapter 3 (Josh)

World Series

Look at that mouth, those perfectly shaped full lips. I got a hard on just by watching her take the shot. Nina's beautiful and sexy. I've fucked plenty and never gave them a second thought. What is it about this girl? Why did she cross my mind all weekend? That gunk she had on her face the first time I met her along with the standoffish attitude she gave me has me intrigued. Well, she's cornered now. I'm not letting her escape until I'm able to take a sneak peak past her guard.

"Wow. No flinching, no gagging, no chaser. You took it to the head like a pro. You're pretty hardcore." I point out jokingly.

"Just a little." She smiles and shows off her perfect white teeth.

I notice Dillon and Nina's friends are focused on the game. I decide to test the water. I question Nina about her work, family, and hobbies, the usual line up of questions, nothing too intrusive. Her answers are extremely vague. Her guard is shielded by heavy armory that I won't be able to get through anytime soon.

A challenge. I'm up for that.

The rest of the evening goes by at high-speed. We continue to drink, enjoy each other's company, and get more comfortable with inquisitions. Oddly enough, the only time tension arises is when the waitress arrives.

"Josh, what do you do for a living?" Kade asks. All of a sudden, all eyes are on me and everyone except for Dillon is hanging on my every word.

"I'm a contractor and own a construction company. My focus is on ecological construction of buildings that are beneficial or non-harmful to the environment, efficiency of resources is a main priority to my business." I manage to reply even though I'm completely side tracked. *Damn. I can't stop staring at Nina's lips. I just wanna taste them! Man...snap the fuck out of it.*

Kade seems genuinely impressed. "So, you're in an eco-friendly trade. Cool! I never would have pegged you as a tree hugger. But it's awesome of you to try to preserve the world some people trash on a daily basis."

I wonder what Nina would do if I were to bite her lip and pull her hair?

"Wait. What? A tree hugger?" I laugh. "That's a first. I've been called many names, but tree hugger has never been one of them. I'll take that as a compliment."

"I'm sure my Cheesecake can give you plenty of compliments." Kade says under his breath as he does his best to contain a chuckle from spurting out. I choose to ignore the comment, but an evil grin plants itself on my face.

"You seem young to own a construction company. How old are you, if you don't mind me asking? By the way, I'm 26, Cheesecake and Em are 25. Cheesecake is a Gemini who actually celebrated the fifth annual anniversary of her 21st birthday. Of course, you already know Dillon is 35."

I turn to Nina. "The fifth annual anniversary of your 21st birthday?"

"She doesn't want to grow up and be an old hag." Kade smiles fondly at Nina.

If looks could kill...Nina shoots invisible daggers with her eyes at Kade. He smiles and blows her a kiss.

I decide it's best to change the subject. "Well, I'm 27. Is everyone ready for another round before the game ends?"

I turn to watch Romo pitch on the flat screen TV mounted to my left. On my right side, I sense some sort of altercation.

"Ow! That hurt!" Kade yells.

I turn to my right and see Nina's angelic smile. She's absolutely breathtaking.

The Giants win the 2012 NLCS and are headed to the World Series. Everyone at the bar basks in triumph. Fans are standing up, overfilled with excitement, and reveling in the victory. Caught up in the moment, we all get up from our booth, and join the enthused fans with high fives. As our group is preparing to down shots to celebrate, Nina turns to me excitedly and throws herself at me with a big embrace. Although I'm taken by surprise, I instantly wrap my arms around her waist. Immediately, I'm overtaken by her sweet, clean, powdery scent...she smells amazing. I lower my head and place it at the side base of her neck, inhaling her delicious fragrance. As she begins to back away from me, I tighten my hold. I can't let go. She feels perfect within my arms. At that moment, I feel as if everyone has disappeared and it's just us left standing. She gently glides her hands from my arms to my hands. Her touch feels heavenly. As I feel her retreating, I slowly move my head and lightly rub my cheek against hers, bringing our lips to a tempting proximity.

"I'm ready for my drink." She whispers. Nina tilts her head back and stares into my eyes with a look of longing, as if willing me to kiss her.

I back away from her. She's kept her guard up all night and now the drinks have taken a toll. I don't want to be the cause of regret the following day. We separate and down our shots with Dillon, Kade, and Emme staring at us with shocked expressions and mouths wide open.

The celebration comes to an end. I discreetly hand my card to the waitress and pay for everyone's tab. We agree to meet on Wednesday at a different bar for the first game of the World Series. I can't get enough of Nina and want to remain by her side, but I grudgingly leave her behind with her friends. Dillon and I are the first to leave and head our separate ways.

Work has never seemed so vibrant and inspiring. Instead of waking up with a hangover, I wake up feeling refreshed, and enthusiastic, eager to begin a day's work. The sooner I commence my day, the quicker it ends, and the faster tomorrow will arrive. And then...I get to see her again. I fall asleep with Nina as my last thought. She's such a mystery, so succumbed to her privacy. I want to peel those layers of armory and unveil her true self.

After work, I decide to check in with my mother. Her home is a condo within the Millennium Tower located in the Financial District. She lives by herself. Early retirement wasn't something she welcomed; she actually put up a fight and refused to go down without kicking and screaming. After persistent orders from her physician, she finally left her position as CFO of my company, E-Con Solutions (ECS). She has always been a workaholic. She's goal driven and doesn't stop until her purpose has been accomplished. Now that she is able to relax and enjoy life, she chooses to sulk in misery.

I call before I arrive. She tells me she's at a nearby coffee shop and requests that I meet her there instead of her home. The place is quaint and smells amazing with a rich coffee aroma. My mother is sitting in a corner reading a health magazine. She looks up and waves me over to her seating area.

I hug her and plant a kiss on her cheek. She's a stunning woman in her early fifties with gracious elegance. Her emerald eyes and fine features are captivating against her short auburn hair. She's a natural blonde, but has always changed her hair since I can remember. I've never seen her with golden, long hair the way she used to have it before I was born. I've only seen pictures.

"How are you, son? How's the company? Did you decide which supplier you'll be purchasing the expanded clay aggregate from? I think—"

"Mom, can you please stop thinking about work? You're no longer Celeste Ryan, CFO of ECS, you're stressing out about insignificant things that aren't a part of your life anymore. Prioritize! You're the only mother I have, so now you need to make your health and well-being your main concerns." I scold her like a child.

"Fine. When are you giving me grandbabies?" She folds her fragile arms in front of her chest and gives me a scrutinizing look.

Fuck. There she goes...

"When will you stop dating floozies? I don't believe I've ever seen you with the same girl twice. Why are you so adamant about not having a family? One day, I'll die and you'll be left alone if you don't get over this relationship phobia you have. I'm not getting any younger, but don't get me wrong, I still have my looks, and admirers from a distance, you know." She says matter-of-factly.

"Mom, I'm gay. So, there goes your dream of being a grandmother." I do my best to distract her.

"Bullshit. Pardon my vulgarity. Gay couples can adopt. I'm aware it can be a long and strenuous process, but it's still a possibility. So, don't give me that nonsense that having grandkids will never be a reality. Try again." She means business.

"I'm impotent." I keep my fingers crossed hoping she'll drop the subject.

"Again...you can adopt. Keep trying." She sighs heavily, clearly losing her patience.

"Woman, I have a criminal record from a few years back. So, I don't qualify for adoption." I try to maintain a grave face. I fail.

"Why did I have to raise such a smart ass for a son? Fine. I won't bring it up again until our next visit. I love you. You know that, right? You're my world and I don't want to see you end up a lonely, old man with women who are only with you for your money." She says with concern deep in her delicate features.

"Mom, that won't happen. They'll be with me for my devilishly, handsome good looks. If I have to endure meaningless sex with beautiful girls for the rest of my life, it's a sacrifice I'm willing to make." I try to remain tactful, but this conversation is a broken record. The least I can do is pull the woman's chain for a bit.

"You expect me to socialize and meet new people. At my age, it's extremely uncomfortable for me. I can handle networking for your company or financial negotiations, but other than that, I'm completely out of my element. But, I'm willing to give it a try to prevent you from worrying so much about me. All I ask in return is that you make the same effort and try to meet a nice girl who wants to build a family with you in the future. I want to see you happy. I'm not asking for much." She maintains eye contact with me and I can see her holding back tears.

"Okay." I lie.

I would promise my mother anything just to see her happy, but she's already asked enough of me. I haven't forgotten.

My tiny fib is enough to pacify her and drop the issue for the moment. We end our visit on a positive note and I remind her I'll be checking to see if she's going out and being active like she assured me.

The next day goes by at a snail's pace. I'm anxious to see Nina later tonight. Due to issues at work, I realize I have to stay over and miss seeing her.

I'm pissed. *Damn it! Why the hell am I so eager to see this girl? Calm down, cowboy. You just met her.*

I end up leaving work fairly late; tonight's baseball game has already ended. Nick, the project manager who stayed over invites me to a game of pool and some drinks. After the day I had today, I'm game. When we arrive at the bar, the first thing that catches my attention is the grungy feel the place has along with the walls covered with pictures of dogs. I could care less about the décor; I feel tense and need to relax. Immediately, I order some beers and head to the back for a few quick games. As Nick and I are preparing to begin our first round, two brunettes approach us. They appear to be in their early twenties. They're both pretty, wearing tight jeans, low cut shirts, and have predatory looks on their faces. They ask to join our game. I have no problem with it since I'd rather be in the company of women than a man's. One of the girls admits to never playing before and requests that I teach her before we officially begin. She positions half her body over the pool table as I come from behind to demonstrate the proper way of holding a cue stick before a shot. Deliberately and in slow motion, she backs up and grinds my crotch with her ass.

Right at that moment, I hear, "Hey, Josh." The sound of my name distracts me from my teaching lesson.

I look up and see Nina and Kade standing right across from the pool table. Kade has a smirk on his face and Nina looks irritated. My heart sinks. The situation between this girl and I just looks wrong. It's not the type of impression I want to make on Nina.

"See ya, Josh." They both say in unison and walk away.

I excuse myself from the girl and hurry to catch up with Nina and Kade. I apologize for not being able to make it earlier to watch the game with them. I also explain that I recently got off work and just met the girl. They both tell me I have nothing to apologize for or explain. They say goodbye, but before leaving agree to still meet up to watch tomorrow's game. *Why do I feel guilty?*

Once I'm done with my beer, I decide it's best to call it a night. Before I leave, one of the girls promises me a good time if I stay or take her with me. She seductively presses her body against mine and wraps her arms around the nape of my neck. On a reflex, I lower my face towards her, allowing her lips to brush against my jawline. Soon, she finds my lips and I go along with her move. As I'm kissing her, I visualize Nina. *What the fuck?* I also notice that I am completely numb to this girl's touch. I don't feel passion, excitement, or the slightest bit of respect towards her. Where's the challenge? During my younger days, I'm positive I would have jumped all over her, but now that I'm older, I need quality in a woman. *Since when?* Without a second thought, I move away from her and leave Nick at the bar with both girls.

Thursday evening, I head over to an Irish Pub in the Mission district. Kade insists he wants to be surrounded by his kin. The place is small with a few high tables by the windows. The baseball fans are quickly getting themselves situated to watch the game. Bowls of peanuts are on every table and peanut shells are scattered throughout the floor. As I enter, I immediately spot Nina sitting by the bar. She looks over her shoulder, sees me, and waves at me. She stands to remove her coat from the stool beside her. She has very subtle makeup on and her long, wavy hair is down...she looks amazing. She's wearing our favorite team's colors. Orange and black have never looked so good. Then, I get a full view of her perfectly shaped round ass in tight jeans. My mouth goes dry. I need a beer.

I greet everyone and take the bar stool next to Nina. I noticed she saved a seat for me right in front of the large, flat screen TV mounted on the wall. Dillon and Emme are seated at the end of the bar to my left. I'm between Kade and Nina. This should be interesting.

Before I sit, an old fling whose name I can't remember rushes me and gives me a big hug. "Josh! Oh, my goodness! It's been forever! I've missed you. We should hook up again soon for some drinks or something." The girl is ecstatic to see me, yet I don't even know her name. It doesn't matter; she needs to go...now.

"Sorry. I can't, but it was nice seeing you again. Take care." I give her a half hug, turn my back towards her in a subtle attempt to dismiss her, and have a seat next to Nina. She gets the hint and walks away.

"Hey, lovely lady...Sorry about that and again for not making it last night. A problem arose at work that required my immediate attention. After work, my project manager and I decided to go out for a game of pool and some drinks to release the tension from our hectic day." I try to explain.

"That's okay. Your loss. You missed a great game." Nina smiles as she takes a sip of her drink.

"That's not all I missed." The words slip out of my mouth before giving them a second thought.

What the fuck? Play it cool, man!

"Is that right?" She gives me a knowing smile. Her beautiful chocolate eyes instantly light up.

"Are you two done eye fucking each other? I want you guys to try these Irish Car Bombs. They're pretty kick ass." Kade is grinning from ear to ear as he interrupts to hand us our drinks.

The rest of the evening goes by at a rapid pace. The bar is packed and extremely noisy. Before the game comes to an end, I have no choice but to invade Nina's personal space so that she can hear me.

God, she smells divine.

"So, are you busy tomorrow night? The next game isn't until Saturday. Feel like doing something?" I hold my breath as I ask her out. *Why am I nervous? Since when do I ask girls out? I'm a 'fuck em and leave em' kind of guy. I don't do dates.*

"No, I'm not busy. But, I'm not going on a date with you, Josh. I don't do the dating thing." Nina replies. She puts a double lock on her guard.

Rejected. A bruise to the ego. But, I'm not a quitter. "Hey. Whoa. Slow down. Who said anything about a date? I just asked if you wanted to do something. Don't get ahead of yourself. I don't do the dating thing either. So, calm down. Since it's not a date, I'll pick you up after work at your house. Is five thirty okay?"

She takes a long moment to ponder on whether she should go or not. Clearly, she's relishing on seeing me suffer. "Fine. I'll go. Where exactly will we be going?" She asks curiously.

"Don't worry about it. Just dress casual. It's not a date. No need for you to get all fancy for me. If you act right, maybe I'll treat you to some tacos. There's a restaurant I know that has a special...two tacos for a buck."

"You're not funny." She pouts making her lips look even more luscious. I need to taste them.

Focus, asshole!

"I never claimed to be and I never said I wanted to take you on a date. Damn, woman...You just love jumping to conclusions. Sooooo can I have your number?" I ask with an evil grin on my face. "I need to contact you for our non-date. I can't wait for all the non-hooking up we'll be doing. I'm looking forward to it. Are you?"

"Yes." She replies and gives me her winning smile that immediately makes me melt and gets me hard at the same time. *How is that even possible?*

The evening comes to an end and it's another win for the Bay Area. Our group makes plans to meet up again on Saturday for the third game of the World Series. Reluctantly, I leave, but anxiously await the following day for my non-date with Nina.

Chapter 4 (Nina)

Non-Dates

"Oh. Hell. No! You are not wearing that stupid turd on your hair tonight. A sock bun? Seriously? What's wrong with you? This is your chance to dust off the cobwebs you have down there." Kade points towards my private area between my inner thighs with no consideration to personal boundaries. "What are you thinking?" He's beyond appalled and is pacing back and forth in the living room.

"This isn't a date. I'm wearing jeans and a fitted white long sleeve shirt. No makeup. And my bun. I'm not trying to impress anyone tonight." I'm holding my ground. This is NOT a date.

Kade gives me an exasperated look. "You're beautiful, but a quick lick wouldn't hurt you any. I'm just sayin'. At least you had the decency to shower after a full day's work." Immediately, he begins to walk backwards with his hands raised, palms facing me claiming he doesn't want to go to war.

I get distracted when my cellphone rings, Josh wants to come in. I deny his request. I gather my hooded sweatshirt, purse, and put on my vans.

Before I leave, Kade asks, "Cheesecake, have you waxed recently? I don't want the poor guy to have to feel the cactuses you call legs or deal with a hairy beaver. Usually you let the hair reach a fur coat status by mid-December, but right now, I just don't know about you." Instantly, Kade takes off running as he sees me grab the remote. I throw it and strike the back of his head. Direct hit. Score!

I go downstairs to meet Josh. This isn't a date. No need for formalities.

He's waiting for me right by the stairs. "Hi." We both say in unison.

He stares at me intently. "Since this isn't a date, I won't be telling you that your natural beauty is absolutely breathtaking. I will kindly ask that you don't put any roofies inside my drinks tonight. If you want to take advantage of me, please do so while I'm not under the influence of any drugs." Josh says matter-of-factly.

"Right. Got it. Thanks for clearing that up." I reply in the same manner.

Josh picks me up in a black GMC pickup truck with a crew cab. He opens the door for me and gives me a hand getting inside since it's pretty high. Right away, I notice the front is a bench seat, overall very spacious. Nice. His truck still has that new car scent and roars loudly as we take off. Although it's early in the evening, the sky is already a midnight blue. I observe that Josh's eyes are mesmeric even in the dark as we drive by the city's lights.

Neither one of us is hungry so we proceed to our destination. He doesn't tell me the location or purpose of our non-date. He junctions on Interstate 80 East, it's quite a drive. We engage in small talk. He insists I provide him with details of my job and not just tell him that I'm a paper pusher. He listens intently as he merges onto Highway 99 North.

"During my third year at UC Berkeley, I began working for local government. I worked in the Human Resources department as the assistant to the HR Director. She advised me to apply to all the job postings that I qualified for. I did as I was instructed. Now, I work for a division within the D.A.'s office as a victim advocate. Initially, I worked in claims and dealt with victims who had accrued financial burdens due to crimes committed upon them. Reimbursements for counseling, medical, and moving expenses are some causes for restitution to be established. My responsibilities now consist of being the liaison between sexual offense victims and criminal court while moderating the effects of rehashing the trauma."

I pause. *Why do I feel awkward talking about my job?* I push the discomfort aside and continue.

"I feel it's imperative that criminals committing these wrongdoings pay on all accounts. I handle my job to my best ability to ensure defendants are held monetarily accountable and completely responsible for their inhumane actions. It's the least I can do." I hesitate again and use that moment to observe Josh. I have most of his attention; his other focus is the road ahead of him. I continue. "Initially, it wasn't my ideal job, but grew to respect my work. This job can be emotionally and mentally draining at times. After I earned my Master's degree, I became a pin-up model to maintain balance in my life. It's a fun, sexy, and exuberant distraction from my overwhelming day job. I enjoy both careers but obtain a different satisfaction at the end of a work day." I feel myself relaxing the more I open up to him. *Weird.*

"What do you mean, it's the least you can do?" He questions with a crease on his forehead. He's serious; the intensity in his features only makes him look more appealing. Wow. I didn't think that was possible.

I ignore his intrusive question. I definitely won't be touching that subject. "I just finished rambling. It's your turn to tell me about your tree hugging tendencies and your company."

Josh shows reluctance for a moment. "Fine. E-Con Solutions originated from a small construction company my mother's boyfriend, John owned. They dated for almost fifteen years. My mother refused to marry despite being in love with him. Since middle school, I used to accompany him on job sites and was sometimes put to work. John was a real craftsman and taught me everything I know." He stops to look at me; I notice a glimpse of sadness behind his entrancing hazel eyes. "In my early twenties, he passed away and left me his company along with several investments. He didn't have kids of his own and considered me family. He also insured my mother was well taken care of. I obtained a Bachelor's degree in Business Management at San Francisco State and a Bachelor's degree in Construction Management through an online university. Upon completion of my degrees, I began making several changes to the business. One of the first changes I made was use eco building materials; they're non-toxic and come from renewable resources. They're beneficial because they have very minimal impact on the environment or help in conserving energy. I'm very proud of how rapidly my perseverance, hard work, and sweat turned this conventional construction firm into a successful eco-friendly one. I care about our environment and its future." He shrugs his shoulders. "See, not much to tell, pretty boring stuff."

This man is many things, but boring is definitely not one of his descriptions.

"I don't think it's boring. It's essential that companies implement ways and techniques that will protect our environment. I think it's pretty cool of you, actually. So, what else are you into? Besides posing as eye candy for Kade, that is." I smile at him coquettishly, completely unintentional. *Yeah, right.*

"Whaaaaat? You think of me as eye candy and want to see how many licks it takes to get to the center of my lollipop? Wow! You don't beat around the bush, do you? I like your style." He raises his right eyebrow twice and gives me his biggest boyish grin he can conjure up.

"Ummm...no. Nice try." I attempt to be serious, but fail. *Did it just get hot in here?*

"Hey! I heard you loud and clear. Posing. Eye candy. I can feel you undressing me with your eyes as we speak." He winks.

Of course you're eye candy, you fine delicious piece of man! But, I'm not going to tell YOU that!

"Hey! This is a non-date, remember? No sugar talk is allowed." I try my best to sound as dignified as possible.

"Sugar talk?" Josh questions.

"Yes. Sugar talk, a conversation sexual in nature including but not limited to flirting, dirty talk, discussing fetishes, admitting kinky desires, sexting, and so on." I feel myself blushing. *Since when am I shy?*

Josh gives me a disbelieving look. "But, you started it with all the talk about wanting me to pose naked over a bear skin rug while you lick Pop Rocks candy off my butt cheeks."

No, he didn't. Sexy AND cute? How will I resist him for the remainder of the evening?

"You're delirious." I laugh.

"What? You want to know if I'm delicious? No need to beg, you can taste me anytime. But, I thought this was a non-date. Why are you throwing yourself at me?" He questions me jokingly.

Adorable. I can feel my heart begin to melt.

"If I were to throw myself at you...as you just put, you definitely wouldn't be questioning my actions." A wicked smirk plants itself on my face.

Josh's expression turns lustful in a matter of seconds.

What if I were to run my fingers through his hair and caress his face lightly with my lips. That wouldn't do any harm, right? Wrong! Get your horny ass together and think of something that won't get your panties in a bunch!

The song, "Kryptonite" by 3 Doors Down starts playing on the radio. "I love this song! I haven't heard it in years." I turn it up, start singing along, and move to the beat. *Perfect distraction.*

Josh stares at me and gives me a sensual smile, making his features look even more alluring.

But, I'm sure he thinks I'm insane. We continue to joke, laugh, and crank up the music when feel good songs come on for the remainder of our drive.

"Hey, so tell me about your family." Josh has a curious expression and lowers the radio.

"There's not much to tell. It's just me and my mom, Victoria. Oh, and Kade...of course. My mom moved to California from Jersey in the mid-eighties. She became pregnant with me and it was just us two until Kade came into our lives and moved in with us about twelve years ago." I reply.

"Tell me more about you and Kade." Josh tries to sound nonchalant about his inquiry, but he's unsuccessful.

"Kade is my best friend, my headache, my sunshine, my partner in crime, my roommate and most important, the brother I never had. I want to run him over and use him as a speed bump sometimes, but I love him. Since we met, we've never been apart. My mom considers him a son. He's family. What about you? Any siblings?"

"Just my mom and I, that's it." He smiles, reaches for the radio, and turns up the music once again.

Hmmm...he doesn't like talking about himself, he's very private. I wonder why?

We're in Elk Grove and finally arrive to our destination. An indoor shooting range? Is he serious?

"We're here! Since this is our first non-date and you were radiating tension this week, I thought shooting a few rounds would make you relax and let loose for a bit. What do you think?" He asks with contagious excitement.

Before I have a chance to reply, he gets out of the truck and grabs a duffel bag from the back seat. He walks over to my side and opens the door for me. *A gentleman.* "I know this isn't what you had in mind. Just trust me. I know what will make you feel good." With his husky voice, his words sound absolutely erotic. I swallow hard. He reaches out for my hand and helps me get out since his truck is fairly high. As I get out, I stumble onto him pressing my body completely against his.

My God, he smells exquisite with a scent of body wash and citrus, his chest feels lean and oh, so manly. I want to kiss every crevice of his body and lick my way down from his neck to his...Stop it, Nina! This is not a fuckin' date!

Immediately, I push myself away from his hold. Reluctantly, he lets me go.

"Nina? Are you ready? Come on. Let's go." He grabs my hand and interlocks our fingers as we walk side by side. *Shit.*

The place is very clean and has a modern feel to it. It has two sides, sales and an indoor shooting range. The store's walls are neatly covered with shotguns. Accessories are organized everywhere. We show our IDs. Josh purchases three cases of ammunition and some targets.

We head over to the range. It's very spacious; we're the only ones there. It has twenty lanes and the shooting distance is about 25 yards. Josh lays his duffel bag, ammo, and targets on a table near the far right wall. He pulls out two silver gun cases, protective glasses, and earmuff hearing protectors. He places twelve bullets into the gun's magazine. His hands are steady and he's in control; clearly, he's done this many times. He tells me the gun I'm about to shoot is a Sig P226 MK25. He explains the components of the gun and safety precautions.

It's finally time to let off some steam.

As I put on my glasses and cover my ears with the hearing protectors, Josh places my target in my lane. I can't help but observe his tall, thick, and lean build. I walk over to him; he positions himself behind me and wraps his solid arms around me, placing his hands over mine as I hold the gun. With his right leg, he separates my legs making my stance widen for better balance. He's tightly pressed against my body. I can feel his bulge against my lower back. It takes all my will power to focus on my civilian target. My right wrist gains tension. I'm too anxious to speak. Slowly, he releases my hands and seductively caresses my arms working his way down to my body until he reaches my waist, gripping it firmly.

Oh, God. His touch awakens every cell within me. Remaining focused proves to be more difficult than expected, but I'm determined to put my raging lust for him and my anxiety about the gun to the side. His presence gives me strength and courage.

The adrenaline rush is pure ecstasy.

I take a deep breath and gradually pull the trigger.

The gun feels like it was made for my hand. The trigger pull has a great balance with little recoil, not too light or too hard. I love it. I continue to shoot until my magazine is empty. Josh observes me reloading. He's confident that I can continue on my own and goes to his lane to shoot.

I discretely take a moment to observe him. Raw sensuality exudes him as he's serious and focused positioned in a wide stance firing his gun. I admire his athletic build with broad shoulders and narrow waist, the black long sleeve shirt he wears defines his upper body nicely. He's wearing loose fitted

Levi's that beg for his ass to be grabbed. Damn...Joshua Ryan is one hell of a temptation who is making my inner thighs long to have him between my legs.

I want him. I want to rip off his clothes and taste every bit of him. I want to get on my knees and swallow him whole. I want to make him weak and hear him moan. Nina! What the fuck? Get a grip! Get your horny ass together and start shooting!

I snap out of my reverie and focus on my target. Between the two of us, we finish off three cases of ammunition. At some point, I noticed Josh firing a shotgun. He must have rented it. I was too entertained with my Sig to want to shoot anything else. Once we're out of ammo, Josh explains it's time to clean the guns.

"Thank you." I say simply and shyly.

"You're welcome." He replies reluctantly and turns his attention back to his task.

He takes his gun apart by removing the magazine, slide, barrel, recoil spring, and guide off the frame. I replicate the steps with my piece. He takes a thin rod with a brush at the end and adds gun oil. His hands are steady as he's in deep thought expertly brushing, stroking, and wiping down each component.

What I wouldn't give to be that gun.

We finish, wash up, and head out. We agree to grab a bite once we're closer to home. We're quiet for a while, it's a comfortable silence. We have close to a two hour drive back home. He turns up the radio to an R&B station. The song, "Adorn" by Miguel comes on. It's nice listening to a soothing song after enduring such an adrenaline rush. I feel relaxed.

"Thank you again for taking me out. It was a very exhilarating surprise. I really enjoyed myself." I'm completely beaming, but I don't care.

"You're welcome. You seemed very focused and gravitated

to that gun as if you've been shooting all your life. You did a great job." Josh praises me with a prideful expression.

"Thanks. I had an awesome instructor." His smile makes me melt, so I turn away from him, and face the few lights we pass along the highway.

"So, tell me, why does Kade call you Cheesecake?" Josh asks nonchalantly. *I wonder how long he's been curious about that.*

"I can't tell you that. It's personal." I fake being offended by his question.

"Please." He begs. "How are we supposed to move forward in our relationship and go on an actual date if you don't tell me about yourself?" He gives me a heartbreaking look, but slowly turns his frown into a shy sweet smile. *Oh, he's good.*

"Umm...excuse you. That look that you just gave me, don't waste it on me. I'm immune to sexy guys giving me guilt trips." *Sexy? Who said that? D'oh! Hopefully, he didn't notice.*

"Sexy?" Josh turns to look at me and raises an eyebrow. *Of course, he noticed.*

"Calm down. Don't get excited. I'm not jumping your bones or anything, so relax. This is a non-date, remember? No sugar talk." My expression is stern.

His jaw drops. "Do I need to remind you that you were the one who mentioned me being so sexy that you would kill to wash your wet panties on my washboard abs?"

"There you go...twisting my words. You're not funny, you know." I can't help but have a cheesy smirk on my face.

"It's ironic how you say I'm not funny, yet you haven't stopped showing me your stunning smile. It's really not fair. It's one hell of a weapon that I'm quickly becoming a victim to." He replies as he hungrily stares at my lips.

Oh, dear God. Look away before you really jump his bones! Focus!

"You...a victim? I don't think so. You're more like the predator or player, whatever term you prefer best." *Why did I say that? Now, he's going to think that I've been overanalyzing him.*

"Player? I've never been in a relationship, so I can't be a player or predator, whatever it is that you think of me. I don't make empty promises to women. I'm not a liar, Nina. I say what I mean. Well, except when I'm speaking to my mom or when I'm rephrasing your statements to mean what you really want them to mean, but that's different." Josh tries to justify himself and his actions.

"Why do you lie to your mom?" I'm curious.

"We'll talk about that some other time. Now, where were we? Ah, yes...you were in the middle of telling me how sexy I am and how you feel guilty for not jumping my bones. What's with being allergic to sugar? You seem so adamant about staying away from that topic, yet you keep bringing it up. Can I interest you in a Splenda chat instead? It's a sugar substitute. I'm all about finding solutions to problems." He has the audacity to say with a straight face.

"You think you're cute and clever, huh?" Oh, I'm onto him.

"Maybe. But, I'm definitely not as clever as you. I never would have thought about driving hours away for our non-date just so that you can spend as much time with me as possible. That's simply genius. And for you to wear your hair in a bun...that's bringing out the big guns. You know how cute I think it looks on you. I love how it exposes your neck, it tempts me to bury my face in it, and rest my head on your shoulder. I'd love to get lost in your sweet, clean scent I've been smelling all evening." Josh turns to me, his look instantly turns lustful.

"Focus on the road, tree hugger." I smile and remain quiet. I allow myself to wonder about possibilities with Josh. The soothing music eventually takes over me. I begin to doze off.

When I wake, mellow tunes are still playing; I notice my head is resting on his chest as he's driving. I feel his arm around my shoulders and his hand touching my skin, caressing my side since my shirt has risen slightly. I feel safe and protected within his arms. His touch is heavenly. As I begin to stir, he tightens his hold on me. I revel with joy in his embrace.

I want him. Fuck the consequences.

My lips find his skin right above his collar. I dab gentle kisses along his neck working my way up until I reach his stubble. His jaw begins to clench, my teeth lightly graze it back and forth. I've altered my position so that I can face him. I'm on my knees with my legs spread apart over his right leg. His hand is all over my body caressing and rubbing every part that he can. As I'm nibbling on his earlobe, I hear him moan. I vaguely realize that now he's driving at a faster speed. His hold on me has become desperate. I begin gliding my hand down to his pants. I feel his thick erection under my grasp, so I rub and massage it. He's ready to be let loose. I start to unbutton his pants, but abruptly stop as I notice we're no longer on the highway. We're in a deserted commercial lot. He stops and shifts the gear to park.

Josh looks at me with voracious eyes. "Since I first saw you, I haven't stopped thinking about you. That's never happened before. You're intelligent, passionate...you're absolutely beautiful." He smiles warmly at me, but with an intense gaze. He grabs me by the nape of my neck and kisses me softly. His tongue enters my mouth as I welcome it anxiously. I slowly caress the stubble on his face with one hand and run my fingers through his hair with the other. I use this moment to straddle him and feel his hardness beneath me.

Slyly he gets ahold of my bottom lip and begins to gently suck. He returns his attention to my whole mouth more aggressively; his intensity beckons me to meet his pace. I eagerly oblige. Our tongues revel in delight as our kisses become more eager. His strong hands grip my waist tightly and gradually work their way underneath my shirt excitedly caressing my bare skin. I bring my body as close to his as possible with our treacherous clothes being our only barriers.

"God you feel so fuckin' good." He breathes into my mouth between kisses. I let out an untamable moan that's been desperate to escape. He lowers his hands and grasps my ass firmly with both hands. His kisses work their way down to my neck enthusiastically. As he's kissing and sucking my neck, on reflex I close my eyes and roll my head back allowing him full access. Our breathing has increased and I vaguely notice the windows of his truck have fogged up. We're in our own little world inside his truck and there's nowhere else I'd rather be at this moment. As I'm basking beneath his touch, he lowers his head and grabs my nipple with his teeth even though my shirt and bra are thin obstacles. The sharp pain feels exquisite and the only thing for me to do is moan louder and bury his face deeper onto my chest. In the heat of our moment, a loud pounding on the window startles us both.

What the fuck?

Reluctantly, I remove myself from Josh and sit beside him. I begin to laugh. I can't believe I was just about to fuck this guy in a parking lot. What was I thinking? Talk about raunchy.

Josh wipes down the window with his arm to get a better view of our hostile visitor. A security guard flashes his light inside the truck and tells us we're in private property and need to leave. Josh lets out a frustrated sigh, reluctantly lowers his window, and pulls out his wallet. "Get that light out of my face." He hands the security a business card. "This is my property, now be on your way and stay as far away from my truck as possible."

The security guard has a look of shock once he reads the

card. "Yes, sir. Right away, sir. My apologies." And takes off in his patrol car immediately.

Now, both Josh and I are in hysterics.

"Damn...tree hugger. You must be loaded if you own this building." I whistle.

"My company just built it; we're in the process of leasing out the offices. Would you like a tour?" He asks with a big grin.

"Not today. How about we get something to eat instead?" I suggest.

"Okay." He looks at me with a sexy, lazy smile and gives me a gentle kiss on the lips. Before he backs away, I get closer to him and prolong the kiss. I can't help myself. His kisses are so good, they're addicting. He enthusiastically matches my pace as we begin to savor each other's mouths once again.

As Josh skillfully strokes his tongue against mine, I can't help but yearn to have him in me, even if it's just for one night. Who cares if our only time together is in his truck? So what if it's raunchy. Sometimes you just need to live in the moment and enjoy life.

"Aren't you hungry?" He asks as he begins to work his kisses down to my neck.

"Maybe we should work up a really good appetite." I reply breathlessly as I bestride him once again.

Josh moans onto my neck, places his hands underneath my shirt to caress my sensitive skin, and pulls off my shirt in a swift motion. He continues to explore my mouth while he unhooks my lacy white bra. "God. Your breasts are per-fect...so full...and silky." He says in between kisses. He lowers his head, licks, and sucks on my nipple. As his mouth is enter-tained with one breast, his hand is stroking, twisting, and pinching the other nipple. His expert touch has me weak. I moan. I can feel myself getting wet.

I need this man inside me. Now.

Our breathing is deep and uneven. Josh unbuttons my jeans and I kick off my shoes. He lays me down on the bench seat. As he moves away, he pulls off my pants and removes my socks. He takes off his black shirt leaving on just a black tank top. *Wow. Seeing his broad chest and cut up arms, escalate my craving for him. Dear Lord...he has a large tattoo on the right side of his chest and shoulder, but I can't make it out. It doesn't matter, knowing it's there just adds to his sex appeal.*

Josh lowers himself and presses his body against mine. He feels so sexy and manly as he hovers on top of me. While kissing me, he slides his hand beneath my panties; he rubs my wet opening and finally inserts his two fingers inside me while rubbing my clit with his thumb. The constant invasion of his fingers feels amazing.

"You're nice and wet for me." He breathes out in a husky voice. "You feel so good. I would have done anything to feel your trigger while we were at the range." He whispers in my ear. His comment along with his continuous expert touch is about to send me over the edge. My body desperately craves it, but before I reach that glorious sensation, he backs away, removes my lacy thong, and puts on a condom.

"I need to be inside of you." He murmurs as he kisses my breast. He slowly enters me and immediately, I get taken by surprise. He feels extremely thick and long. Josh fills me so deep, my body isn't prepared.

"God, Nina...you feel so tight. You're driving me crazy." His voice sounds hoarse, as he says the words by my ear. He thrusts himself inside me over and over, the penetration is blissful, and I can feel myself losing control...I'm ready to explode. The orgasm that ripples through my body is exquisite. He continues to pierce me with his stiffness. I'm in heaven. As he prolongs the mind-blowing experience, my mind goes blank and I simply revel in the sensation. Once I'm back in reality, I become determined to ride him and give him an equally, incredible feeling.

With a raspy voice from all my panting, I say, "Sit upright, I wanna ride you." Swiftly, he does as he's instructed, yet remains inside of me. Once I'm straddling him, I begin slowly grinding my hips on top of him and licking his neck. The combination of his clean scent, delicious taste, and feeling down in my sex feels overwhelming in the most pleasurable way. I continue by moving faster and pressing myself deeper onto him. He kisses me and moans as I aggressively grab his bottom lip with my teeth and begin to suck. I loosen my hold on his lip and invade his mouth with my tongue once again. He tightens his embrace as I continue to ride his thick bulge. Moments later, a gruff moan escapes him as he's fighting to contain himself, but he can't any longer.

"Damn, Nina...you feel so fuckin' good." He groans. And with that comment, I feel myself lose control and feel his body tense as he and I both release ourselves. He remains inside me and continues to kiss me. I can stay like this forever...*No, you can't! Snap out of it, Nina! This was just a one-time thing!*

Eventually, we pull away and get dressed. I put on my seatbelt and assume he's ready to leave the lot. Instead, he unbuckles my belt, reaches for me, and brings me to his side. "I want you next to me. I can't get enough of you. You're an amazing lady, Valentina Moretti." He plants a soft kiss on my cheek that brings a smile to my face. I strap on the seatbelt that's in the center of the bench seat and make myself comfortable.

The drive back to the city feels like a dream. I rest my head against his chest as he keeps his arm wrapped around me. We talk, joke, and kiss all while R&B music continues to play in the background. Since it's pretty late and most restaurants are closed, we grab a quick bite at a drive thru. My burger and chocolate shake have never tasted so good. He asks me to spend the night at his place. I refuse. He persists and begins to tickle me, determined to continue until I cave. I give up and agree to stay with him for the remainder of the evening.

Josh resides within the Russian Hill district at the top of a very steep street. Luckily, tonight we went uphill, but tomorrow when he takes me home, it will be hell driving down to reach level ground. Instantly, I push the thought aside, no need to panic just yet.

Josh drives slowly as he reaches his house surrounded by a wrought iron gate. With a remote, he opens the gate at the entrance of his driveway to the left of his home. Once the gate opens, the house immediately lights up. The Italianate structure is surrounded by a formal garden and has a red brick patio. He enters the deep driveway and parks his truck inside a garage located underneath his detached guest house. We walk over to his three story residence. As we enter, Josh gives me a quick tour. The bottom level is completely empty. He hasn't decided what he wants to do with it yet. The second level consists of an open floor plan with warm, neutral tones and oversized furniture. It has a top of the line kitchen with a nook table towards the back wall, grand dining area, and a living room with a massive flat screen TV. The top floor consists of three bedrooms with their own bathrooms.

"Wow. Your house is absolutely beautiful. Did you decorate it yourself?" I ask curiously. Everything looks very well put together. I wonder if a woman had her hands on the décor.

"Thank you, but no I didn't do much of the decorating. I did add the bamboo and tile floors myself along with the detailed trim work. This house actually belonged to my mom's boyfriend, John. She used to stay here often, but once he passed away, my mom didn't want to live here by herself. Neither one of us had the heart to rent or sell it, so I moved in and gave my mom the condo I had just purchased. Once she retired, she was anxious to stay busy, so I allowed her the opportunity to remodel the entire house. I informed her of everything I wanted and she ran with my ideas, ensuring I felt at home. Of course, my mom used as many recyclable and energy efficient materials whenever possible. They don't call me a 'tree hugger' for nothing." He laughs. As an afterthought, he asks, "Would you like something to drink? Wine? Beer? Are you hungry?" He's attentive. I like that.

"Are you trying to get me liquored up and take advantage of me for a second time?" I giggle. "Well, since I am thirsty, your ploy might just work. I'll have a beer."

"If I recall correctly, you took advantage of me. You used your seduction powers that no human being in their right mind can resist. I was at your mercy to do as you pleased." His easy going self vanishes, he gives me a predatory and lustful grin as he approaches me. "Now, it's my turn." All of a sudden, I feel tiny next to his tall and muscular body. "I'm not strategizing on getting you into bed. I don't need to. You'll do it willingly and enjoy every minute of it. Take off your clothes." He uses an authoritative tone as he hovers over me, immediately my knees become weak.

My jaw drops. So blunt. If I wasn't so turned on by his take charge attitude, I'd give him a piece of my mind. "Feeling pretty confident, I see." I acknowledge sheepishly.

"Our clothes have gun powder on them, they need to be washed. It's not my fault the gun powder is one hell of a convenience." Josh raises his right eyebrow twice while showing off that boyish smirk I've become so captivated with.

Mmm...Sexy.

"Fine. Can I shower and borrow some clothes?" I feel myself getting anxious, my goodness it's hot in here. Why does he have so much control over my emotions? Usually I'm in control, I run shit. Now, I feel like one of those defenseless virgins who has never seen a dick in her life and behaves completely coy. That is so not me.

Josh hands me my drink, bends down, and whispers in my ear, "I'm going to join you. I want to feel your soft, slippery skin against mine. I won't promise you my best behavior, but I will promise you one hell of a fuck." The warmth of his breath and his clean citrus scent drive me in a frenzy.

My mouth goes dry; I lick my lips slowly contemplating a decision. I take a sip of my beer. Josh backs away and stares at me intently with his compelling hazel eyes underneath thick, long lashes awaiting my response.

Who am I kidding? I chug my beer. "Okay." I respond simply. Screw these damn pretenses. I need to keep it real...I'm horny and he is one hell of a fuck.

Josh kisses me along my jaw and slowly works his way to my lips. His hands explore my body as his kisses become more fervent. He takes off his black shirt and tank top. His bare chest is overpowering. I can finally see his tattoo, it's a tiger draped from his mid-back down to his chest taking up all of his left shoulder. It's surrounded by a tribal design that looks like barbed wire. The tiger has a ferocious look, almost as if it's in attack mode. The realism and intricate design of it is astonishing. Apparently, I have a masochistic side I wasn't aware of, since I think the dangerous animal on Josh is sexy as hell. His well-defined chest is cut up with a six pack of rock hard abs as a perfect compliment. His pants hang loosely showing off that perfect V by his pelvis.

No sense in wasting time, I take off my top, kick off my shoes, and socks. He unbuttons my pants and I slide them right off. I'm left wearing just my white lacy bra and panties. He takes off his pants leaving on just his boxers, bends down to kiss me, and lifts me up. I wrap my legs around his waist putting us in a tight embrace. As he's kissing me hungrily, his skin feels soft and smooth as I caress his upper body while he carries me upstairs to his master suite.

Before I know it, we're in his master bath. I continue to straddle him as he turns on the water to his rain shower. I rapidly unhook my bra. We gaze into each other's eyes intently. No words, just raw passion. We attack each other's mouths again with an unexplainable fierceness as the water cascades over us. Soon, I get pinned up against the wall as his lips and tongue devour my mouth, neck, and breasts. I feel his dick caressing my entrance. We're both losing control.

"Wait...wait...what about a condom?" I stammer out.

"I've never had sex without a condom and get checked regularly. I'm good." Josh says as he's kissing my neck eager to be inside me.

"I'm on the pill and I get tested also. I'm good too." I breathe out raggedly.

That's all he needed to hear to adjust his solid shaft from his boxers. He moves my panties to the side, backs up, inserts himself inside me, and begins to thrust hard. It's the best pain I've ever felt. He fills me completely. I can't speak. The water running down my body and his fierce kisses add to the sensation; the feeling is overwhelming. He continues to penetrate me with his rock hard erection, eventually, I lose control and allow the feeling to overtake me. The orgasm ripples through my body making the momentum seem everlasting. He sits on the tiled bench inside the walk-in shower while he's still inside me. I take a quick moment to catch my breath and revel in the thought that I finally get to ride him again. I rub body wash all over my breasts and press my body against his. As our bodies glide against one another, our skin feels silky smooth. I ride him hard and for as long as I can savoring the feel of him until I cum again. He finishes shortly after, but remains inside of me catching his breath.

"You're amazing." Josh whispers as he buries his face onto my neck.

I slightly pull away from him and maintain eye contact with a timid smile. "You're not so bad yourself." I kiss him and laugh as I bask in the taste of his delicious lips.

We finish showering and head over to his bed. He gives me one of his t-shirts to sleep in.

"What are you doing to me, Valentina? I can't get enough you." Josh questions as we're climbing into bed.

"I'm not doing anything, especially right now. We've had a long day, exhaustion finally caught up to me." I give Josh a small peck on his nose and grin shyly at him.

As we lay in bed, he wraps his strong arms around me from behind and falls asleep. I feel safe. I haven't felt a sense of security in years. What is it about this stranger that is making me do and feel the unexpected? I lose consciousness with Josh as my last thought.

I wake up. Josh is lying behind me and is gently kissing the nape of my neck. The room is still dark.

"Valentina...can I have...something...to eat?" He asks in between kisses.

What the hell? I know he didn't just wake me up to have me cook for him. Having sex is one thing, but cooking...that's a whole other level!

As if he read my mind, he says, "I don't need you to cook. Just lay back and allow me to feed myself." He positions himself above me, spreads my legs, and works his way down.

"Oh." *Who the hell needs coffee when I can wake up to this?*

That morning an enticing aroma awakens my senses. I head to the kitchen and see Josh solely in his boxers preparing pancakes and bacon. "Good morning, lovely lady. Can I just say that last night was the best non-date of my life?" He has that cute boyish grin that is quickly becoming irresistible. "Hungry?" His hair is slightly tousled, but he's still clean cut with a slight ruggedness from the stubble on his face that makes him look sinfully mouthwatering.

"Starving, actually. I had a pretty good time, too. Can I give you a hand with breakfast and help myself to a cup of coffee?" I ask as I'm blatantly enjoying the view that is him. Then, I notice that his tattoo has the initials K.O. on the body of the tiger. *KO? What does that stand for? Knock Out?*

"I'm almost done, but thanks for offering. Please make yourself at home. While you're at it, hook me up with a cup too, please." He winks at me making my insides melt.

"So, what does KO stand for?" I attempt to ask nonchalantly.

Josh comes from behind me as I'm pouring the coffee into my mug. "We'll talk about it some other time. Can I see you today, before this afternoon's game? I want to spend some alone time with you and go on an actual date before we meet up with everyone else. I know my truck isn't ideal for dates and I know this sounds cheesy, but I actually bought a 'date car' with you in mind this week."

"You did? That's sweet, but very presumptuous to assume I would go on a date with you. What did you buy?" I ask curiously.

"I'm all about taking chances. Well, not really, but when it comes to you, I'm willing to take a risk." He says earnestly, right away he changes his tone to a more playful one. "I bought a Range Rover. I've never owned anything that wasn't a truck, so this was a big step for me. There was no way I was buying a car; sedans and coupes just don't do it for me." He admits.

I decide not to address the issue of the KO initials again. We can discuss that topic at a later time. "I like your truck, even though it's really loud, it's grown on me. So, your SUV will have to wait to be driven because there won't be a date in our plans this afternoon. But, I will go on another non-date with you. We can just hang out and see what the early day has in stored."

"Why can't I take you on a date? Give me the opportunity to wine and dine you." He gets serious all of a sudden.

"Wine and dine me?" I laugh. He's just too cute. "Oh, you'll wine and dine me, all right. I'll be sure to burn a hole in your pockets. You asked for it." I tease him.

"So, is this a date? Because if it's not, we're going Dutch." Josh smacks my ass as I head to the nook table ready to polish off my breakfast.

"Not a date, but you will be feeding me. Oh, and I'm not the salad eating type so be prepared to spend some money on me." I joke.

"Hey, speaking of...do you cook?" He asks as he scrunches his face.

"Do I cook? Of course! I can't bake to save my life, but I sure do know my way around the kitchen otherwise. Besides, even if I didn't know how to cook, you don't have to worry that sexy little head of yours, I'll ALWAYS have something for you to eat." I wink at him coquettishly and begin to giggle.

"Now, that's what's up!" He puts up his hand for a high five and gives me a cocky grin. He's so sexy.

As we're heading out and are in the car, a fierce panic hits me. Instantly, Josh notices the change in my behavior. "What's wrong, lovely lady?" He asks with concern. Embarrassed I admit to being afraid of driving down the steep hill. To my surprise, he laughs instead of being consoling. Jerk.

"I'm sorry, but I just never pegged you as the scary type. You come across as invincible, as if nothing can touch or frighten you. You have nothing to be afraid of. Forgive me?" He asks with a playful smirk on his face.

I'm so terrified; I'm immune to his flirting and sex appeal. Besides, I'm upset that he laughed at my expense. I cross my arms and stare him down. What do I want exactly? A sincere apology? No. I'm buying time.

"Nina, I apologized already. Stop looking at me all crazy." Now, he's getting serious.

I don't care. I refuse to be in the car as he goes down this hill. Fuck! But I can't walk down this hill either. *What do I do? What do I do?* Panic is rapidly overwhelming my thoughts.

"Valentina Moretti, don't play chicken with me. You don't wanna test me." He says with a stern expression.

What? I can't back down now. Ugh! Why must I have so much damn pride? As I'm contemplating my next move, I hear Josh say, "Okay, you asked for it." Then drives off at a ridiculous speed down the vertical street.

My eyes pop out of their sockets as my whole body tightens. Once we reach the bottom of the street, I turn to Josh and yell, "Asshole! I can't believe—" Immediately, he interrupts my tirade by kissing me with a strong force. I lose myself to the kiss and wonder what the big deal was about driving down the steep hill to begin with. For years, I avoided every vertical street in San Francisco due to panic of having to go down them. With just one moment of being with Josh, he puts my fears to rest. I feel safe with him, a feeling that was stolen from me so many years ago. I disregard the memory. We both laugh in between kisses and then head to my house. He drops me off and states he'll be picking me up in two hours, just enough time for me to ride Lucifer and run a few miles.

As I enter my house, Emme is waiting for me in the living room watching TV. "Hey! Where have you been?" Emme asks with extreme curiosity. "We were supposed to go to your mom's house for breakfast. I ended up going with Kade. Couldn't pass up Victoria's pastries with coffee." She confesses.

I hear a door slam from the hallway. Kade rushes to the living room and yells, "Don't you say one fuckin' word! Let me get comfortable. This shit is gonna be good!" He throws himself onto the couch. "Okay. I'm ready. Shoot. And don't you dare skip any juicy details! First, tell me...where did you go? What did you talk about? Is he a good kisser? Does he know how to fuck? Did you suck his dick? Did you give him something to eat? Come on, woman! I don't have all day! Tell me. My curiosity is killing me!"

Emme interrupts before I have a chance to say anything. "Why the hell must you always be so vulgar, Kade? Don't you have a filter? You're so raunchy. Show some class." She rolls her eyes at him.

Annnnd...they're off.

"Vulgar? Raunchy? Because I speak my mind and don't put up a front? That makes me real, honey. You only wish someone would get dirty and vulgar with you and fuck you right for once. Instead, you live your life uptight with a stick up your ass, always worried about how society views you, and trying to impress people who don't give a fuck about you. Don't play the prissy role with me. It doesn't suit you and I will call you out." Kade laces his next words with venom. "You're so full of shit. You dated a married man who had kids. Were you being classy when you were on your knees sucking his dick and breaking up his marriage?" Kade waits for Emme's response with an evil smirk on his face.

Emme is so furious, her leg is shaking. "I didn't know he was married! What I do behind closed doors is my business. I don't publicize my sexual encounters to others. Some things are meant to be kept private. Don't you worry about who I fuck or how I fuck, that's none of your concern." She replies with a weak attempt at maintaining some dignity.

"For such a smart girl, you sure can be dumb as fuck. I saw you and him weeks later after you found out he was married. You were screwing a married man. That makes you a dirty home wrecker. You're in no position to be judging me. If you're going to point the finger at me, at least make sure your hand is clean. That's beside the point, we're behind closed doors and Cheesecake is my best friend! I'm not asking her to spill the beans in a public setting surrounded by kids. We are in the privacy of our own home! So, if I want to be vulgar and raunchy in private, I have every right to do so!" He yells at Emme giving up the last of his composure.

"Yes, who you fuck and how you fuck them does concern me. If they were to fuck you right, I wouldn't be dealing with your shitty judgmental attitude. Maybe cuming every once in a while might have you more laid back and fun. Instead, you walk around with high and mighty arrogance acting like your shit doesn't stink. Baby, I hate to break the news to you, but your shit...reeks." Kade stares at Emme willing her to continue arguing.

"Josh has a big dick!" I blurt out and pray that I can diffuse the tension.

They both turn and stare at me.

"Do you want to know the details or do you want to continue biting each other's heads off?" I ask annoyed.

"Details." Kade and Emme say in unison.

My Lady

Josh and I make last minute change of plans. Kade insists we all attend tonight's Halloween Pub Crawl where a massive crowd gathers and goes bar hopping within a five block radius beginning in the afternoon. Everyone dresses up in costumes and goes to several different bars participating in this event. Each bar provides drink specials that are too good to pass up. Josh agrees to meet up with Kade, Emme, and me at a bar on Union Street in the middle of the afternoon. I remind him to wear a costume.

Emme shows up at my house wearing a tight fitted black ensemble. Her hair is swept to the left with a turquoise flower on the right side above her ear. She has a sugar skull design painted on her entire face and looks pretty bad ass with the intricate details matching her flower. Kade is in a foam box that looks like a three drawer stand with a leopard print nightshade as a hat, no pants, and knee high white socks...a one night stand. I'm dressed as a pin-up sailor girl. I opted for a sexy blue and white corset with white trousers that have a slight flair at the bottom. My hair is in reverse rolls with a large, red flower as a decorative accessory. Half my face has retro chic inspired makeup with red lipstick and cat eyeliner. On the other side, my face is painted white with a sugar skull design consisting of black and red details to match my flower. Emme and I agreed to implement the sugar skull designs in our costumes in honor of the Day of the Dead which is in a few days.

"Damn, girl! Can you say boobilicious? You've got some wicked curves. Your waist has always been small, but that corset makes your tits, ass, and hips look crazy hot! Fifty bucks says that Josh grabs your ass within five minutes of seeing you. There's no way he'll be able to keep his hands and eyes to himself. Look at you...sex on heels! Rawr..." Kade winks at me and gives me his signature devilish grin showing off his dimple.

I can't help, but giggle. "You're so sick and twisted. I love you. Placing bets about me getting felt up is so us. I love your costume by the way, it suits you. Thank goodness you don't have chicken legs; a man with chicken legs is so unsexy. Yuck."

"Amen to that, sister!" We high five each other. Kade turns and faces Emme who's busy playing Words with Friends on her phone. "Your makeup looks sick! You've got mad skills, boo. You should wear your face like that more often, it's definitely an improvement."

Emme glares at Kade. "Says the one night stand, you might as well write 'DICK with STDs' on your forehead. Come to think of it, yeah...your costume suits you perfectly." Emme gives Kade a sweet, innocent smile that looks creepy as hell.

Kade is unaffected by Emme's comments and replies, "I practice safe sex. I've been tested. I'm good. Can you say the same? So, what if I like to sample the buffet? I don't give anyone false hope of a relationship and I'm upfront about what I expect. Many find my honesty refreshing."

"Why do you always make references to food? And of course, I practice safe sex. I don't want to die!" Emme exclaims.

"Hello? I used to be horizontally challenged a few years ago...remember? I'm used to making analogies with food and all aspects of life. It's more interesting that way. Hey, can I ask you a serious question?" Kade has a somber expression on his face and waits for Emme's response.

"Shoot. But hurry up so we can leave." She replies impatiently.

"When was the last time you had a pickle tickle?" Kade asks with a serious expression then bursts out laughing.

Annoyed, Emme yells, "Kade! You're such a dick!"

That's our cue to leave and meet up with Josh.

When our group finally gathers, we're all more than eager to commence with the partying. Josh is wearing all black; the dark tone gives him a mysterious appeal. He looks good enough to eat. When he sees me, he places a large foam magnet around his neck with baby chicks on both ends...a chick magnet. *Men.*

"You look amazing. Your sugar skull is pretty bad ass." Josh holds me in a tight embrace and gives me a soft, yet sensual kiss on the side of my neck. I smile and back away. As he's releasing his hold on me, he manages to grab my ass, and gives me that lazy, boyish grin that is quickly becoming a weakness to me.

"That's fifty in small bills, please!" I hear Kade yell. *Shit.*

The third game of the World Series begins in the early evening. It's a given that all bars will have the game on. We're more than ready to get the party started.

We attend several bars. All are packed with baseball fans and partiers dressed up in costumes. Josh ends up knowing several people at each bar, mostly girls, of course. The atmosphere remains festive, fun, and full of energy. Within a short while, we're all feeling pretty good. We've had several drinks and our Bay Area team is winning so far. Emme, Kade, and

Josh are getting along. Josh and I have been inseparable all evening. On a few occasions, he pulls me outside just to talk; he wants to know everything about me. Politely, I manage to evade his questions and get him to tell me more about himself. Everything is going great.

We're all at one of the bars. I excuse myself to use the restroom while Josh escorts me. He has his arm around my waist and has part of my body tightly pressed against his as he walks me across the bar. Possessive much? I don't care. I love how he's staking a claim on me. *Wait. What? Where did that come from?*

I wait in line for what seems like forever. Why must women's bathrooms always have a ridiculous line while the men's restrooms rarely have any waiting? Some women can be so annoying sometimes. Just go in, handle your business, and get out! No need to add several layers of makeup or have full blown conversations in there. Get it together, ladies!

It's finally my turn. As I'm leaving the restroom, I immediately start looking for Josh. I'm a bit surprised he's not waiting for me, since minutes earlier he was attached to my hip. As I continue to walk, I see Josh standing by the bar with his back against it. In front of him is Nicole, I recognize her right away as the waitress from the sports bar we attended on Monday. Now, she's completely invading his personal space. Josh sees me, leaves her, and walks over to me. He plants a kiss on my lips and attempts to lead us back to our booth. I come to a halt and press his body against mine. I lean close to his ear, "What were you talking to that girl about?" I feel my body tense and my blood begin to boil. *What the fuck? What's that about?*

"That was the waitress from the bar we went to earlier this week. Her name is Nicole, yesterday she left her résumé at my work for a receptionist position. I was surprised when I saw her at my office soliciting employment since my company isn't currently hiring. She was inquiring about the status of her application. I told her that once a position became available, I would personally see if she met the qualifications for the job. See...nothing important. Come on...let's get back to watching the game." I can sense Josh's unease about the topic, but decide to dismiss the thought even though something doesn't feel right. Nicole has SKANK written all over her face. There's something about her that rubs me the wrong way. I decide to ignore my nagging feeling and choose to continue enjoying my evening.

Our Bay Area team wins. Everyone in the bar is ecstatic and the mood is contagious, the celebration gets taken to a higher level. Several drinks and shots of tequila later, Josh and I decide to call it a night. The sexual tension between us is now radiating and neither one of us can maintain control any longer. Kade and Emme are with a large crowd who is going to an after-party in Castro after tonight's pub crawl.

Josh and I hitch a ride on one of the many cabs that are lined outside and head to his house.

In between the kisses Josh is giving me on the side of my neck, he asks, "Valentina...can we...spend the night...at your place?"

"I don't know if I can wait to have you in me. I'm horny and I'm ready to fuck." I breathe out heavily.

"Oh, baby. You're always sexy, but when you talk dirty to me, you're sexy as fuck. You make my dick hard just by hearing you say you want me." Josh whispers as he grazes his fingers lightly over my chest. "You know exactly what to do and say to make me crave you."

We arrive at his home. I feel hot; I take off my coat and realize the alcohol has definitely kept my body temperature warm. I only have one thought. *Fuck Josh like crazy.*

He offers me something to drink. I choose one of his white wines. As he's preparing our drinks, I step outside onto his balcony. The cool air feels refreshing against my skin. The view of the city is exquisite and I take a moment to savor its beauty.

"Aren't you cold, baby?" Josh whispers as he wraps his arms around me from behind and hands me a glass of wine.

Baby...a second time tonight.

I press my back completely against his body. "No, actually the weather feels nice even though it's a bit chilly."

Josh sweeps my hair to the side, kisses my shoulder, and works his way to the nape of my neck. Soon, his lips find mine at an angle. He releases my breasts from the corset. He massages them passionately and pinches my nipples hard. I unbutton my pants and easily slide them off along with my panties. I'm left wearing just my corset and heels. His kisses become more eager. As he's holding me tight from behind, he slips his hand in between my thighs and massages my sex.

"Oh, baby...you're nice and wet for me. Let me finger fuck you and give you a taste of how good you make me feel." He inserts two fingers inside me, pinches one of my nipples hard, and sucks on the back of my neck. The compilation of sensations is mind-blowing. He continues to mercilessly thrust his fingers inside me. As my sex is tightly grasping his fingers, he removes them, and plunges his thick, long dick inside me from behind. The penetration is intense and I love every moment of it. My nipples and tongue immediately start to tingle simultaneously. *What the fuck? How is he doing that? He's fuckin' incredible!*

Our "sexcapade" on the balcony seems to last forever, I'm completely lost to the responsiveness of my body. Josh moans as he continues to infiltrate himself between my legs. "Baby, you're so beautiful. I've done nothing but crave every part of you this whole evening. I can't believe how amazing your pussy feels. So tight and wet. You're perfect." His words send me over the edge and soon after, he joins me and releases himself. We're both left speechless from the intensity of our passion.

Eventually, we go back inside. Josh is adamant about spending the night at my house even though it's past midnight. He gathers clothes and hygiene products then puts them in his duffel bag. Moments later, he leads me to the taxi cab that's waiting for us outside since we're both still too drunk to drive. He spins me around to face him and kisses me softly. We head over to my house. Anxiety starts to get the best of me during the drive; I've never had a man spend the night. My home is my sanctuary. What am I thinking? I barely know him. Why is it so easy for me to make exceptions for him?

"What are you thinking?" Josh asks as he holds my hand and interlocks our fingers.

I decide to disregard my apprehension. "That I don't want you getting any funny ideas and think that I'm going to let you hit it again. I'm tired. So, none of that kinky business you're so good at. Understand?"

With a huge grin he runs his fingers through his tousled fawn hair. "I'm good? You must bring out the best in me. It must be that amazing pussy you have that makes things for me so easy. But, okay...got it. No kinky business. But feel free to rape me in the middle of the night. I'll only be too glad to oblige."

"You're not funny." I smile.

"Yes, I am. But, I was trying to be a gentleman." Josh pouts with an offended look on his face. Then he asks, "What were you like as a kid?"

His simple question takes me by surprise. "What? Where did that come from?" I reply with questions.

Josh sighs. "I want to know you. You're such a mystery. You seem so guarded sometimes, I just wish you would let me appreciate all of you." He seems to ponder on his last statement.

Instantly, my guard double locks itself. "We just met. The only people who truly know me are my mom and Kade."

"What about Emme? Isn't she a close friend of yours?" He inquires.

"Yes, she is. I've only known her for a few years though. She moved here from Arizona. She didn't know anyone and we had several classes together. We quickly developed a friendship, but even she doesn't know everything about me nor do I know much about her. I respect her privacy because it's what I expect from her." I do my best to make my point without being rude.

"Okay. Your life is in a deserted island guarded by white killer sharks. Got it. Hey, can I finally take you on a date-date?" Josh raises my hand and plants a kiss on it.

"I'm glad you understand. No, tomorrow I'm mean later on today, we're going on our non-date before we meet up with everyone else for the game." I wink at him and rest my head on his shoulder.

"You're so difficult sometimes. I'll have to admit that your feistiness has me intrigued." He kisses the top of my head.

We finally arrive at my house and literally crash on my bed within seconds of arriving.

That morning, I wake up to a wonderful, delicious aroma. Thank goodness Kade can't function without coffee and it's the first thing he makes every morning. I get up and quickly fall back into bed. I wasn't prepared for the head rush. *Stupid alcohol.*

Okay, let's do this again, but slowly this time.

As I leave my bedroom, I hear laughter from two people. I reach the kitchen and see Josh and my mom laughing about something. *What the hell?*

My mom is a naturally beautiful woman with delicate features. She has honey colored eyes, medium length, wavy brown hair that she usually styles in a ponytail or bun. She rarely wears makeup, is all about being fit, and living a simple lifestyle. People often have a hard time believing she's my mom and say she passes more like my older sister. "Good morning, sleepy head. I stopped by to take you out for breakfast, but since you've been sleeping, Josh and I have been getting acquainted." My mom gives me a hug and winks at me as she takes a seat. *Oh, dear God...no.*

My mother is nosey and a worry wart to the tee. She frets about every detail in my life, although lately, she's been getting better. Well, except for last week when she asked me if I'm a "lez be honest chick." She watches too much *Jersey Shore, Mob Wives,* and those housewives from Jersey; she feels it's important to support her Italian people. She's obsessed with my nonexistent love life, not because she wants me to be with someone, but more to ensure I'm happy with the choice I've made to be single. How can I explain that I don't do the "relationship thing" because of trust issues? If I bring it up, I know unnecessary sadness and guilt will consume her. There's no way of letting my mom know I'm getting laid, but not serious about anyone without sounding like a slut. Now that she sees Josh, she's going to devour him and get as much information as possible, knowing her...she already did. *Great.*

"Baby, I promised your mom we would stop by her bakery later today. She insists I try her homemade Italian pastries. I'm only too willing to please." Josh smiles at me and gives me a knowing look.

Don't call me that in front of her! She's going to eat it up and think we're serious! Ugh! You did it on purpose...you jerk!

I try to maintain my composure even though in my mind, I've killed Josh a million different ways. "Sorry, mom, but we have plans. Maybe some other time, right Joshua?" I stare Josh down.

"Going to Roxie's for sandwiches and Mitchell's for ice cream hardly sounds like plans set in stone. We'll either go after we stop by the bakery or we'll go sometime this week. But today, we're going over to Victoria's even if you pout all the way there. I'm not breaking a promise just because you're ready to throw a tantrum." Josh gives me a look willing me to argue back. I turn to face my mom and notice she has an amused expression on her face. *Traitor.*

What the hell? What is it about this man that has me so intrigued? Instead of being upset at him, I'm turned on! Fuck me...it's too early to process my feelings. I need a shower.

"Slow your roll, tree hugger. Fine. We'll go. I'll shower and get ready quickly." I roll my eyes at him. Something tells me, I shouldn't have done that.

Josh stands with an intense look and clinches his jaw. Instantly, his expression changes into a devious one. "Would you like me to join you? I already showered, but I wouldn't mind showering with you again." Josh smirks at me waiting to hear my response.

ASSHOLE! I feel my face beat red. Yes, I'm a grown ass woman, but still...my mom is right here!

My mom interrupts our silent battle. "Okay, so I'll see you two lovebirds in just a few. I'm leaving so that I can check up on the new cashier." She gathers her small backpack as she beams at us.

"How did you get here? Do you need a ride?" I ask before she leaves.

My mom laughs. "I used my bike to get here, silly. But, since you guys are coming over, I asked Kade to take me to the bakery. Besides, you know how Kade will use any excuse to get his hands on some cannoli. I'll wait for him in his car."

My mom must be the only adult who refuses to buy a car. She uses her bike, trolleys, and BART as her forms of transportation. She gives Josh a beaming smile and a quick hug. She turns to me and puts both hands on either side of my face and kisses both my cheeks. My mom gives me such a tender smile that it melts my heart.

As soon as she leaves, I turn to Josh with a deadly glare.

He raises both hands. "What? What's with the scowl?"

"I can't believe you said that in front of my mom! It was rude and completely inappropriate! What were you thinking? Now, she's going to think that I like you, like you. Ugh!" I'm livid! Well, not really, I think my outburst is more for dramatics. But still...his comment was tactless.

"First of all, Victoria didn't find it offensive at all. If anything, she seemed highly amused. So, relax. Second, you do like me...a lot. You like it when I kiss your soft full lips and slip my tongue inside your mouth. You like it when I bury my face in between your legs and lick you dry. You like it when I massage your heavy, creamy breasts with my mouth and finger fuck you at the same time. You like it when I stick my long fat dick inside your small tight pussy. And most important, you like it when I hold you and make you smile." He whispers the last statement and kisses me softly on my lips. "So yes, lovely lady, you do like me and I like you. Now, get your ass in the shower. I'm joining you to remind you why you like me so much." Josh commands and looks at me hungrily.

"Okay." I murmur and slowly lick my lips.

"Dang, Cheesecake! You like a lot of stuff!" Kade walks into the kitchen laughing. "You sure are a freaky one!" He grabs an apple, winks at me, high fives Josh, and leaves the house.

Josh and I use our alone time to our advantage by getting ready and freaky at the same time. Eventually, we reach my mother's bakery which is in the center of San Francisco's own

Little Italy. Her bakery is located across the street from a park that regularly has vendors selling paintings and art pieces, along with the seasonal farmer's market. The area is laid back for the most part with traffic consisting from locals and tourists. I park my classic beauty, Betty along the curbside. I insist on driving to maintain some control. Besides, it's a gorgeous day to drive with the top rolled down.

My mother's pastry shop is unpretentious and full of heart. As you enter, the seating with small iron tables and chairs are to the right while the pastries and gelato are on the left side. The items, prices, and specials are on a large black board written in different colored chalk. Her family in New Jersey and Sicily own Italian bakeries that have been established for several generations. She decided to continue with the family business when she moved to the west coast. She keeps the décor simple, yet inviting allowing the scent and taste of her delicious pastries to overcome one's senses.

"Victoria, this place smells heavenly. Everything looks so good. Making a decision on what to indulge in first is overwhelming." Josh rushes to my mom and gives her a big bear hug. She's thrilled to have him there and quickly leads him to the back to give him a tour of her second home.

"Nina, I just made some cannoli, help yourself, sweetie." My mother's smile is radiating. I grab two cannoli, have a seat at one of the small tables by the window, and sink my teeth into the crispy shell with a chocolate chip filling that's topped with confectioner's sugar. It's an orgasm in my mouth...absolutely scrumptious. Moments later, my mom heads over to me with two plates, one plate is filled with small samples of different cheesecakes. Apple crumb, limoncello, pumpkin, ricotta, amaretto, and strawberry are among the flavors. The second plate has appetizer portions of biscotti, cream rolls, cannoli, pardula, napoleon, fedora, and tiramisu.

Josh is behind her with two pint size milk cartons and a look of excitement. You would think he just won the lottery.

"Mom, you're killing me. What are you thinking putting this tray of temptation right in front of my face? For every pastry I eat, I have to run an extra mile on Lucifer. Today, I'm saving my calories for a sinful lunch." I scold my mom as I shove a large spoonful of fedora in my mouth. The chocolate pastry soaked in rum tastes like heaven, almost as if Jesus himself made it. Since I don't want it to go to waste, I hungrily devour the remaining piece. *It's just so good...and fluffy...and rich...yet, light at the same time...and simply...the best chocolate dessert I've ever had in my life. Absolute perfection.*

"Baby, you're sexy as hell just the way you are, but don't worry, I've got this." Josh winks at me and gives me a devilish grin. Josh proceeds to eat all the samples my mother provided him and even has seconds on some.

My mom and Josh are getting along; a few times they even ignore me during their conversations. He seems sincere with his responses to my mother's twenty questions and genuinely interested when she speaks. As we're heading out, my mother has a look of awe. I notice she really likes Josh and is already seeing him as part of the family. *Great. No, mom, don't get attached. It's too soon. I'm not ready for this! What have I done?*

We decide to pick up some sandwiches and snacks at Roxie's Deli, their pastrami and turkey sandwiches on Dutch Crunch bread with all the fixings are simply bad ass. We head over to palm tree studded, Mission Dolores Park and sit under some shade where Josh and I have a great view of downtown. I bring my Betty Boop rolled up blanket that I always keep in my car's trunk and lay it out. It's a sunny afternoon with a slight chill and no breeze, by San Francisco's standards, it's a perfect day for outdoor relaxation.

"Why did you name your car Betty?" Josh asks curiously.

"Hello? I named her after two iconic pin-up models, Betty Page and Betty Boop, even though Miss Boop is just a cartoon character. It's only common sense." I tease.

"Oh, I see!" He makes an exaggerated expression as if he just unveiled life's greatest mysteries.

"When I became interested in the pin-up culture and modeling, I really gravitated to them. That's why I have so many trinkets and posters of both Bettys throughout my house." I remind him.

"But you don't have any besides the blanket in your car." He points out.

"You're right. I never noticed. I guess I haven't found anything special enough." I turn on Pandora from my cellphone and put on a Lowrider Oldies station. The song, "Don't Let No One Get You Down," by War begins to play. I feel completely relaxed.

"What else do you like?" Josh asks.

"I like fast exotic cars. I think they're sexy." I state with a sinful smirk.

"What have you driven?" Man, he's really probing me with questions.

"I haven't. I guess I just like the idea of them." I confess.

"I'll fix that and take you for the ride of your life one day." He says this with determination clear in his voice and deep in his handsome features.

"If you insist! I'm game." I can't help but have a cheesy smile plastered all over my face. The thought of him making future plans for us delights me.

"Can I ask you a question?" Josh seems a bit hesitant. "It's sort of been on my mind since our first non-date."

"You can ask me anything you want. It doesn't mean that I'll answer, but if you're curious, it doesn't hurt to try to get a response from me." I take a bite of my bomb sandwich.

"Always so guarded, but fair enough. When you were describing your job, you stated that you did it to the best of your ability and that 'it was the least you could do.' What does that mean? Why would you say that?" His face is serious, I have his undivided attention. Immediately, I shut down.

I can't speak, but I want to. No, it's too soon.

"Valentina, I know we just recently met, but I want to know you from the inside out. I can't stop thinking about you. I've never felt like this. You consume my thoughts. I know you're this strong, independent woman, but I get this urge to just want to protect you. When I look at you, I see this beautiful rock hard exterior, but I feel there's something inside of you hurting. I just want to take some of your pain to make things easier on you." Josh lowers the volume to the music playing on my phone. He sits quietly and patiently waits for me to speak.

I can't. I just can't, but I want to. I've never discussed this with anyone! And now, all of a sudden I'm considering pouring out my soul to a stranger? Why this need to want to connect with him on all levels? Why can't I resist this desire to want to feel protected by him?

I decide to go against my better judgment and open up to Josh. My incomprehensible reason to discuss my past isn't about getting closer to him, even though on the surface that's how it appears. Slowly, I realize it's more about seizing the opportunity to face my tragic history, something I've always evaded at all costs. Josh just happens to provide me with the push and strength I desperately need at the moment.

My chest begins to tighten. I take deep breaths.

It's okay. It's okay. Calm down. You can do this. For the first time in over a decade, I relive that shattering experience.

I begin to speak quietly and slowly, afraid to hear my own words. "When I was little, I developed at a really young age.

In the sixth grade, I was a C cup bra size and when I began junior high, I was a size D. The boys couldn't keep their eyes off me and the girls didn't appreciate me getting so much attention even though the stares were unwelcomed. Eventually, I grew to be very shy, began to keep to myself, and became extremely self-conscious about my body. Despite being a loner, dressing in really baggy clothes to avoid the annoying gawking, hurtful rumors began to spread about me being easy and sexually active. During that time, I hadn't even kissed a boy yet. In middle school, the boys saw me as a sexual object and the girls could no longer tolerate the attention I received. Everyone looked at me different and I hated that feeling. I was bullied regularly and had to fight in order to defend myself. Since teachers never witnessed the harassment, nothing was ever done about it at school. I didn't confide in my mom, afraid if she intervened she would bring more attention to my problem, and make it worse.

One day, I was sitting at the school's library during lunch when a boy who was in my math class sat across the table from me. He was really nice and asked if I could help him out with that morning's lesson. I agreed to help him. There was nothing more I craved than a friendship. For the remainder of the week, I helped him study for our math final and was happy that I finally had a friend again. On the last day of school, before summer vacation, he wanted to buy me ice cream as a thank you gesture for my help. We agreed to meet at a corner store that was at the top of a hill near his house. It was a longer distance from my regular route, but I didn't care. I went through a park that was right across the street from the store. As I was walking by the empty basketball court, I heard my name called out. I turned and saw my new friend; he was with two high school boys. I stopped and let them catch up; right away, they started walking with me. I noticed their eyes were red and that they couldn't stop laughing. I felt uncomfortable and decided to go straight home. One of the older boys grabbed my arm and told me I wasn't going anywhere. I yanked my arm away from him and began running. They all caught up to me, stopped me, and kept me in place. All three boys began harassing me by fondling my whole body. I tried fighting them off and managed to kick one in the groin. He dropped to his knees, gathered himself, and struck my face with a closed fist. Another one of the boys pushed me so hard I lost balance and hit the back of my head hard against the pavement. I tried getting up, but I felt too dazed. Someone grabbed my arms and dragged my body behind the bleachers of the basketball court. I was punched in the face again when I attempted to get up. I wanted to yell, but couldn't, instead I was choking. One of the boys was pouring alcohol into my mouth as another was pulling down my pants." I wipe away tears I didn't know had escaped my eyes.

As I relive that experience by telling my story, the tightening in my chest becomes unbearable, but I want to continue.

"I was raped by each of those boys. I was only twelve years old, five days before my thirteenth birthday. I was left behind the bleachers almost naked, beat, full of blood, and too weak to get up. I don't know how long I remained in that position, but it seemed like forever. Eventually, a boy my age saw me and ran to me. He took off his jacket and covered me up. He was going to run off and call the police for me, but I begged him not to. I'm not sure why, I just knew I wasn't ready to speak with the police. He helped me get up and provided me with support as I got dressed. He wrapped his arm around my waist and walked me home down that dreadful hill in silence." I pause for a moment, allowing my words to sink in.

"So, that's why you're so terrified of going down steep hills. They remind you of that dreaded day." Josh murmurs to himself.

I lightly nod and proceed retelling my past. "I was thankful he allowed me to cry in peace. When we reached my house, he asked if there was anything he could do. I couldn't speak or face him. I entered my house, locked the door, and fell to the floor. The feeling of disgust and repulsion was intolerable. I remained in that position for several hours. I have never felt so violated. I trusted the boy who I helped out at school and befriended. I couldn't comprehend why he betrayed me, took advantage of my friendship, and set me up to get raped. I vowed never to trust anyone again so easily. When I realized that my mom was due to come home from work, I gathered up what was left of my will power and took a shower with my clothes still on. I felt so dirty, I couldn't move, instead I cried uncontrollably. Slowly, I managed to take off my clothes and intensely tried to wash off the layers of filth I felt penetrated on every inch of my skin. That dirty sensation I tried so desperately to scrub off...wouldn't. Exhaustion from crying and the endurance of such violence left me feeling spiritless. I fought against it and was ready to get out of the shower. I heard noise outside the bathroom door and realized my mom was home. Panic set in. I had to inform her and recreate that appalling scene all over again. I prayed for strength to endure the retelling of my horrific and traumatic experience.

When my mother saw my swollen face, busted lip, and black eye, she lost all self-control. She cried hysterically, insisted on taking me to the hospital, asked what happened, and demanded to know who had done this to me. Tears I wasn't aware I still had came rushing out. I knew I had to tell her, but couldn't make myself repeat the heinous crime I had just undergone, so...I shut down completely. I couldn't tolerate the thought of my mom looking at me different, just like everyone else. Between my sobs, I lied stating I had gotten into a fight and was jumped by three girls after school."

My body is steady and my face expressionless except for the traitorous tears that flow so easily from my eyes. I focus my sight on our beautiful scenery of the park with its palm trees. Josh attempts to hold my hand and bring me closer to him, but I stop him.

No pity. I don't deserve sympathy or comfort nor do I want it.

"I'm so sorry you had to endure such inhumane abuse. If you don't wanna talk about it anymore, you don't have to. Just know that I'm here to listen and help you any way that I can. Do you want to continue?" He asks me cautiously. I can't face him, but for some unfathomable reason, I want to continue shedding light onto my dark past.

I close my eyes and slowly nod.

"I refused to go to the hospital. I asked my mom not to make an issue of it at school. I reminded her it would be pointless since we were now officially on summer vacation. I asked her to simply transfer me to a different school. Reluctantly, she agreed.

One day, towards the end of summer, I went to a doctor's appointment with my mom due to severe stomach aches. I was informed by my pediatrician that I was pregnant. My whole world came to a halt and shock took over my body. My mom was in the waiting room. She wasn't informed of my situation since I hadn't provided written authorization.

The next few days were filled with thoughts of the baby. I was just a kid myself. I knew immediately that I couldn't kill this baby growing inside of me; after all, it wasn't the baby's fault. I read the pamphlets on different choices I had regarding the pregnancy. The decisions that had to be made were overwhelming. I knew it was time to talk to my mom. I waited for her to come home from work. Throughout that day, I had felt sick and towards the evening, I was experiencing severe cramping. I dragged myself to the restroom and held onto the sink due to the excruciating pain I was experiencing while I sat on the toilet. Too soon, I felt big clots of blood being released from my body. The twisting of my insides was unbearable. Moments later when I attempted to get up, I saw the large clumps of blood and knew I would be flushing down my baby's lifeless body.

When my mom finally arrived, I was lying on the bathroom floor. I don't remember much after that. I simply recall waking up in the hospital. Apparently, I had lost an excessive amount of blood when I miscarried the baby. My mother was in tears. She asked me who had done this to me and if it was consensual. I couldn't face her. She pleaded for me to say something. All I could say was that I had been forced. After she overcame the initial shock, her first reaction was to notify the police. I begged her not to say anything and cried profusely. She wanted to discuss the situation. Every time I tried, I felt as if I was reliving that sickening encounter all over again and cried uncontrollably. Eventually, she stopped asking.

Since that day, I made it a point to move forward with my life with a hope that my mom would never bring up that subject again. She took the remaining days of my summer vacation off and we spent every moment together, never touching that forbidden topic. When it was time to return to school, she changed her work hours to reflect my school schedule."

I sigh. I have never thought back to that day, especially with so much detail. Now, it feels as if that loathsome incident just occurred. I can smell the outdoor musty scent each boy possessed, I can taste the liquor that was poured into my mouth, and I can even savor the metallic flavor from my blood. All my senses were awakened by retelling and reliving that experience. I even said the word "rape," I have never used that word to pertain to myself. I recreated that nightmare and still managed to survive. Slowly, I feel my spirit relax and a tremendous weight lift off my shoulders.

"Did you ever see the boy who helped you out again?" Josh asks quietly.

"Yes. When I transferred to my new school, I saw him on the first day. We didn't speak to each other. Actually, I didn't speak to anyone. A week passed by and one day during lunch, he sat by me, pulled out a brown paper bag, and in the form of a question said 'cheesecake?' I smiled, but didn't speak. He handed me a plastic fork and we both ate the cheesecake in silence. The next day, I brought him two different flavored cheesecakes from my mom's bakery. I handed him the container that morning and walked away without saying anything. For a whole month, we sat together during lunch in a comfortable silence. I finally broke my muteness by saying a simple 'thank you.' To this day, we have never spoken of that incident. Kade is my life saver in more ways than one." I turn to Josh and smile.

I think back to how Kade respects my privacy and has never questioned me regarding that incident. Since the day I broke the silence between us, Kade and I have been inseparable. The repulsive experience I endured made me become completely closed off to people, with the exception of Kade, that is. I used to hide behind dark baggy clothes and did my best to remain inconspicuous. As I grew older, I was settled on not allowing my past to hinder my present and future any longer. I began embracing color again and shortly after, started wearing fitted clothing. During my early college years, I was determined to feel confident within my own skin and embraced the sexuality that was pinned up inside me. I resolved in not letting anything or anyone victimize me again. I was determined to be in control of my life and not feel ashamed of who I was...a survivor.

Unfortunately, the guilt I feel about keeping quiet regarding the rape and failing to hold those boys accountable for their malicious actions overwhelms me at times. I wonder if others were victimized because I failed to speak up. I pray that I was their only victim. Although I try to be strong minded, deep inside I am well aware that my past will always remind me of my insecurities, my lack of strength, and my mistakes.

"You're such a strong and amazing lady. You managed to survive being bullied, a rape, pregnancy, and miscarriage at such a tender age. You—" I interrupt Josh.

"Please, stop. I'm a coward. I should have informed the school of the bullying I was enduring. I should have notified the police of the rape, but I couldn't relive that experience. Others may have suffered similar situations because I was too afraid to speak up. I would be to blame for not doing something about it when I had the opportunity. I could have said something later, but I chose not to. I was too weak and frightened even though so much time had already passed by. I don't deserve anyone's compassion or praise." I state with hurt set in my facial expression.

"You were just a child! How can you hold yourself responsible? You were the victim. You work with victims of sexual crimes and do your job to the best of your ability. Every day you attempt to give back those victims a sense of what you lost and that's worthy of anyone's respect. But, you're trying to make up for something that wasn't your fault. You can't blame yourself, that's not guilt for you to carry. You need to take a good look at yourself and see all your astonishing qualities. You truly are a remarkable lady." Josh kisses me lightly on my cheek and holds my hand. After several moments of silence, he lies down on the blanket we're sitting on. I do the same.

I remain quiet, I've said more than enough.

I notice Josh grabs my phone, puts Pandora on shuffle, and increases the volume. We continue listening to music. A salsa song, "Siete Vidas" by El Gran Combo comes on. Immediately, it relaxes the tension in the air. The title of the song couldn't be any more perfect, "seven lives" I feel I've experienced in my short life.

Josh abruptly gets up and brings me up with him. *What the hell?*

He pulls me into an embrace and starts moving to the beat. He spins me around and does a side step, he moves forward, and backwards with just his lower body. His upper frame is in full control as he directs each spin, sharp movement, and crisp turn. I keep up. Damn, this man can dance. At that moment, I feel like the world is revolving around us.

I get caught up with the music. I feel a sense of relief and happiness that I've never felt before. "Oye, papi...you can move." I say as I start giggling like a teenage girl. Josh comes to a sudden halt. His eyes stare down at me full of lust. He changes his grasp and holds me with intensity. I expect a passionate kiss, but instead, he gives me the most tender and sweetest kiss I've ever experienced. For the first time in my life, I feel all my barriers crumbling down.

We finish our food and continue relaxing in the picturesque park. An hour later, we return to my house to freshen up and switch vehicles. The fourth game of the World Series is this evening; we're in a hurry to meet with Dillon, Kade, and Emme at a sports bar downtown. Even though, we're anxious to watch the entire game, we make some intimate time for each other in the shower.

As we're leaving the house and approaching his truck, I ask, "Are you sure you want to drive your truck? I can just call a cab. I don't want you drinking and driving."

"No worries, I don't feel like drinking. Besides, I have a busy day at work tomorrow. I need to be on my A game, not hungover." Josh states nonchalantly.

"Good, then I'll drink for the both of us and let you take advantage of me." I give him a sex kitten pout.

"Baby, you know just what to say to make my dick tingle." He gives me a kiss and opens the door for me. I can't help but have a huge beam on my face. Before I get in his truck, I walk around it. "Hey, tree hugger! This truck isn't a hybrid. What happened to you being all about saving the environment and wearing your cape on nice and tight?"

"Sorry, baby. I'm not perfect. But, I'm glad you're into role playing and dressing up. Awesome. I'm game!" Josh raises his eyebrows twice and gives me my favorite lazy grin that makes him look effortlessly sexy.

"You have a one track mind and very selective hearing." I laugh and get in the truck.

We arrive at the bar just as the game is starting and find it's incredibly packed. If our Bay Area team wins against the Tigers tonight, they'll be the World Series champs. A lot of pressure is riding on this game. That explains the large and energetic crowd on a Sunday night. I search for Kade since he usually stands out, all I see is orange and black on everyone except one man. Is he really wearing a white Tiger's jersey in San Francisco during the World Series? He stands out like a sore thumb, either he's really brave or extremely stupid. He catches me looking at him and licks the rim of his beer bottle then smiles, not a nice kind of smile, but a perverted typed of smirk. Immediately, he gives me the creeps, not because he's a Tiger's fan, but because he has an evil vibe to him. *Ewww.*

We see Kade who is waving at us from the middle of the bar. Josh holds my hand and leads us through the crowd. We reach the booth and find our friends drinking Hurricanes, clearly Kade ordered the drinks which means he's in an extra fabulous mood, and plans to party hard. Before we sit down, Kade sees me holding hands with Josh.

"Sup guys? Where's Dillon?" I catch myself yelling with a big grin on my face.

"Dillon went to the east coast for a last minute gig. He'll be back next week. But, check you two lovebirds out. Are you two going steady now or what? Were you busy LIKING stuff today?" Kade laughs uncontrollably. "Cheesecake, did Josh give you his letterman's jacket and pin you yet? Never mind, don't answer that last part. I can tell you've been pinned several times today. Rawr..." Kade chuckles making his laughter contagious.

"No, we are not going steady. We haven't even been on a date yet. Did you watch the movie, *Grease* today or something?" I ask curiously since his choice of words is a bit odd.

Josh interrupts. "We haven't been on a date because she won't let me take her on one. Only non-dates for us."

"I haven't heard you complaining." I move away from Josh.

"That's only because our non-dates are AMAZING!" Josh brings me closer to him, puts his arm around my shoulder, and kisses my forehead.

"Not only did I watch *Grease*, Em also made me sit through the movie, *She's the Man* for the billionth time. I swear, I don't know what's wrong with you girls. Watching a movie one or two times I can understand, but seeing it countless times and saying the words along with the actors...you girls kill me every time!" Kade says with a disbelieving look.

Emme smiles at Kade. "You know how much I love torturing you. It's the highlight of my day." She says with an angelic smile.

"My highlight of today was seeing you drenched in sweat from trying to keep up with me at the gym. It was my payback and I enjoyed every minute of it." Kade sneers at her.

I'm confused. "Wait. You two spent the whole day together without me and didn't kill each other?"

Emme laughs. "I didn't feel like going to prison today. Tomorrow being locked up for murder might not seem so bad though." Kade puts up his hand and Emme gives him a high five.

"Babe, do you want a beer?" Josh asks.

The man licking the rim of his beer bottle comes to mind. "Ummm...No, thanks. I don't feel like drinking anymore."

Josh leans over and whispers in my ear, "I thought you said you were going to drink for the both of us and that you were going to let me see how flexible you can be."

I whisper back, "Don't worry, babe. I don't need alcohol to be a freak in the sheets."

He tries to contain his smile, but fails. "There you go making my dick tingle again."

❧

It's the seventh inning and the score is tied. I realize I left my phone in Josh's truck.

"Can I have your truck keys? I need to get my phone." I explain.

"What do you need your phone for? You can use mine. Or if you want, I'll go with you. It's dark and I don't want you walking out by yourself." Josh says in a serious tone.

"Calm down. I'll only be gone for a bit. I'm a big girl. I can take care of myself. I need to take pictures of us once the Giants win to post them on Instagram. I also want to tag Romo to let him know he did an awesome job." I wink at him.

"Romo? The pitcher?" Josh asks.

"Yes, Romo. I like him." I state nonchalantly.

"Do you like him, like him, or just like him?" He asks with

no trace of humor behind his words. *Oh, my gah! Is that jealousy I sense? It's too cute!*

"I just like him." I say shyly, but deep down inside I'm doing flips over this new found revelation.

"Good. I don't want any other man making your panties wet. That's my job." He declares.

I give Josh a grave look. This is as good a time as any. Emme and Kade are involved in a serious discussion about the game. I take a deep breath and sigh. "Josh, we need to talk. You're not the only man who makes my panties wet. Several...scratch that...more like countless men make my panties wet." I confess.

Josh gives me an incredulous look and waits for me to continue. "I'm involved with numerous men, sometimes even a girl or two catch my attention." I take a long pause. "Yes, they're all in books and are fictional characters, but our relationships are real. I'm a book whore. If you see me with an open book, I suggest you don't bother me, especially if you can tell that it's an intense part of the story. Lord forbid you breathe loud while I'm reading...I will cut you." My expression is humorless. There are some things in this world that you can't take lightly; my relationship with characters is one of those things.

Kade interrupts. "Oh, God. What are you two cupcakin' about? Whatever sweet lovey dovey crap you guys are discussing is giving me cavities."

Josh tries to maintain a somber focus, but fails. "Nina was just informing me about her book obsession."

"Oh, hell no! I have put up with YEARS of her fascination with books. It's pretty sad, actually. For a while, she was head over heels in love with a sparkly vampire. If that shit isn't gay, I don't know what is." Kade fakes repulsion.

"You leave Edward out of this! Don't you talk about my first love that way!" I grab an ice cube from my water and throw it at Kade.

He completely ignores me and continues to focus his attention on Josh. "Oh, and don't get me started on the Dom who had serious mommy issues...Fuuuuck! This girl had it bad. She used to have a heart attack whenever she saw Audi R8s, grey ties, and walked around saying, 'Laters, baby.' Who the fuck does that shit?" At this point, Kade is laughing so hard he has tears. "My bestie. That's who!"

"You wash your filthy mouth when you mention my Christian!" I yell.

"For someone who has such an 'adult' job during the day and a sexy, fun profession as a pin-up model, you sure can behave like one of those teeny bop girls when it comes to your fictional loves." Kade winks at me.

"Baby, you truly are cuckoo. You know that, right? I don't care if you do have a few screws loose; I still like you and think you're sexy." Josh smiles sweetly at me and kisses my nose.

"Okay, but don't say we didn't warn you." I can't help but laugh. "So, can I get your keys?"

"Fine, but hurry back." He gives me a peck on the lips.

As I leave the bar, immediately, I feel the cold crisp air brush against my skin. My poorly lit surrounding gives me a restless feeling as I'm walking to Josh's truck. I turn around and realize no one is nearby, everyone is indoors watching the game. I'm not sure why I feel so paranoid, but decide not to question it and start walking faster to my destination. The truck is parked slightly over a block away from the bar. Luckily, the truck's inside light automatically turns on when I open the door so I'm not left searching in the dark. While I'm standing outside the truck stretching my arm underneath the seat trying to find my phone, I feel Josh grab my ass. *Shit! He scared me. Asshole!*

I turn to face and go off on him. *What the fuck? The Tiger's fan? Creepy pervert dude? Huh?*

"What the hell? Get the fuck away from me...NOW!" I yell at the stranger as my mind is running a mile a minute.

Creepy pervert dude doesn't move. Instead, he just leers at me with a lewd and lascivious expression planted on his face. He continues to block my exit. He's about six feet tall, with a burly build, light skin, and has stubble along his jaw. He appears to be in his mid-thirties. As he gets closer to me, his eyes immediately catch my attention. They're a light blue color, but his pupils are extremely dilated. *Fuck. He's on something.*

Besides the keys, I don't have anything that I can use as a weapon. He's in too close proximity to kick or punch him with as much force as I can conjure up. I get creative; I close my fists and position the long part of the key to come out between my middle and ring fingers. If things get physical, I'll kick and punch him, making him feel the key first with every hit I land. Assuming I actually make contact, that is. Hopefully, the situation won't escalate to that, but one never knows. *Get him talking. Kill time.*

Once again, he moves closer to me no longer leaving any space between us. I'm completely backed up against the inside of the truck. I panic and lose composure. "I guess you didn't hear me the first time, get the fuck away from me!" I scream in his face and try to push him away.

"You sure are a pretty and feisty little cunt." He breathes heavily along my ear. His breath is foul and reeks of hard liquor. "Why are you being a dick tease? I saw you checking me out earlier." He runs his eyes slowly from my face down to my chest.

"Get the fuck away from me, you delusional prick!" This time, I yell from the top of my lungs. Instantly, I feel a blow to the left side of my face causing me to feel dazed.

No. Not this again. Please, God...help me.

89

I feel a hand on my neck and the rapid pressure and squeeze of it. I try to fight him off, but he's too strong. I fail. Terror consumes me as I'm gasping for air.

"I'll give you a reason to scream, you fucking cunt!" I think I hear him say.

Within moments, my neck is released. Although my neck is in pain, that first breath of air is overwhelming, yet the best feeling in the world. I try to stand, but my body is still in shock and I can't seem to move or focus. Slowly, I manage to sit up. Vaguely, I see two figures, one in a white shirt and the other in black fighting. I close my eyes and open them gently in an attempt to clear my view. That's when I see Josh throwing the dirty creepy bastard on the ground and slamming his head against the concrete.

Alarm strikes me and realize that Josh is about to kill this guy. "Josh! Get away from him! Get in the truck and let's go!" I yell out with a raspy voice.

Josh slowly stands, gives the guy a few final kicks on his ribs, and leaves his limp body on the ground. As he gets in the driver's seat, I hand him the keys. We take off; the roar of his truck surprisingly brings me relief.

"Are you okay? Do you need to go to the hospital?" Josh asks extremely agitated, but with concern deep in his striking features.

"No, I'll be fine." I can't face him; instead, I look at the busy city life we're rapidly evading.

"Damn, Nina!" Josh runs his fingers through his hair while clenching his jaw. "Why can't you fuckin' listen? Why must you always insist on things being your own damn way? You're so fuckin' stubborn!" He yells.

His words and tone feel like a slap on the face that won't stop stinging. Although he's right and has every right to scold me for not listening to him, I can't help but feel hurt. I'm afraid to say anything. The tension in the car is unendurable.

As we continue to drive in uncomfortable reticence, Josh appears to be searching for something or someone. Finally, while we're on Mission Street, he pulls over, gets out, and uses a payphone briefly. Then, he makes a call using his cellphone. *That's strange.* I use this time to text Emme and Kade to let them know that Josh and I left so they wouldn't worry.

When Josh gets in the car, he's silent. He drives for a while, parks at a marina, and finally speaks. "When I used the payphone, I left an anonymous tip with the police regarding that piece of shit. I'm so sorry for not protecting you, baby. I shouldn't have let you walk out by yourself. I knew better, yet I let you go out alone. I hate myself for not going with my instinct." Josh says with great sorrow.

I'm confused. "What? None of this would've happened had I listened to you. This whole situation is my fault! You feel bad for not protecting me? You did! You should be mad at me. I thought you were and that's why you weren't speaking to me."

"Valentina, this man put his hands on you. So, no. I didn't protect you in time. I became restless as soon as you left, I had to make sure you were okay. That's when I heard you screaming and ran towards the truck. When I saw him choking you, all I saw was red. I wanted to kill him. Seeing him touch my lady—" Josh's cell rings and interrupts our conversation. *My lady.*

Josh is on the phone for several minutes. He finally gets off and faces me. "The guy was taken to the hospital. He has a serious concussion and fractured ribs. An officer ran a check on him due to an anonymous tip indicating he attempted to rape someone. The police found out that he's a parolee from Michigan, violated parole, hasn't registered as sex offender since his release from prison, and has a bench warrant out for his arrest. He had meth on his person and high blood alcohol

91

content in his system. Upon his release from the hospital, he'll be taken into custody, and most likely, extradited back to Michigan. The police aren't too concerned with his assault."

Thank you, Lord. My jaw drops. "How do you know all this information?"

"I know people in high and low places." Josh winks at me.

Relief washes over me. "I was worried about you getting in trouble. I hope nothing comes of this situation and that we can leave this night behind us."

"Again, I'm sorry you had to go through such a traumatic experience." Then, Josh gives me a perplexed look. "So, wait...You were worried about me and not concerned about the guy?" Josh asks with a curious smirk on his face.

"No, I wasn't nervous for him. Fuck him! During the past hour, I've been contemplating different scenarios I could tell the cops to leave you out of this whole mess. You defended me, you've done enough, I wasn't about to let you get caught up in this problem because of me." I'm dead serious.

"You'd lie to the police for me?" He looks at me with awe.

"Of course. I didn't wish that man any harm, but he crossed me, so now he can go fuck himself and rot in prison for the rest of his life. I definitely won't lose sleep over what he did to me. Fuck his bitch ass; I refuse to give him that satisfaction. I'm just glad you were there for me. I'm sorry for being so vulgar, but the thought of you being arrested has me restless." I lean closer to Josh and softly caress his jawline.

"Hey, all will work out just fine. Please don't worry. Use all the profanity you want, I think it's sexy when you're all riled up. If I had to do this again, I would. You're mine and I will do everything in my power to always protect you. Do you understand that?" His gaze is intense. I feel my heart beat rapidly. *Oh, my...I could get lost in those entrancing hazel eyes forever.*

I snap out of my reverie. "I'm yours?" I question as I swallow hard, trying my best to contain my enthusiasm and confusion for willingly wanting to give myself to him.

"Yes. You. Mine. End of discussion." He pronounces without giving me the opportunity to debate his claim.

"Wow. You sound so barbaric, like such a caveman." I smile. *I like it!*

He gives me that boyish grin while slightly showing off his perfect white teeth. "I don't hear you complaining. I'm a rookie when it comes to relationships. I've never been involved in one, but I can't stand the thought of seeing you with someone else or allowing them to touch you. I want to be a part of your life, make you happy, know you inside out, and be the only one who gets to savor your body." He pauses and then asks, "So, will you be my lady?"

He makes my heart melt. I unbuckle my seat belt and respond by giving him a long passionate kiss. In between kisses, I say, "Yes. Now...let's go back...to your place." I slightly back away and ask for confirmation, "So, it's just us now?"

"Yeah, baby. Just us." He replies and gently kisses the bruise on my face.

I'm beaming with joy. I feel ecstatic knowing we're committed to each other even though we just recently met. I'm with him because I want to be with him, not because I need him. There's a difference. He makes me feel safe and secure, although I love the feeling and appreciate his protectiveness, I take comfort in knowing that I can still hold my own if necessary. I never want to be a woman who's with someone because she needs them or loves them more than she does herself. I won't let that happen. With that in mind, I embrace my relationship with Josh and open my heart to him.

Driving back to his house, we listen to the radio and find out the Giants won the World Series. We're both thrilled; I move closer to give him a kiss, celebrating our team's victory.

It was meant to be a quick peck, but immediately turns hot and heavy. I can't wait to be all over him. The radio station starts playing the song, "Superwoman" by Lil' Mo featuring Fabolous. I back away from him and slightly lower the volume. "I know you want me to be your lady, but for this moment, can I be your dirty whore?" I ask.

"Whaaaaat? Baby, I swear, I love it when you make my dick tingle. You can be whatever you want as long as you're just mine. I don't fuckin' share." *Mmm...territorial. Why does that turn me on?*

"Good. Because I want you to fuck my mouth while you're driving. I want to feel the tingle for myself." I slowly lick my bottom lip and grasp it with my teeth. "Besides, I brought a treat." I pull out a packet of Pop Rocks candy. "I clearly recall you mentioning something about me licking this candy off your butt cheeks. Well, instead I'll be sucking you while the candy explodes in my mouth."

His jaw drops slightly from the bluntness of my words. I laugh at his expression. I turn up the radio, unbutton, and unzip his pants. I position myself on my knees hovering above him. I've never done this before, but I rise to the challenge. I eagerly caress his hard erection and release him from his boxers. I open the candy packet and pour the crystal-like sweet particles into my mouth. Immediately, the candy begins to sizzle and pop on the top of my tongue. Hungrily, I work my way down. I lick his shaft from the base up and twirl my tongue around the tip while the candy continues to fizzle. I take all of him inside my mouth, feeling the tingling sensation, and begin stroking his base with my right hand as I suck. I back away for an instant and spit on his dick. Although the left side of my face is in pain from being struck, I'm still enjoying the moment. All I want is to please him, I continue sucking him up and down while stroking and twisting his base. His moans become more intense.

"Babe, I love having your fat dick inside my mouth...You taste so good...My lips can't get enough of you...I want you to cum in my mouth...I want to savor every drop of you." I say in between sucking him.

"Baby, your mouth feels like heaven. I absolutely love fucking your mouth and pretty soon you're gonna make me nut." He has my hair twisted around his fingers and his palm over my head directing me to go lower down his shaft. I increase my speed, feel his body tighten, and hear his breathing escalate. I revel in the power I have over making my man weak with just the touch of my mouth. I feel the explosion of his warm, milky juice and swallow. Once he's done, I back away from him licking my lips.

"You're amazing." Josh pulls me close to him and kisses my lips. I can't help but smile. "As soon as we get to my house, it's my turn to devour you all night."

He keeps his word by relishing me until dawn.

The next morning, Josh drops me off at home on his way to work. I call my supervisor, inform her I'm not feeling well, but will be in the office by noon. It isn't really a lie; my body feels sore from all the good fucking Josh gave me and the left side of my face is now black and purple due to the hard punch I endured from the piece of shit. Mondays are usually busy, so I force myself to work at least half the day.

I shower and put on some shorts and a tank top. I want to relax for the next two hours before I get ready for work. I decide to check up on Kade to ensure he arrived home safely. I knock lightly on his bedroom door. Since there's no answer, I open it. Shock consumes my mental state and body. It takes a few seconds to register and comprehend the scenario in front of me.

"What the fuck? What did you do?" I yell.

Kade is taken by surprise and instantly sits up. He's completely naked and covers himself with his sheet. "What the fuck happened to your face, Cheesecake?"

"What were you thinking, Kade? Ewww. This is like incest! Is there no one you will fuck?" I'm appalled with the scene in front of me.

"Did Josh do that to you? Tell me, Valentina Moretti...NOW! I swear to God, I'll kill him!" Kade is beyond enraged.

I hear a thump on the ground and realize that Emme fell off the bed. Kade and I both stare at her naked body as she's desperately trying to cover herself up with a blanket.

"Fuck! Can you two please keep it down? My head is pounding!" Emme says as she's climbing back to Kade's bed refusing to make eye contact with either one of us.

"Valentina Moretti, if you don't fuckin' tell me what the hell happened to your face right now, I'm taking my ass to Josh's work and going psycho on his ass." Kade threatens.

"Calm down. Josh didn't hit me. Some asshole did, Josh kicked his ass afterward. But enough of that, tell me what happened between you and Emme last night? Hello? You two are worse than enemies and siblings who hate each other and constantly fight. Excuse my shocked reaction, but I feel like I just stepped into the *Twilight Zone*." I admit.

Kade continues sitting up, but covers his face. He remains silent.

"Hurry up and explain, I'm not getting any younger." Irritation is clear in my voice.

"Okay, good. We'll get back to your story since you're just dying to know mine. The Giants won last night, so of course, we had to celebrate. We had already been drinking since the early evening, so by the time the game ended, we were drunk. Add several shots of tequila to our already wasted state and you get full blown madness." He takes a few deep breaths.

"Fast forward, Kade." I'm just itching to know.

"Em was running her mouth throughout the night; I got

frustrated and somehow fantasized about shutting her up with my dick in her mouth. When we left the bar, I told her to come with me because I didn't want her catching a cab by herself. When we got home, I smacked her round, firm ass and kissed her." He shrugs his shoulders, as if indicating he couldn't help himself last night.

"You know, you really shouldn't be giving me all the details, but since you already started, you might as well continue, I don't want to be rude and interrupt your story." Part of me feels guilty for being nosey, yet the other part of me wants to know every juicy detail. It must be the Gemini in me.

Kade rolls his eyes at me before he continues with his story. "Thank you for not being a 'nosey Nancy' and allowing me to give you every disturbed detail. Like I was saying, well you know how sometimes I just want to choke Em? Well, I did and Miss 'I have a stick up my ass' liked it! We both got rough with each other, but in a hot way, nothing violent. Well, maybe just a little. I simply wanted to give her a good fuck to shut her up and make her relax a bit. So, I did...on the kitchen floor, on the couch, on my bed—"

I interrupt him. "Okay, Kade! I get it. You're a fuckin' freak."

"I couldn't help myself. The more she yelled out my name, the harder I kept thrusting myself inside her. I'll give her props, she can fuck. I fucked each and every one of her holes and enjoyed every minute of it." Kade has a huge evil smirk planted on his face.

"Hello! I'm right here!" Emme yells and sits up. "A gentleman doesn't kiss and tell, Kade!" She gives him an irritated look.

"Lucky for me, I'm no gentleman and you're no lady, you're more of an undercover freak!" He blows her a kiss and then turns his attention to me. "Cheesecake, seeing Em on her knees sucking my dick was a dream come true—"

Emme interrupts Kade by throwing her naked body onto him and attempts to suffocate him with two pillows. I take that as my cue and walk out.

That was weird.

A few minutes later, both Emme and Kade meet me in the living room fully dressed. They both want details of last night's assault. Initially, retelling that experience is difficult, but when I think back to how Josh defended me, I immediately feel a sense of security. Emme and Kade can't understand why I'm smiling. I have to explain that I'm not happy because of what that man did to me. I'm in a blissful state because I now have someone who cherishes me and wants to protect me just as much as I crave for it, even though I never wanted that before. I always took pride in being independent, self-sufficient, and being able to fend for myself. Now that I've had a taste of his protectiveness, admiration, and lust I want to cloak myself within his arms and never let him go.

"So, are you two a couple now or what?" I quickly change the subject to avoid talking about feelings and my future, things I hate discussing.

"Hell no!" They both yell out simultaneously and give me a disbelieving look as if I'm speaking in tongues.

"Fuck buddies?" I'm perplexed regarding their latest actions and want clarification as to how this will affect our trio.

"No. This was a one-time deal. Once is enough. Let's just forget it ever happened and move on." Emme instantly crosses her arms in front of her chest and stares down at Kade.

He ignores her glare. "All I know is that I'm NEVER going to drink that much again. Well, until next weekend, that is. And no, we didn't just fuck one time, I tapped that ass four times last night. You're a nymph, don't get it twisted. As for wanting me to forget about it, you must be cray cray! You talk shit all day, every day, and for the first time, you bowed down to me. If you think I'm ever going to forget that, you must not really know me. I'm bringing it up every chance I get."

"You're such a prick, Kade!" Emme looks as if she has a demon inside of her and is ready to rip Kade's head off.

"That may be so, but I'm a prick whose dick you had willingly inside your pussy, mouth, and ass. So, you can go ahead and call me all the names you want because I'll just be thinking of how you kept calling out my name and telling me how my fat dick felt delicious in your wet pussy." Kade is relentless.

"Cabron culero!" Emme shrieks as she curses him out in Spanish.

"Now, now my little Mexican bean burrito...Don't start getting all native and riled up, unless you want me to give you more spankings." Kade continues to taunt her.

If looks could kill Emme would shoot daggers at Kade with her eyes. "I'm out of here. I'm going home. I'm glad you're okay, Nina. I'll see you at the parade on Halloween." Emme grabs her purse and slams the door behind her.

I turn to face my bestie. "Kade, you're such an ass."

"Tell me something I don't know." He has a big grin on his face completely unremorseful.

There's no sense in trying to reason with him, he's clearly relishing in tormenting Emme. I get ready and head out to work. I spend Monday and Tuesday evening with Josh getting to know more about his playful side, desires, and everything else that he's willing to share. Although, we're both still reluctant about discussing certain topics, our lines of communication have definitely improved.

It's Wednesday, Halloween, and the celebration of the World Series win for our city. The parade is being held downtown. I call in sick; no job is worth missing such a grand festivity. Josh and I make plans to meet with Kade and Emme. Since I've been spending time with Josh, attempting to get to know him on various levels, I haven't seen them since Monday morning, the day my eyes were made susceptible to their freaky shenanigans.

When the four of us finally meet, I notice that Kade and Emme act as if nothing sexual ever occurred between them. Things are back to normal. We position ourselves near City Hall, towards the end of the parade since moving around is particularly difficult due to the massive crowd. Emme, who is wearing a cute panda hat and I are pleased with our morning drink, a cherry Slurpee with tequila in it. The men stick to rum and Coke. Yes, it's still morning, but it's the evening somewhere in the world, and even if it weren't...who cares! Our Bay Area team won the freakin' World Series! It's time to celebrate!

We're surrounded by an extremely diverse fan base. There are people in Halloween costumes, parents with their young children (clearly they allowed their kids to ditch school), original Giants fans from when the team arrived to San Francisco from New York in 1958, adults who called in sick from work, and every other type of fan in between. The streets are covered in orange and black from the team's loyal supporters.

The parade ends and now it's time for the victory rally, but we decide to remain at the same location. The overpopulated crowd makes it a vast obstacle to get any closer. The four of us get comfortable on the front steps of a building enjoying our drinks and listening to the ceremony. I'm relaxed, leaning on Josh, and in good spirits, until I see Nicole, the loose waitress skank who can't seem to stop throwing herself at Josh.

Nicole approaches our group; I sit up as Josh stands up to greet her. He extends his arm for a handshake, but Nicole dismisses it. Instead, she gives him a hug and a kiss on the cheek.

What the fuck?

I sense Josh's awkwardness. I continue to focus my attention on the skank who is so quick to violate my man's personal space. Immediately, he introduces her to our group and makes sure to announce me as his lady. She waves hello, but is fixated on Josh. Nicole asks him if she can speak to him in private. He appears confused, yet curious, and agrees to have a quick talk. He informs me he'll be back in just a few moments and gives me a peck on the lips. Josh and Nicole walk just a few feet away from us, they're still in plain sight, but I don't like it.

"Cheesecake, what the fuck is that about?" Kade asks. Clearly he noticed Nicole's touchy ways.

"I don't know, but she rubs me the wrong way. She's like a leech that you can't get rid of." I indicate with resentment.

"Is this history in the making? Is thee Valentina Moretti actually jealous over some girl?" Emme asks in a taunting manner.

"I'm not jealous! My blood may be boiling slightly and I might be contemplating ripping her throat out, but I don't envy that cheap slut. I just don't like how she's all over Josh, completely dismissing me. Stupid bitch. Before Josh introduced me as his girlfriend, she blatantly threw herself at him every chance she got, whether I was with him or not didn't matter to her. She's practically handing her rotten cookies to him on a silver platter!" I'm pissed.

"The question here is...Will Josh take a bite?" Kade sits in deep thought pondering his own question.

"He can do whatever he wants. He just needs to be honest with me." Without delay, my guard goes up.

"Dang, Cheesecake, you've never liked a guy this much, not including your fictional loves, that is. Wow, you must really like him to allow yourself to get all worked up." Kade has a genuine look of surprise on his face. "I assumed you two were just fucking and having a good time, it didn't cross my mind that you are actually developing real feelings for him."

Serious feelings? No, it's too soon for that. "Calm down, it's not like that." Instantly, I try to shake off that jealous and clingy girlfriend persona, it's never been my style.

"Yes, it is and it's okay for you to have feelings for someone and actually instill trust in them. Take a chance. I can tell this guy has strong emotions for you. Whatever you do, don't get upset with him. It's not his fault 'loose lips' is trying to sink her teeth into him. He made it clear to her that you're his lady. Don't let her win by allowing her presence and actions to ruin the rest of your day." Kade rarely gets serious, so when he does, I listen.

"Okay." All I can do is agree with my bestie.

"And if she doesn't back off, I'll be more than happy to intervene and teach her a good lesson." Kade winks at me. "Rumor has it...I'm pretty good at pounding sense into people. Right, Em?"

"Shut the fuck up! You're such a prick. Ugh! I can't believe we fucked! You're never going to let this go. What the fuck was I thinking?" Emme says with pure disgust and regret.

Kade starts laughing. "Hey, Em...remember when you had my dick in your mouth? Because I do! You're so cute when you're on freak mode. Why can't you be like that more often?"

"Shhhh!" I notice Josh is done with his conversation with Nicole. He heads back to me and puts his arm around my shoulder.

Kade and Emme back away from us and pretend to be focused elsewhere. I know better. Those two are hanging on our every word from their distance.

"So, what did that girl have to say that was so important and private that she couldn't say it in front of us?" I probe.

"She inquired about her application at my company again. I told her we currently weren't hiring, but that if something became available and she was qualified for the position, I would be in touch with her. This is the second time I tell her the same thing. She's very persistent." He seems annoyed.

"Yeah, well...persistent isn't all she is." I say with a much more bitter tone than intended.

"Valentina Moretti, are you jealous?" Josh asks with a bewildered look.

"She sure is! Don't let her fool you!" Kade says loud enough for several people to hear.

I can't help but give him and Kade an appalled look. "No."

Josh leans in closer to me and whispers, "Baby, you're so fuckin' sexy. I swear, the minute we get back to my place, I'm gonna tear you apart and show you how good you just made me feel." He puts his hands on either side of my face and gives me an intense expression. "I don't want anyone else. Understand?"

"I can't believe you're turned on because you think I'm jealous. You're sick and twisted. You know that, right?"

"Yes." He kisses me lightly on the lips. "Remind me to stop by the store on our way back to my house. If my lady wants to play naked Twister, who am I not to fulfill her wishes." He hugs me tightly before I have a chance to protest.

Chapter 6 (Josh)

Familia

few weeks have passed since I asked Nina to be my lady. I can't get enough of her. In such a short timeframe, she has monopolized my thoughts and my heart. I never thought I would fall for anyone. I'm used to hooking up with random girls at clubs, bars, anywhere really, and simply having one night stands to fulfill my needs. I never craved a connection to one specific person. Monogamy is a term that was irrelevant in my lifestyle. Until now, that is.

Nina and I have been staying at each other's place every night since we made our relationship official. We both feel comfortable enough to wander about freely without a sense of invading private spaces. We have quickly fallen into a domestic routine which I surprisingly take great comfort in.

Tomorrow is Thanksgiving Day and I decide to let my staff off early today so they can begin their four day weekend on a positive note. I use my afternoon wisely and meet with my mother to check up on her and discuss tomorrow's gathering. We meet at her favorite café shop around the corner from her home.

"Hey, mom. You look great. I've missed you. You've been awfully busy lately. What gives? What have you been doing? Every time I stop by, you're never home." I casually observe her appearance. She's lost weight, looks tired, and definitely appears more fragile than the last time I saw her, but one thing that never fades is her beauty. "How do you feel?"

"I feel fine. I've been busy socializing, just like you demanded of me. Don't you remember? I've made friends in my building and many nights we meet to complain about our overprotective and nosey kids." She indicates straightforwardly.

"Don't sass me, woman. I can't help if I worry about you. You're the only mother I have. I don't like you being out so late and with people I've never met." I scold her halfheartedly.

"Since when is the early evening considered late? You need to remember that I'm an adult and not some old senile fool who needs to be cared for. I'm more than capable of taking care of myself." She raises her head in a dignified manner.

"Have you been taking your medications? What did the doctor say during your last visit? Why won't you allow me to go with you?" Her fragile state has me concerned.

My mom sighs deeply. "My goodness, I never realized how much of a worry wart you are. Stop it. I have a male friend, he accompanies me to my doctor's appointments, and I'm diligent about taking my medication, so please stop with your obsessiveness over me. You're coddling me and I don't like it. Now, onto more important things, when are you giving me grandbabies?"

"Woman! Who is this male friend you speak of? And mom, do you have a one track mind? Grandbabies...that's all you think about. How about asking me how I'm doing or what my latest interest is?" My mother can be draining at times.

"I'm the parent. I ask the questions around here. Don't you give a second thought to my friend. Yes, I have a one track mind. The day I die, I want to know that you won't be left alone. It's a fear of mine. As for asking you how you're doing, well, I don't need to ask. It's written all over your face, you're happy. I know you. Now, tell me what or who brings you this joy?"

"That's what I want to discuss with you today, mom. Tomorrow, I was planning on bringing (cough, cough) my girlfriend (cough, cough) to our Thanksgiving lunch." *Please, please, please don't start with your never ending inquiries.*

My mother's eyes are practically out of their sockets. *Too late.*

"You have a girlfriend? Who is she? What's her name? How old is she? What does she do for a living? Where does she live? How long have you known her? How long have you two been dating? Oh my goodness, is she pregnant? Do you love her? Why is this the first time I hear of this girl? Why haven't you brought her over sooner? Why—"

"Woman, contain yourself!" No wonder my mom looks so fragile, she's been saving her energy to bombard me with questions! "I haven't brought her over because I'm afraid your interrogation will scare her off. She's a very private person and doesn't like her personal life being intruded upon. You have to be on your best behavior tomorrow and respect her boundaries. We've only been dating about a month, but she means a lot, mom. Please don't scare her away with your obsession of grandbabies. We haven't discussed that yet. I've never even thought about being a father. Please don't bring it up and make her feel uncomfortable." I plead with her. "So, what do you say? Will you agree to be on your best behavior?"

"Oh, my goodness! You're going to get married and one day have kids! You've made your mother extremely happy!" She's smiling and I can see her mind already planning my future nonexistent wedding.

Why do I even bother? I'm sorry mom, but I can't do this for you. Not after all you've already asked of me.

My mother quickly becomes serious. "How much does she know about you? About us?"

"She doesn't know anything, but she does ask about my past. There isn't a way for me to tell her about myself, without discussing you, and your history. In my opinion, it's not my story to tell. Just know that I've never felt like this towards any woman. I can't keep anything from her if I want her in my life. In my heart, I feel I can trust her." I confess.

"Do you love her?" My mom asks with pure warmth in her eyes.

"I've never been in love. I don't know. I think it might be too soon for that. All I know is that she makes me feel complete; she's my first and last thought of the day. She's a good person with a great heart; she's passionate, strong, feisty, intelligent, and beautiful. Mom, this girl takes my breath away."

She's completely ecstatic about my new relationship. I leave when two women who are also residents in my mom's building, join her and make plans to play cards tonight. I depart with relief knowing my mother has promised to be on her best behavior.

I arrive at Nina's home to pick her up, she's spending the night. Before I have a chance to get out of the car, she's already out of her house. I walk towards her, give her a kiss, and take her overnight bag. She's wearing red heels along with a black coat that's fitted at her waist and then spreads loosely to her knees. The red lipstick she has on makes her already full and luscious lips stand out even more. Her hair is styled the way she had it on the Bentley photo shoot. She looks amazing.

"Baby, you look incredible. I thought you didn't want to go out and just wanted to watch a movie at home. Don't worry, it'll only take me a few minutes to change clothes so that I can take you out, you just tell me where you wanna go."

She smiles at me. "I don't want to go out. I wanna go to your place and hang out like we planned. Why would you think otherwise? You can order a pizza, we can watch a movie, and drink beer."

"You're so sexy. Come here and give daddy some sugar."

"Mmm...gladly." She gives me a soft kiss and lightly traces my lips with her tongue.

"Let's go, babe. The sooner we get to your place, the faster we can get down and dirty." She commands with a devious grin.

That's all I needed to hear. I turn on the ignition and bring my truck to life. We drive by the city's dynamic streets with their lively ambiance. We finally arrive to my house. When we enter, she coquettishly smirks at me and leads the way to the living room. I'm right behind her when she turns around, takes me by surprise, and grabs my dick under my jeans. *Whaaaaat? So straight forward. I love it.*

She grabs me by my shirt, presses her body with mine, and against my lips innocently asks, "Mr. Ryan, would you mind putting on some music then having a seat on the couch?"

"Whatever you want, baby." I gaze at her eagerly doing my best not to rip off her coat and throw myself on her. Instead, I do as I'm instructed while she heads over to the kitchen and brings me a beer.

As she hands me the bottle, she leans in and whispers in my ear, "Just in case you get thirsty. It might get a little hot in here." Her words along with her sweet breath against my skin awaken all my senses. She gradually backs away maintaining eye contact with me and slowly begins unbuttoning her coat as she's swaying to the music. She's seductively keeping me in a trance, desperate to see her every move. Her face is beautiful as she gives me a lustful and taunting gaze. When she finally undoes the last button, she has a sensual, yet wicked grin.

Fuck me.

Nina unhurriedly removes her coat still in rhythm with the music. Gradually, she reveals her bare shoulders and eventually, her completely naked and glorious body underneath her coat, leaving on just her red heels that emanate raw sex. Immediately, my mouth goes dry as my attention is fixated on her perfection. There's nothing that can deteriorate my longing or make my eyes stray from her, not even a fire. She continues to enticingly dance for me to the beat of the song. I'm too mesmerized by her beauty to pay attention to the music. Nina looks astonishing with her long, silky hair flowing down her back, her spellbinding dark eyes full of desire, and her flawless ivory skin yearning for my touch. She rubs her full, creamy breasts and pinches her pink, aroused nipples. I swear, they're craving my mouth, but I maintain control. Her alluring curves and ass are a work of art; I can't wait to run my tongue along every crevice.

As Nina is seducing me with her looks, body, and moves, she flirtatiously asks, "Do you like my heels?"

I observe her up and down, lusting after every inch of her figure. "I love them. They're fuckin' sexy."

"I'm glad. I bought them today thinking solely of you. I envisioned wearing them as you're fucking me with my legs over your shoulders. I thought these heels made sexy FMSs." She smirks.

"FMSs?" I ask, not familiar with the acronym.

"Fuck Me Shoes, babe." As she walks over to me, I unbutton, and unzip my pants. She begins by gently massaging my bulge, then pulls it out and strokes it in vertical and circular motions using my pre-cum as lubricant. Nina gives me a sweet beguiling smile, gently grabs my beer bottle, and takes a drink. Without hesitation, she lowers her head and puts my dick in her mouth while she still has cold beer inside it. The shock of the chill sensation is mind-blowing. As her hand strokes and her mouth devours my dick, the wintriness feeling fades and is replaced by a hot awareness. I study my lady's fascinating body as her face hovers between my legs, without a doubt, this woman is absolutely exquisite. I sit back and enjoy my beer as my lady is on her knees swallowing me whole. I'm in heaven...I'm one lucky bastard.

After a long night of intense foreplay and amazing sex, I wake up with Nina in my arms. My emotions feel perplexed. I'm not sure when or how it happened, but somehow Nina has managed to make me see my life and future in a different perspective. I once shone away from intimacy and commitment, now I relish in it with her. I never thought I would enjoy something so much I never once craved for in the past.

It's dawn, still too early to get up. Nina starts to stir, she tightens her hold on me, and gives me a kiss on my chest. I can get used to this.

"Morning, babe. Why are you up so early?" She asks as she's rubbing her eyes.

"I woke up seconds before you did. Go back to sleep, we have a long day ahead of us, you should rest." I kiss the top of her head.

"Tell me something about yourself that I don't already know." She requests in a sweet manner.

Without thinking, I blurt out the first three things that come to mind. "I don't like milk, I love Mexican food, and my mom is very overprotective. There, now it's your turn."

"Not so fast, tree hugger. I already knew about the milk and Mexican food, so please elaborate about your mom. I know you two have a close relationship, but you rarely talk to me about her. I'm meeting her today. Tell me something. Anything. I know that you love her, but it's clear you resent her. Why?" Now, Nina's giving me her undivided attention.

Damn. Just suck it up, talk, and get it over with. "When I was younger, I used to play baseball. Since I joined t-ball at the age of four, my dream was to become a Pro-ball player. I soon realized pitching was my niche; to say that I was good is an understatement. I don't mean to toot my own horn, but I was pretty bad ass. I used to live, breathe, and sleep baseball. I always had my mom's support, until I became a high MLB (Major League Baseball) draft pick. College scouts, MLB teams' top scouts, some regional supervisors, cross checkers along with scouting directors all came to see me play late in the high school season."

I pause to reminisce on those days and then continue with my story. "Yeah, I was that good. My mom knew I was talented, but never imagined I would be offered a contract to go Pro right out of high school. Instantly, everything came to a halt. She wouldn't allow me to sign, not because she wanted me to go to college or because she wanted me to be better prepared, she had other reasons for not consenting. At that time, she became very sick and I didn't have the heart to go against her. Although, I resented her, I knew she had her reasons. Seeing my dream slip away was difficult, to say the least. After high school, I refused to continue with my education. I partied and worked with my mom's boyfriend, John. When I turned twenty, I went back to school with a goal to major in criminal justice. I wanted to follow in the footsteps of my grandfather who was DEA (Drug Enforcement Administration) Chief of Operations. We're pretty much anti-drugs in my family. Well, once again, my mom didn't allow it for the same reason she didn't consent to me playing Pro-ball. When John became ill and requested that I take over his business, I knew it was time to grow up and make him proud. He was the only father figure I had. I wanted to show him that I was capable and ready to take on the responsibility."

I pause and look at Nina intently. "Now, my mom wants to see me married and with children, I can't give her that. She's already taken and asked too much of me. I love her dearly, but I can't allow her to control any more aspects of my life. I won't marry or give her the grandkids she wants...ever."

"Oh." Nina looks at me with comprehension in her eyes, but curiously asks, "So, what's her reason for interfering with your goals and dreams?"

I bring her closer to me and embrace her tightly. "That's not my story to tell. I'm sure you'll find out soon enough."

"Thank you for your honesty and opening up." Nina returns the hug and kisses me softly on my neck. Sleep quickly captures us until the late morning.

As we're preparing to leave my house for our first Thanksgiving stop, I take a moment to observe Nina from a distance. She looks gorgeous in the beige dress she's wearing. It's fitted at the top with a daring cut out detail on her chest and a white fold over on the back. The dress flows from her waist to her knees as a circle cut. Her high strappy sandals show off her neatly manicured toes. *Damn, she has pretty feet.* Her hair is down and swept to the side. Her makeup is so subtle, it's almost nonexistent. She looks perfect. *And there goes my hard on.*

"Baby, I can't even look at you without wanting to fuck you." I confess.

"Soooo are you saying that I look nice?" She questions me teasingly.

"Nice? Nice can't begin to describe your beauty. You're radiant! You look so delicious I just wanna pound you like crazy!"

"Awww...babe, you're so romantic." She laughs. "You look

pretty tasty yourself. I'd do you." She coquettishly smiles and winks at me.

I sit back on the couch with a wide grin on my face.

This girl brings me so much happiness, I just want to savor her all day. Since we have three stops to make today, I decide to behave myself and devour her at a later time. "You can bet your sweet ass you'll be doing me tonight. Now, let's get going before I rip your dress off and fuck you on the kitchen table."

With a sinfully astounding look, she replies, "Whatever you say, Papi."

Fuck me!

"Take your dress off...NOW. I need to be in you." I look at Nina hungrily. There's no way I can wait to be inside her until tonight.

"Yes, sir. Your wish is my command!" She says enthusiastically.

God, how I love this girl! Wait. What?

My mother resides in a two bedroom condo located in the Millennium Tower. It's actually a condo I purchased when the building was still in the construction process. After John passed away, my mother didn't feel comfortable living alone in John's grand home. I didn't feel at ease leaving her unaccompanied with her health and medical state being so delicate. When my condo was completed, I handed the keys over to her. The Millennium Tower is luxurious and has several amenities including 24 hour concierge service and security. Since she insists on living by herself, I at least take comfort in having her reside here.

We arrive at the blue-gray glass high-rise building. As we enter, Nina is taken aback by the tower's opulence. I take her hand

and lead her to the elevator. My mother is anxiously awaiting our visit and greets us as soon as the elevator doors open.

Instantly, my mom enfolds Nina in her fragile arms with genuine warmth and happiness behind her lovely emerald eyes. "It's such a pleasure to finally meet you, Nina. My son has said so many wonderful things about you. His compliments did you no justice, you're beyond stunning."

Nina gives my mom a sincere smile. "Thank you, Ms. Ryan, you're an exquisite woman. I'm delighted to meet you as well."

As we walk into my mother's spacious condo with its open floor plan, we get overtaken by the magnificent view of the city and Bay Bridge from her living room. The décor of my mother's home is white with neutral beige colors, it's contemporary, yet has a comfort, and inviting feel to it.

Nina is captivated by the view. "I absolutely love your home, Ms. Ryan. You have your own escape from the reality beneath you and have a peaceful retreat with absolutely breathtaking scenery."

"Thank you, dear, but please call me Celeste. I feel old when people refer to me as Ms. Ryan. This condo actually belongs to my son. He's obsessed with taking care of me." My mother laughs and gives me a discreet wink.

Nina and I spend the early afternoon attacked by my mother's interrogation. She wants to know everything about my lady and our relationship. Nina doesn't seem to mind and answers most questions, the ones she feels are too intrusive she casually dismisses and changes the topic. My mother is genuinely interested when Nina discusses working with victims of sexual crimes and her interest with forties and fifties inspired fashion. Once my mother is satisfied with her inquisition, we eat our catered Thanksgiving lunch at her nook table overseeing our eminent city in a more relaxed and blissful state.

"Please pardon my invasiveness, Nina. I'm just fascinated by you and want to get to know you, that's all." My mother smiles at Nina remorsefully.

"It's okay, no need to apologize. You know, Celeste, when I look at you, I feel as if I've seen you somewhere before. I just can't seem to recall where or when that may have been." Nina looks at my mother with deep concentration.

"So, you're saying I have a common face and I'm not worth remembering?" My mother gives Nina a serious expression.

"Oh, no...that's not what I meant at all. I—" Nina gets interrupted.

I glare at my mom. The woman I refer to as my mother starts hysterically laughing. "I'm sorry, sweetie. I couldn't help myself. I just had to."

"Oh. Now, I see where Josh gets his humor and selective hearing from!" Nina joins in on the laughter; I can't help but be amused by the two women in my life.

After lunch, we head over to the living room to relax. "Son, will you be visiting Delia this afternoon? I spoke with her earlier this week, she misses you and would really like to see you."

From the corner of my eye, I notice Nina's bewildered expression.

"Of course, we're headed there after we leave here. I've been busy lately and haven't had a chance to stop by her house. Won't you be going also?" I ask.

"No. I'm a bit tired, but I'll be meeting with her for lunch this weekend. Please say hello to everyone on my behalf. Later this evening, I'll be meeting with my male friend." My mom states casually.

I glare at her. "What's your male friend's name? Where does he live? It's kind of creepy of you to keep referring to him as your male friend. The man has a name mom, so spit it out."

My mother takes a deep breath. "His name is Michael and he lives in this building. Now, stop asking questions about him, unless you want me to come up with some of my own." Her taunting look wills me to question her further.

I don't take the bait. "No, I'm good, no more questions regarding this Michael guy. But if you ask me, he sounds like a gigolo, I don't like him."

"Well, it's a good thing no one asked you. A gigolo? That's absurd!" The woman who brought me into this world and Nina begin laughing at my expense. I roll my eyes. *Women.*

The remainder of our visit with my mom is full of laughter. The conversation is kept light and everyone is at ease. My mom and Nina are getting along and agree to get together real soon. Right before we leave, I pull my mom to the side, "Woman, don't forget to take your medications, I'll be going with you to your next doctor's appointment whether you like it or not, and mom, I love you." I kiss her forehead and embrace her fragile body. "You're the best. Since you behaved today, I'll cancel your reservation at the old folks' home."

She smacks my arm with her delicate hand. "Insinuate that I'm past my prime again and see what happens." My mother gets closer to me and whispers, "I would love to know what Nina thinks of the names I have picked out for my grand-babies. Call me old again and I'll be sure to find out." She quietly threatens.

"Mom, have I told you today how young and flawless your skin looks? You look absolutely radiant!" I eagerly compliment her.

"That's what I love about you son, you're so wise and observant." She gives me a beaming smile.

Nina says goodbye and gives my mom a final hug before we depart to our next destination.

As I'm driving to South City, I thank God for allowing my

mother the opportunity to spend another year with me. I don't know what I would do if she were to leave my side. Her health and delicate state are a daily concern. I can't lose her, I just can't.

Nina interrupts my thought. "Hey, tree hugger, can you tell me about our next visit? It would be nice to have a head's up. By the way, thank you for introducing me to your mom. I really enjoyed our time with her. You two are so alike! It's pretty amusing, actually."

"I'm glad you had a good time, I did also." I kiss the back of her hand slowly and savor her skin against my lips. Her presence brings me joy. "Next, we're headed to Delia's house. Delia is a friend of my mom's who used to take care of me growing up. She's from El Salvador and her husband from Mexico. He passed away over two decades ago. When my mom moved to California, she was a few months pregnant and didn't know anyone. Delia and her husband formed such a close friendship with my mom, they considered each other family. When Delia's husband passed away, our families became closer than ever. Since my mom was busy working, all my home cooked meals came from her. I grew up eating pupusas, pan dulce, burritos, whatever she cooked, I ate. Her cooking is amazing! I love her and her family; they treat me as if I were one of their own."

"I'll have to admit, at first I was confused about Delia when your mom mentioned her name." Nina admits shyly.

"Yeah, I noticed. I could tell you were ready to mud wrestle over me. That's pretty hot. You're so gorgeous when you're ready to claw someone's eyes out over me." I tease.

She laughs out loud showing off her perfect white teeth. "Slow your roll, tree hugger. I'm not sure if there's enough room for you and your ego in this truck."

We arrive to Delia's house in less than half an hour. It's a two story yellow house with a red brick front porch, the home is inviting with its flower gardens on both sides of her door and the grass neatly trimmed. I'm excited to introduce everyone to Nina. *Shit!* I forgot to give everyone the head's up. Delia is like a second mother to me and just like my mom, she's been eager for me to settle down. I grab the wine bottles and prepare to be amused.

As we enter, I greet everyone in Spanish and make the proper introductions. I've never seen so many jaws drop at once. Nina is surprised to hear me speaking fluent Spanish and everyone else in the house is shocked to find out I have a girlfriend. *This ought to be interesting.* Although everyone in the house speaks English, Delia has always insisted on every person solely speaking Spanish in her home. Today, she makes an exception.

"Mi güerito! I'm so happy to see you! Why you don't come visit me sooner? Let me tell you somesing, I missed you so much!" *She has the sweetest accent. It warms my heart when she refers to me as her little white boy in an endearing manner.*

Delia is an older woman in her mid sixties. She wears bright colors and plenty of jewelry that compliment her sweet and loving personality. Delia excitedly rushes and embraces me in her arms showering me with love.

For the first time since I can remember, I speak to Delia in English. "I'm so sorry, I've been really busy at work and spending time with this lovely lady." I put my arm around Nina and kiss the top of her head. "Delia, let me introduce you to my lady, Valentina Moretti." I'm beaming. I can't help it. Immediately, I notice Delia take in a deep breath and make her best attempt at containing her excitement.

"Oh, Valentina, you are so beeeeautiful! Let me tell you somesing, I'm so pleased to meet you. This is your house. Make yourself at home." Before Nina has a chance to respond, Delia gives her a hug and gives me a subtle wink.

"Mucho gusto, Delia. Please, call me Nina. Thank you so much for such a heartwarming welcome. Yo hablo español un poquito. Me permite practicar?" Nina states her knowledge of the Spanish language and asks if she can practice with a genuine smile.

"Of course! Claro que si!" Delia is delighted and eager to continue introducing Nina to the rest of the family.

Delia has a full house, all her adult five children and their families are there along with several other family members celebrating Thanksgiving. The dining table consists of two turkeys, one baked and one fried both filled with stuffing. There's a honey ham with pineapple ringlets and maraschino cherries on it. In the center of the table are three bowls with Mexican styled pork tamales, Salvadorian chicken tamales, and corn tamales. The table is filled with side dishes and desserts; all together it's a feast to feed a city. Although I recently ate, I can't wait to dig in. But first, a prayer is led by Delia.

The afternoon consists of everyone reminiscing, catching up, and being interrogated regarding my new relationship. Nina easily dodges personal questions. The family is welcoming of her and quickly fall into simple topics of conversation. Every so often, I glance at Nina from a distance and admire her beauty along with her wit, strength, and charisma. *She's one hell of a package.*

As we're saying our goodbyes, I give Delia an extra-long hug, thank her for everything, and remind her that although I may not always be around, she is always in my thoughts and in my heart.

Once we're driving to our third and final Thanksgiving stop, Nina turns to me and gives me a disbelieving look. "Well, well, well...aren't you full of surprises, Mr. Spanish tongue!"

"What do you mean?" I ask.

"You speak Spanish and never told me. That's pretty cool actually, but why never tell me?" She questions curiously.

"It never came up." I state nonchalantly.

"Does your mom speak Spanish also? Isn't she Scottish? Is she mixed?" Nina's mind is quickly going into overdrive.

"Yes, my mom is from Scotland, but she speaks Spanish also. My mom used to work long hours in my early years; she was determined to ensure our financial status was up to par with her standards. She paid Delia to watch over me while she worked. Since I spent so much time with Delia and her family, Spanish became the first language I learned to speak. My mom understood Spanish better than she spoke it back then due to classes she had taken and a friend who had taught her. Now though, she speaks the language fluently. What about you?" I ask.

"From school, Emme, and latin soap operas I watch. The first things Emme taught me were all the bad words. I'm definitely not fluent, but I can get by. So, tell me, are you completely Scottish like your mom?" Nina's curiosity is quickly reaching a forbidden topic for me.

"Umm...no. I'm half Mexican." *No more questions, baby.*

She's genuinely surprised. "Really? Wow. Me too. I'm Italian and Mexican. It's weird how this topic never came up. Would you like to talk about your dad?"

"No."

"Me neither." She replies.

We change the topic, listen to music, and head over to Nina's house where her mom and Kade are waiting for us. She calls Kade to let him know that we're on our way. I take comfort in slowly letting Nina into my life and knowing that she respects my privacy by not probing me for answers.

When we arrive, we quickly greet Kade and Nina's mom, Victoria then head to the kitchen. I'm surprised to see that nothing has been cooked. Instead, there's Chinese takeout, pizza, buffalo wings, a batch of brownies along with two large bags of Doritos. I guess Nina saw the perplexed look on my face and immediately starts laughing. "What's so funny?" I ask.

"Your face! Were you expecting another full blown traditional meal?" She's still laughing.

"No. I'm just surprised to see such a sinful, yet tempting spread, that's all."

"We haven't had a traditional Thanksgiving meal in several years. My mom, Kade, and I regularly have meals together, so doing it on Thanksgiving wasn't very special to us. Instead, we do the opposite. We don't slave over the kitchen all day preparing a grand feast. We take the easy route by buying junk and fast food. The whole day we lounge in our pjs, have a movie marathon, and pig out. On Black Friday, as an alternative to shopping and freezing our butts at the crack of dawn, we sleep in and hit the gym for a two hour workout. We're weird like that, but it works for us and keeps us close. It's our own unconventional tradition that we have grown to love. Today, you get to join us." Nina's smile lights up her exquisite face. As an afterthought, she asks, "Hey, have you ever had regular Doritos topped with lemon juice and hot sauce?"

"No, but I like experimenting." I don't even have to try, inappropriate thoughts just come naturally whenever I'm near her.

"You're missing out! Come on. Let's change into some comfy clothes so that we can truly relax the way this day is meant to be spent in this house. I'll hook you up a plate and get you a beer while you're changing." She gives me a devilish grin that makes me want to tear her apart. Damn, this girl is sexy.

Once we've made ourselves comfortable and Nina has

changed into shorts and styled her hair into a loose bun, we join Kade and Victoria in the living room.

"Soooo how did it go?" Kade casually asks. I can tell that he and Victoria are impatiently waiting on Nina's response. They're dying to know what happened during the visit with my mom. "By the way, I'm going to pretend like I don't notice that turd on your head. For the billionth time, it's not cute."

"Well, I'll have you know that my man does think it's cute. So, you can drink that hater-aid juice all by yourself." Nina states before she feeds me a Dorito chip topped with lemon juice and Tapatio hot sauce. Instantly, she begins giggling.

"Mama V, I suggest you cover your ears because I'm going to do quite a bit of cursing in the next few minutes." Kade warns Victoria.

Victoria completely ignores him and simply stares at her daughter with a wide eyed expression. *I'm confused. What's the big deal? What's with the shocked reaction?*

Kade directs his attention to me. "Sweet. Baby. Jesus! Where is my Cheesecake and what have you done to her?" Kade asks, but continues talking before I have a chance to respond. "What the fuck is with the 'my man this and my man that' talk? And never in my whole entire life of living have I seen my Cheesecake get all lovey dovey with a man. I know you two are a couple and all, but this behavior my girl is displaying is weird as fuck. That's some trippy shit! Now, I've seen it all! Hell is soon to freeze the fuck over!" Kade begins hysterically laughing. Soon, we all join in as his amusement of the situation quickly spreads to everyone.

Nina theatrically replays today's events. An hour later, we finish catching up, get ourselves situated, and are ready to begin watching a movie. Just then, Emme joins us and has a surprised look on her face when she sees me lying behind Nina on the extended couch. I guess Nina in a relationship and being affectionate is just as much of a shock to her friends and family as it is to mine.

"Hi, sweetie. How was your Thanksgiving? Did you have a good time?" Victoria asks Emme.

"It was fine. Not much to tell." She responds.

"You know Em, it's pretty strange how we've known you for about five years or so and we've never met any of your family or friends. What gives?" Kade asks. Emme becomes uncomfortable in her stance. Kade catches on and decides to lighten her mood. "Boo, is it because you're ashamed of me? Even I know how to conduct myself in public...for the most part." He chuckles.

Emme remains silent. She's clearly not amused.

"Glad you made it, hun. We were just about to watch a movie, just can't seem to agree on one." Nina states as she's looking through her blu-ray collection.

"How about we have a *True Blood* marathon?" Emme suggests.

"I don't get what's with you girls and your damn fascination of vampires. You're lucky the Viking vampire and the werewolf are serious eye candy." Kade looks at everyone to see if we're all in agreement with Emme's choice.

We all agree. Before the first episode begins to play, I head to the kitchen to grab a beer. As I'm munching on some chips, Victoria spots me. "I'm glad you came into my daughter's life. It's been years since I've seen her this happy." She takes a long pause. "Whatever you do, please don't hurt her. If you do, she will remove you from her life for good. I would hate to see that happen. You two really compliment one another, it's like you've known each other forever and simply belong together."

"Victoria, I care about Valentina. I never knew I was suffocating until I met your daughter. She's my breath of fresh air. All I know is that when I'm not with her, she consumes my daily thoughts. When we're together, I can't seem to get enough of her laughter and affection. Even when she's upset with me, I find her feistiness amusing. I'm not perfect, but you have my word that I won't purposely hurt her." I look Victoria in her eyes and will her to see the truth behind my words. She responds by giving me a hug.

The remainder of the evening is spent completely relaxed. Kade argues a few times with the actors on the show, but for the most part I enjoy everyone's company. Victoria leaves after watching a few episodes since she has to be at her bakery early in the morning. She's anticipating a very busy day ahead of her.

Nina falls asleep in my arms while we're watching *True Blood*. My intention is to get up and carry her to bed, but her peaceful appearance puts me in such a comfort state that I fall asleep right along with her. Even though we don't have sex, the evening feels perfect and I'm able to have a good night's rest.

On Black Friday, we sleep in, continue to lounge around, and agree to avoid the mall along with all shopping centers. In the afternoon, the four of us head to the gym to burn off some calories by getting in a kick ass workout.

That evening, Kade has plans to go out with some friends while Emme has plans of her own. I'm thankful for having Nina all to myself. We head back to my place for another relaxing night. Nina suggests we play poker. We agree on Texas Hold'em and decide to make it a drinking game. If she loses a round, she'll be taking blow job shots; if I lose, I'll have Satan's vagina shots (per her request). Nina thinks she's funny, so I go along and humor her. We set up our game, alcohol, and shot glasses on the coffee table in the living room and position ourselves on the floor.

We stray away from the rules. We both have one hundred chips; each is equivalent to one dollar. We agree not to have blind bets and no limit betting. If a player loses a round, they have to take a shot. Once a person is left with no chips, the loser has to do whatever the winner demands.

After I shuffle the cards, I deal her starting hand face down and do the same for myself. Then, I lay out the flop; three community cards face up in the center of the table between Nina and I, a nine of spades, a jack of hearts, and a queen of spades. I take a sip of my beer and observe Nina as she's biting her lower lip, completely focused on our game. She bets one chip.

I laugh. *Clearly, she's afraid to lose her chips and have to submit to me. No, no Miss Moretti...you will lose and you will be mine even if you choose to play at a snail's pace.*

I call her bet and raise her four chips. She sees my raise. Nina squints her eyes and gives me a pouty look. She knows I won't allow her to play so conservatively. I deal the turn, the fourth community card which is a seven of diamonds. I stick to betting five chips. She matches my bet, but doesn't raise me.

Awww...she's so cute.

I lay down the river, the final community card on the table, an eight of spades. She turns her serious expression into a beaming smile. She bets ten chips. I call her bet and raise her ten more chips. She matches my raise. If I lose, I won't mind meeting her demands. The more I look at her, the harder it is for me to restrain myself from shoving my dick into her tight, slick pussy.

And...there goes my hard on...again.

Simultaneously, we both drop our cards face up. She has a seven of diamonds and a ten of clovers. My hand consists of a two and four of spades. Since a flush beats a straight...I win. Immediately, I sense my horns pop out of my head.

"Baby, it's time for you to drink up and remove a piece of

clothing." My devilish smirk matches perfectly with my invisible horns.

"Hey! We're supposed to be playing a drinking game, not strip poker!" She makes a feeble attempt at sounding appalled.

"My house, my rules." I'm all balls out.

Nina sighs dramatically and follows it with a sinful grin of her own. "You're lucky I'm hot...otherwise, I'd keep my clothes on." Slowly and seductively she removes her jeans. "If I would've known we were playing strip poker, I wouldn't have taken off my shoes and socks as soon as we entered your house." She gives me a sly sneer. "You wanna play dirty?"

Is it just me or did horns just come out of her head too?

"Fine, we'll play dirty." Nina replies to her own question. She's left wearing a tight black t-shirt and leopard print panties with black lace.

Nina gets on her knees and slowly stretches her upper body across the coffee table to get the shaker that already has her mixed blow job drink inside. She stays in that position, shakes her drink, and pours it into a double shot glass. While she remains in this pose, her panties ride up her round, sweet ass. Her back curves make my mouth water. Right away, I crave to spank that soft, silky skin and caress it with my hands and my tongue.

Nina straightens and pounds her blow job shot. She smiles at me. "See something you like?"

"More than you can imagine. That ass of yours is amazing." I gaze at her up and down. "I'd love to have your vagina."

"What?" Nina asks.

"I'll have the shot you made for me, Satan's vagina." I clarify.

Nina hooks up my shot. I take it to the head and chase it with my beer. "You know...I usually only drink cognac when I gamble, so know that I'm making an exception for you." I wink at her. "Are you ready for the next round of our game?" I ask.

"But, of course!" Nina replies enthusiastically.

The next round Nina plays more aggressively, but still loses. *Forget being a gentleman and allowing her to win, I want her naked!* This time she removes her bra from underneath her shirt. Her nipples instantly peek through. She massages her large breasts over her shirt then takes her second blow job. Knowing her breasts are free makes me crave her even more. Since I can't have her sex, yet...I have Satan's vagina once again. The next round of our poker game, I lose. I remove my t-shirt and remain in my grey sweats and black tank top. I take my shot and surprisingly, Nina takes one also. The next game, Nina goes all in with her chips. She has a full house which is a pretty good hand, except when your opponent has a four of a kind. I win. My horns are now flashing and a lewd expression is clearly written all over my face.

Nina smiles and removes her shirt. She's left wearing just her leopard print satin panties. Her ivory breasts are exquisitely full and silky with bright pink elongated nipples.

Funny...I don't feel a draft. Yes, my baby wants me just as much as I crave her.

Nina maintains eye contact with me as she's about to take her shot. She seductively licks her lips and "accidentally" drops a bit of her drink onto her breasts. She drinks the remaining of the blow job, grabs one of her breasts, and slowly licks it clean. She locks her gaze with mine, inserts her nipple into her mouth then grazes it with her teeth.

Fuck me.

My dick is rock hard at a full salute stance. I need to be in her. Immediately, I stand. "Get up." I command her.

"Yes, sir!" She excitedly replies and does as she's instructed. I bend down slightly, pick her up, and throw her over my shoulder. As I'm headed upstairs to my room, I smack her sweet ass like I've been craving to since the beginning of our game. She squeals when she feels the pressure and sting of my hand on her sensitive skin, then moans, "Oh, do it again, daddy!" So, I smack it again.

As I reach my bedroom, I toss Nina onto my bed. In record time, I remove my clothes and her panties. I spread her legs and position myself right by her entrance ready to savor her slick and sweet sex. First, I rub it with my hand, then I lick, and relish in her taste, slowly I insert two fingers into her hot, wet opening. While I'm stroking her insides with my fingers, I flick my tongue and gently suck her clit. Instantly, Nina starts to whimper as her body tenses up. Soon, I feel a gush of her juice on my fingers and in my mouth. I delight in every drop. I can't contain myself any longer. I back away from her and without warning; I thrust myself deep inside her. I grab both her hands and stretch them above her head. I hungrily devour her mouth as she eagerly responds to my kiss. I keep my hands interlocked with hers and continue to penetrate myself deep inside her tight, welcoming entrance while her legs are possessively wrapped around me. Her body feels like heaven and I can't get enough. I keep on thrusting her deep and hard as she moans and tells me how good my fat dick feels.

I don't want this feeling to end, but I abruptly stop. "I wanna taste you again. Sit on my face." I order. I back away from her and roll onto my back. Nina obligingly follows my command, positions her body above my face, and slowly lowers herself to rest right on my mouth. She holds onto the headboard of the bed, I squeeze her thighs tightly and begin to savor her delicious nectar. After moments of ravenously tasting Nina, I feel her body stiffen as she rejoices in the feel of her second orgasm.

She quickly moves away from me and straddles my dick. "Baby, it's my turn...to ride you nice and hard." She says in between heavy breaths. As she's gripping me with her tight pussy and moving in vertical and circular motions, she's massaging her breasts, twisting, and pinching her nipples. I caress her thighs. The feel of her silky skin adds to the sensation and makes me want to lose control. As she grinds my dick relentlessly over and over again, I let the thrill possess me. Nina's head is leaning back as she moans that she's cuming once again. I join her and release myself inside her.

We remain in that position for a few moments longer, neither one of us wanting to separate. I roll Nina to her side, but still stay inside of her. "Baby, don't think that I forgot about winning. The rules clearly specified the loser has to do whatever the winner demands." Since Nina's head is resting on my chest, I'm able to hide the smirk on my face.

"What exactly is it that you have in mind, Mr. Ryan? Please don't tell me that you're going to run with this?" With the sound of her voice, I can sense her rolling her eyes.

"Well, you did give me a hard time in the beginning." I remind her.

"Spit it out, tree hugger." Nina laughs.

I close my eyes and visualize my request. "What I want is for you to ride me while I'm driving." I say cautiously.

"What? You've got to be kidding me." She responds with a disbelieving tone.

"Nope. Not at all. We can do it any day this week, late at night while there aren't too many cars on the road or highway. You're a smart woman, I'm sure you'll think of a way to fuck me while I drive and still manage to keep us safe." I say matter-of-factly.

Nina raises her head to face me with a stunned look. "You're crazy. You know that, right? But...I'm up for the challenge."

Now, that's my girl! How is it that she always finds a way to surprise me? I'm so glad I didn't ask her to cook for me and instead opted for one of my fantasies. Damn, just thinking about it makes me want to fuck again.

The next morning, I drop Nina off at her place right before I head to the office. It's Saturday, but I have a few things I would like to get resolved before the beginning of the new week. We agree to meet later in the evening and go to a dance club downtown.

As I'm driving to my office, I reflect upon my past choices. I never cared about any of my one night flings and treated women as objects. Before I gave up playing ball, I was young, horny, and chased after every skirt that walked my way. I was having too much fun to give up my freedom for some clingy high school girl. Once I reached the age where I started fucking women, the thought of marriage became repulsive since I valued my free will.

I always ponder on how my mother refused to marry John; she was terrified of such commitment and afraid to lose herself. Years ago, she willingly gave herself to the wrong man, since then, she refused to repeat that mistake. I conveniently clung onto her views. When John passed away and she became ill, her perspective on life and love changed. Since she felt it was too late for her, she was determined to change my views of relationships and marriage. For the past few years, she has been persistent with talking to me about marriage and her fear of leaving me alone in this world. Recently, she's changed her approach and has made being a grandmother her ultimate priority. Whether her grandbabies come out of wedlock or not is the least of her concerns. I love my mom, but have always resented her for making me give up on my life's aspirations. As a result, I have been determined not to fulfill her wishes of seeing me with a family of my own. It's disturbing how I never considered marriage simply to spite my mother even though I love her unconditionally.

With Nina in my life, my negative perception of relation-ships has transformed into something positive. I long to be with her whenever we're apart, she's become my first, and final thought that runs through my mind each day. She truly is an astounding woman. When we're together, I sit and admire her qualities. It's more than just the mind-blowing chemistry between us, it's deeper than that. I can't describe the sensa-tion I experience when I'm with her, but I do know for certain that I don't want to be without her. The empty void I've felt from not having a father and not being able to fulfill my dreams has quickly diminished since the day I met Valentina Moretti.

After a long day at the office, I finally get to spend quality time with my lady. When I arrive at Nina's house, I knock on her door and get greeted by Kade.

"Hey, what's up? Check you out all dark and handsome, yet still managing to appear bad ass at the same time. That combination really suits you." Kade pauses for a moment. "Before you go inside, I'd like to talk to you here, outside if you don't mind."

"What's up?" I ask, curiosity quickly overcoming me.

"If you break my Cheesecake's heart, I'll cut your dick off and make you eat it." Kade's expression is serious, something I'm not used to seeing. *What the fuck?*

"Where did that come from?" I ask, still too stunned to punch his face.

"You seem like a cool guy and all, but I've realized that my Cheesecake has feelings for you. I don't wanna see her get hurt. Let's be real, you and I both know that you fuck girls and leave them. That's fine. I'm definitely no one to judge, but now I see that my girl really likes you and you seem to feel the same towards her. I just don't wanna find out that you're still playing the field." Kade maintains a somber look as he continues making his threats. "You may be bigger, but don't underestimate me. Cheesecake is my family and if you fuck with her, I'll fuckin' come after you and release every demon I have bottled up inside. Trust me, it's a shitload." Kade warns.

"Kade, because I know that your threats are simply to protect Nina, I'll let them slide this time...and this time only. Don't ever come at me sideways again. Next time you make any threats, you'll be seeing my fist pounding your face regardless of your intentions. With that in mind, know that I care for Nina and the last thing I wanna do is hurt her. I'm well aware of all the shit I did in the past. You don't have to remind me. Nina has changed my view of women and relationships. I want to be a better man, someone who is worthy of her company. Don't crucify me for something I haven't done. Nina means a lot and there's nothing more I want than to see her happy and safe." I reply gravely.

"She's my sister, Josh. You can't blame me for having 'the brotherly' talk with you. I'll do anything to protect her." Kade extends his hand as a gesture for a peace offering.

"I respect you for that, Kade." I shake his hand in return.

As I enter the house, Kade offers me a fireball shot. I decline his drink since I'm planning on driving to the club. He insists. He already has the tequila poured into the shot glass, adds tabasco sauce and sambuca then ignites the drink. It's too cool for me to pass up. Immediately, I change my mind and decide to take a taxi to the club so that I can enjoy a night of drinks. I extinguish the fire and down the shot. Kade has one also. After we hit another round of drinks, Nina joins us in the kitchen.

Fuuuuck...

Nina is wearing a sexy, black halter dress. It's knee length, skin tight, and shows off every curve of her silhouette beautifully. Her hair is completely pulled back in a perfect, sleek bun. Her face looks flawless, her full, red lips...luscious. She approaches me since I'm too stunned to move towards her direction. She lightly kisses my lips and tells me that she's missed me.

"I've missed you too, baby. You look gorgeous." I whisper as she's backing away from me.

Slowly, she spins around for me, showing off her dress in its entirety. *She's the epitome of sexy.* Her dress is completely open from the back. How her dress is remaining in place is beyond me. And she's wearing FMSs. I don't think she could possibly look sexier even if she tried.

"Damn, Cheesecake! You're letting the twins hang out freely tonight AND you're going commando?" Kade whistles. "You don't fuck around, do you? For once, I actually like the turd on your head."

Nina starts laughing. "Nope. I sure don't and thanks. I plan on getting real freaky with my man tonight." She smiles and flirtatiously winks at me.

Hell yeah! "Awww baby, you're too good to me." I respond. Nina fills me with so much joy, it's hard to contain. "That's why I lo— care for you so much." I manage to catch myself just in time. I'm not ready to verbalize that sacred phrase. Those three words have so much meaning; I don't understand how people can speak them so freely. As I'm holding in my breath from the shock of my own words, I notice Nina and Kade staring at me stunned with their mouths wide open. Everyone is at a standstill.

"Whaaaaaat? That's one hell of a statement, Josh. Remind me not to give you anymore alcohol. You must be a light weight if it has you speaking prophecies of 'caring.'" Kade says the last word with quote signs.

Nina maintains eye contact with me. "Go away, Kade. Now!"

"Fine. You're lucky I can still hear from the hallway, otherwise I'd be throwing a serious fit." Kade walks away leaving Nina and me staring at each other.

"I care for you, Valentina. In this short period of knowing you, you've grown to mean a lot. Since I met you, you have filled an empty void in my life and made me feel whole once again. I can't get enough of your touch. You're more than I could have expected from an ideal woman. You complete me." I confess.

Nina closes the gap between us and kisses me gently on the side of my mouth. "You give me a sense of comfort and trust that I now revel in. You're an amazing man who has sacrificed so much. When I'm in your arms, I feel cherished and protected. I've told you of my past which I've never spoken of to anyone else. You've made me see myself in a new light." Nina pauses, backs away and slowly raises her head making eye contact with me once again. "What I'm trying to say is that...I care for you too, Josh."

Such words have never sounded so sweet and tender. Nina makes my heart melt, yet fills my being with lust and excitement. I take her in a tight embrace and kiss her hungrily. She responds to my kiss with the same passion.

Slowly, Nina moves away from me. "Mmmm...babe, let's forget about going to the club. I'd rather go back to your place and show you how good you make me feel." Nina caresses my dick with a huge grin planted on her beautiful face.

Kade interrupts our intimate moment. "Oh, hell no! I know you're not flaking on me just because you two are a bunch of horny asses. I'm dressed, looking mighty fine, and ready to party the night off. Em will be waiting for us there and so will some of my friends. If you're not there, she'll hang with me. I don't need her cock blocking me tonight. So, I suggest you put your raging hormones on hold and release them later on tonight."

Kade is serious, but slowly smiles and walks over to us to enfold us in a group hug. "I'm so happy you two found each other. You truly make a beautiful couple, but I'm still not letting you off the hook. You're both coming tonight and dancing your asses off! I'm gonna make some drinks to get us all in the partying spirit."

Kade stays back waiting for his friends to pick him up. After a few drinks, we're feeling the buzz and can't wait to head over to the club, so we take a taxi. While we're in the cab, I look over at Nina and remember she's not wearing any panties. Right away, I want to bury my face between her legs. She gives me a knowing look and smiles. I notice that we're close to arriving at the club, I get as near to Nina as possible and slide my hand up her dress. She gives me a wary look, but doesn't stop me. The driver is focused on the road and can't see what I'm doing from behind. Nina instinctively opens her legs, welcoming me inside. I play with her entrance, make her wet, and insert my two fingers inside her hot, tight sex. I stroke her several times and feel her body tense up. She fights herself to contain a moan from escaping her. Moments later, I feel her juice as her orgasm clenches me. Slowly, I remove my fingers and place them in my mouth to savor. "Damn, baby...you have such a sweet pussy. I can't wait to tear you up tonight." I whisper in her ear.

Nina roughly massages my dick to let me know she's just as anxious. We get dropped off at the club; I walk up to the front of the line and meet the bouncer, who's an old acquaintance since high school at the door. He waves us in and allows us to enter. I thank him and place a bill in his palm as I shake his hand. We walk in; I take Nina's coat along with mine and check them in at the coat check. We stroll deeper into the dance club holding hands with me leading the way.

The main dance floor consists of house and techno music combined with radio songs. The place is dark with strobe lights flickering among the packed crowd. I stop at the first bar we encounter and get Nina and me two double shots of Patrón along with two beers. After we pound our shots, we take our beers, and search for Emme. Right before we arrived, she sent Nina a text stating she was already here. As we're walking through the crowd, I notice a Latin room to my right with red and gold lights. The dj is playing a mix of merengue and reggaeton for the crammed dance floor. I make a mental note to come back here later tonight. We go upstairs with Nina leading the way. Her bare skin feels like silk as I place my hand at the small of her back. I guide her through the second level to reach the V.I.P. lounge. I speak with the bouncer, inform him of everyone who will be joining us, and hand him a tip. The dance floor has a blue light setting; everyone here is swaying to the song, "Swimming Pools (Drank)" by Kendrick Lamar. Nina takes a seat in one of the half circular booths and sends everyone a text of our location. Moments later, Emme joins us at our table and asks Nina to accompany her to the restroom. The girls leave. I use this time to walk over to the bar to place an order for more drinks. As I'm waiting for the drinks, Nina comes from behind me and covers my eyes. I place my hands over hers still maintaining my eyes closed as I turn around. Instantly, I feel her lips pressing hard against mine. I open my mouth and welcome her tongue. I remove my hands from hers while she's still covering my eyes and place both hands on her firm, round ass. Her kiss feels rough and desperate. Soon, she removes her hands from my eyes and places them around my neck. I open my eyes and to my surprise realize I'm kissing Nicole. I'm dumbfounded and alarm rapidly sets in. But, it's too late, as I look past Nicole, I notice Nina's shocked and hurt expression.

Chapter 7 (Nina)

Drunk Ass

That mother fucker! I can't believe he's swapping spit with that dirty cunt! Fuck him! I urgently walk away leaving him with that piece of shit waitress to do as they wish. I'm beyond livid. I can literally feel my blood boiling. As I'm exiting the V.I.P. lounge, I feel someone yank my arm.

"Baby, let me explain. It's not what you think." Josh attempts to justify the scandalous scene I just witnessed.

"Don't call me 'baby' you lyin' ass, punk bitch! Don't fuckin' touch me ever again! Go swap spit with that loose whore! Leave me the fuck alone!" I yell in his face and manage to say all in one breath.

"Shut the fuck up for one second! I don't blame you for being upset, just let me fuckin' explain!" He grabs me, willing me to listen.

His touch repulses me and riles up violence I didn't know I had. The hell with a slap on the face, I want to hurt him. So, I attempt to swing at him. Josh's reflexes are quick and grips me in a bear hold pinning my arms to my side. Somehow, I manage to lower my body and take off my right heel while Josh is still holding me tight.

"Let me go!" I demand.

"Promise you'll stop swinging at me and hear me out!" He orders.

"Yes." I lie.

As soon as I feel him releasing his hold on me, with all my might, I hit Josh with my five inch stiletto heel on top of the right side of his head. Immediately, blood begins to gush down his face. He releases his hold on me and grabs my wrists in an effort to stop me from hitting him again. The strong pressure he has on my wrists makes me drop my shoe. When I turn my focus on my stiletto heel, I realize that everyone in the lounge is staring at us. *Great.*

"What the fuck is wrong with you? I didn't kiss that fuckin' hoe! She kissed me! Don't get all psycho on me without having your damn facts straight!" He squeezes my wrists and clenches his jaw. Even then, I observe he's holding back and doing his best to maintain his composure, but nonetheless, he's hurting me and he's pissed.

But...so am I! Fuck him and his lies.

Emme quickly intervenes as a bouncer is following behind her and tries to be the voice of reason. "Josh, let her go. You two have been drinking and are making stupid decisions. You can both talk about this situation tomorrow or another day once you've calmed down and have had time to think things through."

Josh hesitantly lets me go and instantly, I rush out. I can't believe I allowed myself to be a part of a dramatic outburst for the amusement of bystanders. I hate drama and usually avoid it at all costs. It's pretty pathetic if you ask me, yet here I am being no better. I feel myself suffocating in the crowded dance scene. My body feels sticky from sweat. My mind is congested with bad thoughts of Josh and the dirty waitress. I need fresh air for clarity.

As I'm exiting the club, Kade is walking in. One look at me and right away he knows something's wrong. He says goodbye to his friends, leads me outside, and waves a cab down. The cool, crisp air feels like heaven against my senses. Instantaneously, I stop being mad at Josh and turn the anger onto myself.

I know better than to trust or believe in strangers. I fell for his lies and wished them to be true when he spoke of his feelings for me. I allowed him past my guard. I've resorted to violence out of hurt and anger. I should've walked away. To top things off, I've made a fool of myself from the disturbing spectacle I displayed in front of several people. I'm disgusted with my behavior.

During the cab ride home, Kade and I remain silent. When we enter our home, we both sit on the floor by the coffee table in the living room. Kade patiently waits for me to speak. I can't get the words out. I feel emotionally drained.

"Do you want me to make you a drink? Or does this occasion require ice cream instead?" Kade asks cautiously.

"A drink. A really strong one." I emphasize.

"Okay. Put on your pjs first and we'll get shit faced drunk together as you tell me what the hell happened tonight." Kade gets up and walks over to the kitchen to play the role of a bartender.

I change into comfy clothes and check my phone before I begin my night of drunkenness. Fourteen missed calls, two from Emme and the rest from him. My violent actions tonight originated from his betrayal. That doesn't justify my behavior. How I handled the situation was wrong, it felt good at the moment, but regardless, it was still a mistake. My pride is hurt, but I still contemplate on texting him an apology. As I'm holding my phone, Emme calls to inform me she's right outside. She thought I wouldn't open the door, afraid I would think it was Josh. Hearing his name mentioned, sends me in a frenzy again. Instantly, I decide not to apologize for my actions. *Fuck his cheating ass.*

Emme walks into the house completely dramatic. "Hey, you'll never guess what happened seconds after you left! Shit hit the fan! Josh and the bouncer got into a fight! When you left, Josh was gonna come after you, but the bouncer stopped him. So, Josh threw the first hit and soon they were both throwing blows. Well, Josh knocked his ass out and took off. Man, he was pissed! I'd hate to be the poor soul who crosses him right now."

"Not my problem. That's on him." I state indifferently.

Emme settles in and the three of us begin drinking. I tell Kade my animated version of tonight's events. I make Kade and Emme promise they won't allow Josh to enter the house for any reason. I make it clear that Josh is no longer welcome in my home. They both agree.

Just then, a violent pounding on the front door startles me and makes me spill my drink on the floor.

"Open the fuckin' door, Nina! I didn't do shit! It's not my fault that bitch is thirsty and won't get off my nutsack! Open the damn door and let me explain what you saw!" Josh continues beating the door forcefully waiting for my response.

I'm shocked. I wasn't expecting him to come here. I notice Kade get up and head towards the door completely agitated himself. "Fuck that shit! I know he's not getting all psycho on you!" I grab Kade's arm and stop him from opening the door. I pull him back into the living room.

"Please don't open the door. We've all been drinking and the last thing I need is for you and Josh to get into a fight. Let him be." I plead.

"Cheesecake, I can't let him intimidate you!" Kade argues with a flabbergasted expression.

Emme interrupts, "Don't worry, I just called the cops. He scared the shit out of me! He won't be out there for long." She states with a smirk on her face.

"What the fuck? Why did you call the cops, Emme?" I'm too buzzed to understand my emotions. Part of me wants to get him back for hurting me, but my rational side understands that what he did isn't cause for him to be arrested.

"Please just go away, Josh! Just go!" I beg.

"Fuck that! Not until you hear me out! Open the damn door!" He demands. His voice sounds menacingly deep and husky. Instantly, it runs chills throughout my body.

Minutes later, Josh yells, "I can't believe you called the fuckin' cops! Are you serious? That's bullshit!" Within seconds, I hear him arguing with the two officers who responded to Emme's call.

I can't handle the situation and escape to my room turning on the music loud enough to drain out any thoughts of Josh. Within a short timeframe, Kade enters my room. "The police took him, boo. He got aggressive on their asses. Do you want me to make you another drink?"

I feel my heart ache and my chest tighten. "Yes, please."

As the night progresses, we're all wasted in the living room. We begin adding different Spotify and Pandora radio stations on Kade's phone and attach it to the stereo that's hooked up to our surround sound. Kade hides my phone afraid that I'll drunk dial Josh or the police to find out Josh's whereabouts.

While I'm lying on the floor, "Be Without You" by Mary J. Blige comes on. *Oh, hell no!* I love me some Mary J., but there's no way I can handle this song right now. Next. The song, "I Need Your Lovin'" by Teena Marie begins to play, so I crank up the volume and start to sing along. *Why? Because apparently, I have some masochistic tendencies while I'm drunk and heartbroken. At least, this old school song has a cool and fast beat.*

I begin to sing. *"Love's fever comin' on strong...I don't want the fire without the flame no..."* I stop singing the disturbing lyrics. I face the stereo and warn Teena. "Fire? Girl, you'll get burned! Fuck that." *Girl power!*

I continue to sing. *"Ask me what I need...I need your lovin'...And that's the bottom line...I need your lovin' or...Just a little time, this will do..."* I stop singing.

"I don't need shit, Teena! (hicc-up) Especially his fuckin' (hicc-up) love! Screw him! I'm better off!" I yell out. I don't understand why Teena's trippin'. She's clearly sending me the wrong message.

I disregard the negativity and continue projecting my wonderful vocal skills. *"Love's comin', so glad you're mine...I don't want your rhythm (hicc-up) without your rhyme, no..."*

"Shut your face, Teena! Whatever happened to girl power? I've had enough (hicc-up) of you. I'm stitching the station. See, Teena...I can't even talk straight. I'm speaking crooked because of you, girl. Ugh..." And then I pass out in the living room drunk off my ass.

Vaguely, I think I hear Kade say, "Oh, for the love of all that's sacred, shut the hell up! If birds were flying around, they would be dropping dead from your horrible singing! Lady T doesn't deserve her song being massacred."

I'm sure I'm dreaming because I know I can sing.

I wake up the next morning with a vicious hangover. I can usually hang with liquor, but yesterday, I mixed my drinks which ended up in disaster for me. Too soon, I recall last night's heartbreaking and embarrassing moments, Josh sucking face with the cheap waitress, me hitting him with the spiked heel of my shoe causing him to bleed profusely, and him getting arrested. Emme and Kade are still asleep. I search for my phone and find it on top of Kade's nightstand. I check to see if I have any more missed calls. None.

Part of me is glad, I don't want to talk or think about Josh even though guilt is surprisingly consuming me. The other side is disappointed that he isn't attempting to explain his actions. I know he can't still be in jail, he has money and I'm sure he's already been released. Who am I kidding? There's nothing to clarify. He was all over her! He was holding onto her tight and was rubbing her ass as if there were a genie inside who was about to grant him three wishes!

Let it go, Nina. Just let him go.

When I return to the living room, Kade is awake and heading to the kitchen to prepare some coffee.

"Hey, Cheesecake. How do you feel?" He asks with concern deep in his features.

"Like shit. Sorry you missed going out last night and dealt with my drama instead." I feel it's necessary to apologize for my foolish behavior.

"You should be apologizing for your singing. It's dreadful!" He laughs.

"What? You're crazy! I sing all the time." I'm offended. Clearly, he's grouchy because he hasn't had his cup of mojo this morning.

"Just because you do it all the time doesn't mean you're any good. Next time you sing, you need to focus on all the mirrors shattering around you. That's not a coincidence." He chuckles.

I give Kade the evil eye. "You're such an ass. But regardless, I don't care. I'm going to keep singing whether you like it or not. At least, I'm not completely clueless and sign up to audition for *American Idol*. I feel sorry for the ones who truly believe they can sing and sound like donkeys, poor things."

"I would never let you go on *American Idol*. You're my best friend and if you look bad, then I do too. And we can't have that! I have a reputation to uphold!" He's so silly.

I sigh. "I love how you turn everything about you."

"Thank you. It's a gift. Now, let's get down to the nitty gritty. What are you gonna do about Josh?" Ugh. It's the last question I want to hear, especially from my bestie.

"There's nothing to do. He played me, I'm done with him, and I'm pretty sure he's finished with me too. Hello? He was practically fucking a girl right in front of me and I busted his head open. I'm pretty sure those two things justify our breakup." I remind him.

Kade gives me a look of pity. "You know that I'll always be on your side no matter how psycho and wrong you can be, but I do think you and Josh should talk things out first. Something doesn't seem right. I feel like he really likes you and wouldn't do something to sabotage your relationship, let alone right in front of you. He was pissed as fuck last night, I don't think he would've been so adamant about explaining himself if he didn't care. If you still feel like he belongs in hell after you speak with him, than you and I can go to a gay bar and write his name and number indicating he's ready for a good time all over the men's bathroom. Does that sound like a plan?"

"Awww you're so sweet. I love it when you have your thinking cap on. Still not sure about talking to him, we'll see." I say in deep thought.

The rest of the day is uneventful. I lounge in my pjs and substitute two of my meals with two Ben & Jerry's ice cream pints, Phish Food and Chunky Monkey. Along with my frozen treats, I also eat three cannoli, two biscotti, half a pan of brownies, a large bag of Takis chips, and wash my food down with a large diet Coke because I'm on a diet and don't need the extra calories. Kade gets sick of seeing me moping around and forces me to release my negativity onto Lucifer by running at least five miles. I surprise myself and run seven and a half. I feel slightly better and prepare for the work week ahead.

My Monday morning is off to a bad start. I'm running late, don't have breakfast or time to gather up snacks. Work is extremely busy and chaotic, more than usual. Today, my voicemail box is maxed out with solely victims' calls. By lunchtime, I'm mentally drained after speaking to the victims or the parents and discussing their cases.

As I'm headed to the vending machine for a quick snack, Chris, a young attorney invites me to lunch. I'm so hungry, I agree without giving it a second thought. In the past, he's asked me out a few times, but I've repetitiously declined his requests. I simply refuse to date someone from work, it complicates things. Today, I just need a distraction. It's not a big deal, just lunch with a coworker. Besides, he's pretty easy on the eyes with his bright blues and flawless, tan skin. He's tall, handsome, and clean cut. Usually, I don't like attorneys since sometimes they come across as super dull and geeky or even worse, arrogant and full of shit. But this guy seems nice enough for me to spend the next hour with.

We walk across the street to a Greek restaurant. During lunch hour, the place is packed. I order a Mediterranean salad; guilt still overwhelms me from recent poor food choices. Having special treats on occasion is fine, but everything I ate yesterday combined was full blown madness. I'm enjoying my salad and company with Chris. He's venting about the two cases he just received. Both are about single women who allowed strange men into their homes and as a result, their kids were molested. A single mom has every right to continue living her life. The issue is that the women in our caseloads brought in any Tom, Dick, or Harry into their house, completely disregarding the security of their family. Then, they have the audacity to act shocked once they find out these strangers they've been with for a short period are only with them to prey upon their children. We also discuss a specific case where the man molested his child and the wife's sole concern was her husband and his freedom. She didn't care that her own flesh was the victim; her main concern was finding ways to free her husband. It's a sad, disturbing, and infuriating case. We rant about the justice system and the politics behind it. We're both deep in conversation when I hear, "Valentina."

I almost choke on my food when I hear the sound of his voice.

"Who's this?" Josh directs the question at me as he points to Chris. *Oh, my goodness. I'm so not in the mood for this right now.*

"Josh, this is a coworker, but that's none of your concern. Please leave." I beg. The last thing I need is a dramatic spectacle like the one that occurred this weekend.

"Get up." Josh commands sternly. "We need to talk."

As I'm sitting, looking up at Josh, I feel intimidated. He looks enraged in his tall and manly stance. His deep voice makes my body shiver. Immediately, I sense my nipples harden as they long to be in his mouth. *What the fuck, Nina! Focus! He's not your man anymore and he's going to cause a scene!*

"We were just about to leave and go back to work. My lunch break is over. Our talk will have to wait." I do my best to hold my ground.

"You can be a few minutes late. We need to talk. Now." He reiterates with an agitated expression. I notice he's taking deep breaths and is trying to calm down, but is failing miserably. *Is that steam coming out of his ears?*

Chris intervenes. "Clearly, you didn't hear the lady. She's going back to work and doesn't want to speak with you."

Oh, shit.

Josh faces Chris and lowers his body, positioning himself slightly above Chris. "I heard MY lady just fine. I suggest—"

I cut Josh off and grab him by his arm. "Come on, let's go. Sorry, Chris. I'll see you in the office later."

Josh slowly backs away from Chris, but maintains eye contact with him. I attempt to lead Josh out of the restaurant with as much force as possible, yet still remain inconspicuous. I feel so embarrassed with Chris. Once we step outside, I do my best to remain focused and not allow Josh to manipulate the conversation, but I feel so small compared to him as he hovers over me. I disregard the feeling and use all my pent-up anger to glare at him.

"I don't have time to play your little games, Josh. I have to go back to work. I would never go to your office and behave the way you just did right now. It's pretty psycho of you and you're behaving like a stalker. To be honest, it doesn't suit you." I'm afraid to give in to him, so I do my best to push him away and keep our conversation short.

Josh gives me an evil laugh. "I'll admit to the stalker part, but psycho? You busted my head open and called the cops on me! That's some fucked up shit! That pretty much qualifies you for psycho of the year if you ask me."

"Well, I didn't. Now, leave. I have to go back to work." I'm getting restless now.

"We need to talk about what happened this weekend. Also, I don't want you hanging around that guy." His stare is uncompromising.

"Are you fuckin' serious? Are you aware that you were practically jumping that dirty whore's bones right in front of me? You have absolutely no say in anything pertaining to my life. I don't give a fuck if you don't want me hanging around him. I didn't care for you being with that cheap slut, yet that didn't stop you. I suggest you check yourself before you start making demands from me." Now, I'm furious.

"Damn you, woman! Nicole is a dirty hoe. You can't penalize me for her actions. Can you please just fuckin' talk to me and let me explain without getting yourself worked up?" Josh runs his fingers through his hair and clenches his jaw; he tries to remain calm, but fails.

"I'm not ready. Give me a few days and then maybe we can discuss things like mature adults. Right now, I'm not there yet. Please leave and give me time." I don't know what else to say. I have an array of mixed emotions.

"Fine. I'll be waiting for you. Even though you're psycho, I still miss you." Josh tells me as he tries to get close to me.

"Don't." I reply.

Chapter 8 (Nina)

Gifts

When I arrive home, I inform Kade of my latest drama. He insists that I communicate with Josh as soon as possible to clear the air between us. I'm simply not ready for such a confrontation. I decide to put the situation in the back of my mind and not dwell on it. It's definitely easier said than done.

A few days pass, now it's Friday, the end of the work week. I meet with Emme for lunch. I inform her that I've finally built the courage to speak with Josh. We agree that I should surprise him and show up at his house after work unexpectedly. He has a set routine for himself. On Fridays, he usually leaves his office early to hang out at the gym for a long workout. By the time I get off work, he should be home. I thank Emme for hearing me out and putting up with me. I love her.

I reach Josh's house and notice that his truck is parked in his driveway. The gate is open, so I'm able to walk into the premises and ring the doorbell even though I know he has a key above one of the light sconces by his door. I ring the buzzer again. Still no response, but decide to wait a bit longer.

Right as I'm about to leave, the door opens. Instantly, I feel my stomach turn and vile liquid rise up my throat when I see a half-naked woman answer the door. Nicole. *The whore.*

"Yes? Can I help you?" She asks with a devious leer. She's hiding most of her body behind the door, but I can clearly see her open shirt displaying her bra and bite marks throughout her breasts. Her hair looks disheveled and her breathing is at a rapid pace.

I'm too stunned to move or speak. Eventually, I manage to lace my words with venom and say, "You dirty cunt. I hope that when you kissed him, you were able to taste my pussy's juice all over his mouth and dick."

I know I'm being vulgar, but I don't give a fuck. I know I should be classy and not sink to her level, but all I see is red. I can't comprehend rationality at this point. I want to smash her face in with my foot, but I won't. I refuse to give Josh the satisfaction of seeing me fight over him like some fuckin' dog.

"Is that why he tastes so damn good?" Nicole has the audacity to ask, striking me back with her own poisonous words.

I can't believe this conniving bitch just said that! Walk away, Nina. Just walk away.

"I see you finally sank your claws into him. Well, you can have him." I state as I turn my back to leave. Just then, I hear a noise behind her, I notice Josh wet and naked with just a towel wrapped around his waist.

"Nina!" He yells.

Seeing them next to each other shatters my heart and spirit. It's over. I wasted my feelings, trust, and hope on the wrong person. *Let him go, Nina. He's not worth another second of your time.*

"Don't come after me ever again, Josh. I'm done. You and this dirty slut belong together." I feel my eyes burn as they swell up with tears, but I'm determined not to shed them, especially in front of Josh and his whore.

I walk away as fast as I can until I reach my car.

"Nina! Wait! I can explain!" Josh tries to chase after me, but I'm already in the car.

"Fuck you and your explanation!" I yell out as I drive away.

The hurt from seeing them together is overwhelming, but now I have another reality to deal with first. I'm terrified of driving down this hill, usually with Josh by my side, I feel safe and conquer my fears. But now, that anxiety is at a full force. I refuse to let him hinder my progress. I don't need him; I can do this by myself. With determination and all my will power, I slowly drive down the hill. Once I reach level ground, I take off as if my ass were on fire.

Within moments, my cellphone goes off continuously, missed calls and text messages all from him. I pull over and disregard his messages. Instead, I send him one of my own demanding that he doesn't bother me again since he has hurt me deeply enough.

I head home and drown myself in sorrow and regret, the song, "Rehab" from Rihanna comes to mind. I'm hurt by him and disappointed in myself. I'm not sure which feeling bothers me most. I trusted him and believed his words when he stated he would never hurt me. I knew better than to open myself to him so easily, yet I did. I recognize I should have kept my guard up and not made myself so vulnerable. Lesson learned.

A few weeks have passed by with no word from Josh. I've been in a melancholy state since I saw HIM with HER. I've canceled two photo shoots since then. I just haven't been up to getting dolled up and being under scrutiny for several hours. I usually conduct myself in a professional manner, but lately, my heart just hasn't been in my work.

It's the weekend before Christmas, I decide to do some final shopping and stop by my mom's shop for some baked goods before Kade and I head home. My mom is at the register closing up today's sales. I see the back of a tall, muscular man in a black baseball hat wearing a grey tank top right behind her working on the trim of the doorway to the kitchen. His broad shoulders and cut up arms are well defined as he works. It takes me a moment to register that this man has a tattoo taking up his right shoulder and backside. It's not just any tattoo, it's the back of a tattoo I've kissed and caressed with my tongue countless times.

My mom looks up and has a shocked expression on her face. "Nina! Kade! Hey, loves. What brings you by?" She asks with guilt consuming her delicate features.

At the sound of our names, the man working on my mom's shop turns around and faces me.

Seeing Josh after so many weeks takes me by surprise. First of all, he looks hot as hell. His tank top shows off his muscular upper body. He's wearing loose fitted Levi jeans, he's slightly sweaty, and now his stubble is more evident along his jawline. He looks rugged and absolutely sexy. There's something extremely appealing about a man who's isn't afraid to get down and dirty while he's working. It takes all my willpower not to throw myself on top of him. Then, it hits me. What the fuck is Joshua Ryan doing at my mom's bakery? I can see that he's working, but why him? After the shock begins to fade, I direct my scowl at Victoria Moretti. I'm so pissed, I can't even speak. I walk away and drag Kade with me.

"Wait!" My mom yells.

She chases after us and catches up to me right before I get

in my car. "Nina, stop acting like such a child. You need to speak to the poor kid."

"Why the hell is he working in your bakery, mom?" I'm fuming!

Nervously, she responds, "He comes over all the time. He has a serious sweet tooth. He's depressed over you, Nina. One day, he suggested that I expand the doorway to the kitchen and make other changes behind the register. He stated that he would do it for free on the weekends as long as I fed him Italian dishes and pastries. How could I pass that up? We've had long talks about you and the reason you two are no longer together. You should really talk to him, Nina."

I'm beyond shocked with her words. "My own mother on the side of the enemy?"

My mom laughs. "Calm down, drama child." She gets serious. "He's a good man who has made several mistakes, but has real feelings for you."

"I don't wanna hear it, mom. I can't believe you're siding with him! Let me know when he's done with this project and it's safe for me to get some pastries." I tell her with annoyance clear in my voice.

Kade intervenes. "Cheesecake, I think you're being rude. Sorry, Mama V. You know how stubborn your child can be. I would hate to leave all those baked goods to get stale. I wouldn't mind taking them off your hands."

"Kade!" I yell and give him a disbelieving look.

"What? I've been craving cannoli all day. If you wanna starve, that's on you." He says insensitively.

Just then, Josh approaches us. "I can't believe you're throwing a tantrum on my account. Grow up. I'm helping your mom. This isn't about you. If my presence bothers you so much, ignore me." Josh's aggravated expression and indifference has me bewildered. *Why the hell is he upset with me?*

Josh directs his attention to my mom. "I'll be back shortly to finish up." He walks away without giving me a second glance.

"Wait here. I'll be right back with a box of your favorites." My mom kisses Kade on the cheek and gives me a stern expression. *Is she serious? Whose team is she on anyway?*

She returns with a box of baked goods for the both of us. I'm so pissed; I know those treats won't make it to the house. I'll be shoving them down my throat, eating away my feelings. If Kade even thinks about saying one inappropriate comment, I'm punking him for his cannoli.

On the ride back home, he's quite as he devours his sinful dessert that he allows himself once a week.

Christmas finally arrives. In the morning, Kade, my mom, and I eat our customary holiday breakfast consisting of eggs, waffles, bacon, hash browns, toast, and a fruit salad. *Yum!* We wait for Emme to arrive so that we can open our gifts. She usually celebrates Christmas Eve with her family and opens presents at midnight. On Christmas day, she spends it with us. When she finally arrives, we're anxious to unveil our gifts. As the years have progressed, we've made rules to our gift exchange. We each give five presents to each individual. One present is a nice gift not to exceed fifty dollars, three presents can only cost ten bucks per item, and the final gift has to be sexual in nature with no dollar limit. Seeing my mom open up the sex toys she gets for Christmas always has Emme, Kade, and me dying from laughter. It never fails, it's the highlight of the year.

After we exchange the typical Christmas gifts perfume, clothes, gift cards, and cool trinkets, it's finally time to open up the sexy (in Kade's case...raunchy) goodies. My mom wants to hand out her gifts first. She still feels a bit uncomfortable about purchasing sex toys for her "kids," so she maintains the sexiness level to a minimum. Emme and I get two pretty satin and lace nighties. Kade gets silk boxers with the initials KD on them. Right away, Kade, Emme, and I start giggling. My mom isn't aware that Kade's alter ego (yes, he has one) is KD, which represents "Killer Dick," not Kade Daly, like my mom meant for it to stand. She's completely out of the loop. Kade turns to my mom and gives her a big hug and kiss on the cheek.

"Mama V, you will never know how inappropriate the gift you just gave me is." He says while he's laughing. "It's by far, one of my favorite presents ever!"

My mom slaps Kade's leg. "Ugh! You kids and your perverted inside jokes." She does her best to contain a smile, but fails. That just makes us laugh harder.

She continues handing us the last of her gifts, edible massage oils. Okay, at least she tried. Emme's next. She gives my mom her elegantly, decorated present, a three DVD set of variety porn with several hours of fucking.

"Victoria, I don't really know what you're into, so I decided to give you a sample of everything." Emme smiles warmly at my mom as if she just gave her a scarf for Christmas instead of movies with the covers of open vaginas on them.

"That was very sweet of you, Emme. Thank you." My mom replies. Kade and I can't help but chuckle. She's my mom, not only is it slightly awkward, it's hilarious too.

Emme hands Kade his gift. It's a spanking paddle with the word "SLUT" cut out of it. Without hesitation, I notice Kade's expression change.

"Mom, cover your ears!" I order. In the past, she's asked us to tell her when to wear her "earmuffs," the last thing she wants to hear is something that will completely traumatize her.

Kade can't keep his eyes off Emme. "Well, well...I see you've been a naughty girl and need to get spanked. You want me to mark that sweet ass of yours, you dirty slut? Tell me and beg for it." The look he gives Emme is lasciviously sinful.

"You two stop it! I can't believe you're thinking about fucking during a family event! Get your heads out of the gutter! Emme, I can't comprehend why you would set yourself up like that. You know if you two fuck again, he's going to run his mouth." I remind her.

"I couldn't help myself. I've been horny lately." She confesses shyly.

"That's okay, boo. Daddy will be sure to smack that ass nice and hard the next time I get a chance." Kade winks at Emme.

"Ewww. Stop that. You two are too much. Behave!" There's no way I could maintain being serious. "Okay, mom! Earmuffs off."

"Sorry." Both Kade and Emme apologize without the slightest bit of regret and with smirks on their faces.

"Oh, forget about it." My mom replies with her Italian twang that slips out every once in a while. "I swear...there's never a dull moment with you three around." She says with an exasperated tone.

It's my turn to open Emme's gift. It's a clear glass dildo with a red wavy design inside, it's really pretty. "Awww...thanks, hun. I love it! You so know me." I give her a hug.

I get up and distribute my gifts. I give each of them a trilogy book set, it's time they get to know all about "Mr. Fifty Shades of Fucked Up," they may not appreciate the books now, but they'll definitely thank me later. Since they're the only people on this planet who haven't read this series, I chose to buy it for them. I make them promise to give the books a chance. They do and that's good enough for me.

Kade is more than anxious to give us his presents. He hands us gift bags filled with "goodies." I take the first item out, a set of Ben Wa balls with a cheetah print design on them. "Cool! Thanks, but I thought they were supposed to be silver?"

"The lady at the store recommends that you start off with the bigger ones first, the ones the size of quarters. Then you can work your way down to the smaller, heavier silver balls that are the size of pennies. See...I listen to you." Kade says with a thoughtful expression as if we're discussing a heartfelt topic.

"Awesome." I look at my new toy with wonder.

The next gift is a small tube, China Shrink Cream. It's a vaginal muscle tightening cream. It takes me a moment for it to register. Then I become distracted from Kade's laughter.

"It's cream to make your coochie nice and tight!" Now, Kade's laughing so hard, he's holding onto his stomach and has tears.

"Hey! What are you trying to say? I've never had any complaints! How would you know if I need this cream?" I'm appalled.

"I don't know if you need it, but it's the best ten bucks I've spent. The expression on your face is priceless! Don't worry ladies, I bought you all the same things I got my Cheesecake. And before you start talking shit, Em, know that I bought the cream before you and I did the wild monkey dance. So, please don't get offended." Now, Kade is taking deep breaths doing his best to be serious. He fails miserably.

My mom glares at him. "Little boy, I swear. How is it that after all these years, you still manage to shock me?"

"He's a pervert, Victoria! I don't know why I even feel surprised anymore when it comes to him." Emme adds.

"Let me finish digging into my bag of goodies." I interrupt. The rest of the gifts are nipple clamps, flavored lubricants, and playing cards with sexual positions on them.

"I swear, you can be such an ass sometimes, but even your cream joke shows me how much you think of us. I love you, Kade. You're the bestest bestie ever!" I throw myself on top of him and give him a big hug. I walk over and sit between my mom and Emme, putting my arms around them. "Mom, Emme you two ladies rock and I'll love you always. Thanks everyone for the gifts. How does a movie marathon sound?"

"It sounds lovely, sweetie. But, ummm...you still have one last gift." My mom looks nervous.

"From you?" I ask with confusion clear in my voice.

"No. It's from Josh, but it's technically not for you since he knew you wouldn't accept anything from him. It's for Betty. I told him not to go overboard because I knew you wouldn't take it if that were the case."

"Oh." My feelings are in turmoil just from the sound of his name. I can't allow him to have such an effect on me. "Well, if it's for my car then let me see what it is before I decide whether or not I should keep it." I open up the small gift box. I pull out a bead chain with two silver dog tags surrounded by tiny diamonds. One of the tags has a picture of Betty Boop and the other has one of Betty Page lightly engraved. I love the thoughtful gift. Because it's the Bettys, I decide not to return his present.

"Josh thought you could put the chain around your rear view mirror." Mom says quietly.

"Tell him I love it and that I'll accessorize Betty with his gift." Is all I can say past the lump in my throat.

I lie to everyone and tell them I'm craving candy to go along with the movies we'll be watching all day. They remind me it's Christmas and most stores are closed. It doesn't matter, I grab my jacket and head out in a t-shirt and pj bottoms. I've done one hell of a job containing the hurt I feel, but Josh's gift was the last straw that might send me into crying hysterics. Rapidly, I fight back my waterworks. I refuse to shed a tear over him. Instead, I place the beaded chain with the dog tags around my rear view mirror, crank up the song, "Black Betty" by Ram Jam and put it on replay. I repudiate my weakness and go for a drive. As I'm behind the wheel, I wonder which direction I should head towards, the Golden Gate or the Bay Bridge. Hmm...

CHAPTER 9 (NINA)

DRIVING

Almost two hours later, I return home with a clear mind. I don't want to be a girl who dwells in misery. I take pride in not throwing a pity party for myself. Instead, I was able to conjure up a perfect distraction. When I plop myself on the couch, everyone turns to stare at me.

"Where's the candy?" Kade asks slyly.

"I had to go for a drive. I feel much better now that I came up with the best solution to uplift my melancholy state." I admit.

"So, what did you come up with? Strippers always make me happy." Kade states nonchalantly.

"Vegas for New Year's Eve! Who's down?" I ask even though I already know the answer.

"Hell yeah! Cheesecake, you know I'm game! Time to act a fool!" Kade is beyond enthusiastic, gets up, and starts to do a little dance for us.

"I'm down, Nina. I've never been there." Emme confesses.

We all turn to look at Emme with bewildered expressions on our faces. "You're a Vegas Virgin?" I ask completely shocked.

"How is it that I didn't know this? Oh my goodness, I'm such a shitty friend. If I had known, I would've taken you a long time ago! Honey, we're gonna hit it up big!" I'm determined to make Emme's first time in Sin City wickedly fabulous and full of corruption.

"Okay, kids. Behave yourselves, don't go accepting drinks from strangers and be careful. Make sure you stay together. There are too many sickos out in the world. I can't believe they have date rape drugs. Some people's thoughts can be so sickening." My mom interjects. We try to convince her to go with us, but she refuses. She's a homebody and prefers it that way.

"We're gonna pop Em's cherry! Can't wait!" Kade says with an evil grin.

The past few days had me looking forward to our mini vacation. It's finally Saturday night and I'm packing for our road trip tomorrow that begins at dawn. Surprisingly, my phone has been going off all day with missed calls from Josh along with voicemails and text messages that I quickly delete. It's been weeks since we last spoke. I miss him. I miss his lips and his touch, but I can't allow myself to think of him. I'm not about to let Josh ruin my sinful getaway which is just what the doctor ordered.

Initially, we made plans to fly out Friday morning and sight see before the big New Year's Eve celebration that takes up the whole Vegas strip. Since Emme had a family function today, we decided to take a road trip and sight see during the first days of the new year instead.

Kade is in the kitchen preparing veggie snacks for us to take on our trip. I decide to let him know about Josh. "Hey, you know what's weird? Josh has been calling me all day. I haven't spoken to him in a while. I think it's weird that all of a sudden he's been continuously thinking of me." I say as I start munching on raw sugar snap peas. "We better take chips and cookies with us too. Vegetables and fruit aren't going to cut it for me."

Kade scowls at me. "You'll be drinking the whole time you're there. You can't pig out AND consume alcohol too. I won't let you. Seeing you eat healthy snacks reduces the guilt from knowing you'll be intoxicating your body with liquor the next few days. I know it doesn't make sense, so just humor me." Kade pleads. "As for Josh, I kind of, sort of spoke with him this morning when I saw him at the gym. He seems heartbroken. He really wants to talk to you, but he's been giving you space. He knows you hate him, but doesn't blame you. He just wants to be heard."

Just as I'm speaking to Kade, my phone rings and there's a knock on the door. Kade lets Emme in and helps her with the luggage.

"What's going on?" Emme asks. "Why the glum faces?"

"Josh has been calling Cheesecake all day, he just called a few seconds ago too. She refuses to speak with him and hear his version of the story." Kade explains.

"Fuck him! Let him keep calling you, Nina. He wasn't thinking of you when he was fucking that dirty waitress, so why should you waste your time and energy hearing him out? Let him suffer as a consequence. Do not answer his calls!" Emme is all about the girl power today.

"You're right." I'm determined to get Joshua Ryan out of my mind.

We finish packing and loading up Kade's BMW X5. In the morning, we'll simply get dressed and head out. It takes us almost ten hours to arrive to our destination due to several pit stops along the way. We arrive in Vegas early Sunday evening. Emme and I started drinking prior to our arrival, so by the time we reach our hotel room, we're both pretty buzzed. I don't pay attention to the hotel we're staying in; I just know it's modern, elegant, and expensive. Our room is actually a two bedroom tower suite with a full stocked bar. That's all that matters at this point.

Both bedrooms have an astonishing view of Sin City. Kade gets a king size bed in his room while Emme and I have two full size beds in ours. Instantly, Kade begins to catch up on his drinking. During our trip, we made him be a gentleman by driving the last half of the trip. Emme and I used that time to our advantage and experimented with drinks. I get another text message from Josh. I feel too good to allow him to ruin my buzz. Delete.

Kade tells us he has a surprise, so Emme and I get ready in record time. I'm all about the pin-up look this evening with retro inspired makeup and a rockabilly hairstyle. My ruby lips match the bright red flower on my hair. The skin tight, turquoise wiggle dress appears to be painted on my silhouette while the twins make a bold appearance tonight. Kade is wearing khakis with a black button up shirt. He looks handsome and well groomed as always. We're at the bar located in our suite when Emme steps out.

"Okay. I'm ready. Kade, can you make me a drink?" Emme asks.

Both Kade and I ignore her request. We're too stunned to look away. Emme is wearing an extremely short black dress with five inch stiletto sandals. Her hair has subtle waves to it and is pulled to the side. She's not wearing her glasses and has on red lipstick. She manages to pull the look off exquisitely. In the past, she has always toned down her look. Today, she finally came out of her shell and embraced her sexuality. She looks amazing.

I'm shamelessly gawking at her. "Oh, my...you look sexy as fuck. If I were bi, I'd so do you." I can't help but stare. She's beautiful. Don't get me wrong, I've always thought she was pretty, but right now she looks confident in her own skin. The assurance in herself compliments her beauty.

Kade clears his throat. "Yeah, you look pretty good, Em." The look he gives Emme is completely predatory and lustful, naturally she gives it right back to him.

"Will you two please stop eye fucking each other? I'm trying to have a good time and not be a witness to your sexual shenanigans. Besides, I thought we were pressed for time and had to leave?" I ask getting back on track.

Kade hands Emme a drink, she pounds it and we head out. Kade surprises us by having a limo pick us up. Inside is a bottle of Armand de Brignac Champagne for us. We're ready to live it up in Sin City. Our trio arrives at a gentlemen's club, but we remain in the car until we're done with our ridiculously, expensive champagne. Usually, we wouldn't indulge in such luxury, but tonight we make an exception. We exit the limo and get hit by a cool breeze that instantly takes our buzz to a drunken state. That's what happens when you mix your drinks with fresh air, regardless, we're all feeling pretty damn good.

When we arrive at the entrance of the club, we're told the male strippers are performing for the next hour and the women strip afterwards. It doesn't make a difference to us and happily walk in. Kade pulls out a wad of bills and hands us money to use for our enjoyment. The male strippers are handsome and have incredible bodies, but they just don't do it for me. I can't help but think of Josh and his sinfully delicious cut up chest with his arms of steel. *Yum!*

Oh, shit. I sense myself falling back into my dark hole and refuse to go there. I hand Kade my phone, afraid of drunk dialing Josh. I've remained strong and kept my distance for this long, I can't quit now. Emme buys us all lap dances from the men. Instead of it being a sexual encounter, we mess around by dancing for them and each other.

The female strippers soon begin to put on a show. Again, we put on an act of our own. Most of the girls are cool and even show us some moves; some are catty, but we just ignore them. Unfortunately, in the dress I'm wearing there's no way I can stretch in certain positions. The men and women are all over Kade. He loves the attention and humors them by slipping bills down their thongs.

Emme and I focus our attention on a group right next to us. Since we're drunk, we don't bother with discretion. One of the girls is with her boyfriend, they're pretty loud so we're able to hear them just fine. Apparently, the girlfriend bought her man a lap dance and now that the stripper has her bare chest all over the girl's man, she's getting herself riled up. We hear her ranting about how she's a real woman and if that's what her man likes than he can do whatever the fuck he wants. She emphasizes how she doesn't need him and can handle things on her own. The girl throwing the tantrum is so cute, I smile at her. Clearly, she was trying to be a cool girlfriend, but jealousy mixed with alcohol are getting the best of her. It took courage for her to come out of her shell, bring her man to a strip club, and allow a strange woman to plant her fake boobs all over him. I don't know if I could have done that with Josh. Any other man...Yes. But with Josh, I highly doubt it. The stripper finally backs away from the boyfriend, all I see is relief across his face. He didn't seem to enjoy that as much as the girlfriend assumed. She finally relaxes once her friends have calmed her down.

Awww...they're cute together. I hope they last. I miss Josh. Stop it, Nina!

Once we've had plenty of tits and ass action, we head over to a dance club. We party the night away with good music, plenty of drinks, and the best company, each other. I wake up in the morning still drunk. I look at the time and realize that it's past noon. I wake up my roomies; we get ready and head down to the cabana for some food and relaxation. We're still slightly drunk after we've had our light lunch, but we continue to drink mojitos.

"Damn, Kade. You sure had those strippers eating out of the palm of your hand last night." I tease.

"They thought I had money. Yeah, I have some, but little do they know that you're the millionaire among the group." He laughs.

"What?" Emme appears perplexed.

Kade turns to me and gives me an apologetic look once he realizes he's said too much.

"Yeah, I have money. I just don't see it or use it, so it doesn't count. Out of sight, out of mind." I state nonchalantly.

"Money as in thousands or millions?" She asks, still confused.

"Millions." I answer simply.

"You must be the most modest and humble millionaire I know. I had no clue." Emme looks at me with wonder.

"I don't like to talk about it. It's nothing really. By the way, Kade, which one of my credit cards did you use to pay for our suite?" I casually change the subject.

"About that...I actually used my card, but remember how I accidentally told Josh that we were coming to Vegas? Well, he wanted to pay for our room. So, I canceled the room I had reserved. He arrived this morning, he's actually staying in this hotel. I've been dying to tell you. Damn. I finally feel like I can exhale." He admits.

"Kade! How could you? You know the whole purpose of this trip is for me to forget about him! I can't believe you!" I'm pissed.

"Calm down, Cheesecake. I thought burning a hole through his pockets would be a good way of getting him back for hurting you. I thought it was funny, besides he really wants to apologize for his actions and give you an explanation. I know it sounds like I'm not being a friend to you, but I am. You need closure to move on. Set your terms when you speak with him. He'll respect them. He flew out here just to be with you. Doesn't that touch your heart in the slightest bit? Speak of the devil; he's walking right towards us." Kade warns.

I literally feel my eyes coming out of their sockets. I want to kill Kade Daly! Josh soon approaches us, so I get distracted on my murder plot.

"Hey." Josh says quietly to the group.

"Hi." We all reply in the same tone.

"Okay. So, this feels awkward." Kade states the obvious. "Em, how about you come with me to get more drinks? Cheesecake needs to give Josh a good ass chewing for not knowing how to keep his dick in his pants."

"No. You two stay right here. Josh, have a seat. We won't be talking. I'll be the only one speaking." I mean business.

"Josh, I don't want to hear about what happened between you and that dirty skank, Nicole. I could care less about your explanation. I'm not interested in an intimate relationship with you anymore." I will those words to be true.

"I don't want to live with hate in my heart. It's not healthy. I forgive you even though you haven't asked for my forgiveness. I'm aware I haven't given you the opportunity to apologize; I simply don't care to listen to it. Be aware that I will never forget the hurt you put me through. You have to promise me you will never make a sexual advance towards me again, especially when I'm drinking or try to explain yourself regarding Nicole. If you can do that, we can begin a friendship once again. If you break any of the terms I've set, I will cut you off for good." I stare at him intently, he needs to understand that I'm serious, but that he shouldn't take my kindness for granted and see it as weakness.

"Okay. I'll abide by your terms even though they're bullshit." He says with a solemn expression.

"Good! Now that the air has been cleared between you two, it's time for some shots! That shit was intense for a quick second. I don't know about you guys, but I'm about to get twisted on the last day of the year. Who's with me?" Leave it to Kade to break the tension. I love him.

We all raise our hands. The rest of the day is spent checking out various hotels on the strip with a consistent buzz in our system. In the evening, we return to our rooms to freshen up. Josh's room is conveniently located right next to our suite. Coincidence? I think not.

Since we'll be outside for the remainder of the evening, our attire for the night is casual. No one is in the mood to dress up and be cooped up inside. The streets of the Las Vegas strip are closed for the year end fireworks display. The crowd is quickly growing. We decide to have our last meal of the year at Dirty Dick's. Surprisingly enough, Josh and I are getting along with hardly any awkwardness. I feel comfortable within our group, there's no need to end the year on a negative note. After dinner we head out to the strip, by this time, the streets are much more packed with festive crowds. Half an hour before the strike of midnight, we position ourselves right by the dancing fountains in front of the Bellagio Hotel. Unexpectedly, I become anxious. It dawns on me that in a few minutes Josh and I will embrace to welcome and celebrate the New Year. Maintaining my distance has proven to be quite a challenge, but being in his arms even for the slightest moment might be treacherous against my will. Without realizing it, I finish my drink. By this point, my mouth feels numb and I can't seem to get Josh off my mind. Leave it to Kade to refill my cup.

Too soon, I hear people doing a countdown. "Five, four, three, two, one...Happy New Year!" Our group toasts to a new beginning.

Kade and I hug first. "Happy New Year! I hope it brings you nothing, but joy. I love you, Cheesecake!"

"You're my heart, Kade. I hope you find happiness also." I'm glad we're all together.

I give Emme a big hug and tell her I love her. I turn to Josh and notice him staring at me with a look of awe. Is that how he's observing me? With admiration? I can tell he's confused and doesn't know whether he can approach me or not, so I walk towards him and close the distance between us.

"Happy New Year, tree hugger." I whisper right by his ear and place my hands on his shoulders. As I begin to back away, he holds me firmly from my waist.

He lowers his face to rest right by my ear. "Happy New Year, Valentina." He remains in that position for several glorious, yet heartbreaking seconds. He doesn't want to move away from me either. Being in his arms, smelling his clean scent, having that feeling of security, and being protected makes me want to lose myself to him. I feel his embrace tighten. I've missed being within his arms and now that I'm here, I don't want to leave. For that moment, it feels as if it were just the two of us on the street with no worries, no past, and no regrets. With all my will, I slowly start to step away as the realization of our relationship gradually registers in my mind once again. *Valentina, you have to step away. As much as it hurts, you can't be with him anymore. Josh doesn't belong to you.*

Traitorous tears run down my face, there's no stopping them. Vaguely, I hear the loud fireworks; somehow I managed to tune them out along with everything else. Josh places his index finger below my chin and raises it. When he sees my tears, he grabs me with a strong force, and buries his face by my neck. "I'm so sorry, baby for hurting you. I'll make it up to you one day, I swear it." He speaks rapidly knowing that I'll quickly be pushing him away.

"Please stop. You promised." I remind him.

As he moves his handsome face away from my neck, I feel the stubble along his jawline caress my cheek. Every sense in my body is awakened by his touch. When he faces me, his hazel eyes appear red around the rims. I place my hands around his neck, give him a soft kiss by the side of his lips, and wipe away my tears. His eyes remain locked on me; I look up and take comfort in the fireworks that are right above us. The colorful display in the dark sky is truly a mesmerizing sight. I don't bother looking back at him. I can't. I simply step away from Josh as he unwillingly releases me.

I take deep breaths and gather my thoughts, once I feel I'm able to move forward, I search for Kade and Emme. Shock instantly strikes me. Kade is holding Emme while she has her legs wrapped around him. "Oh, hell no! I know you aren't about to fuck in public! What's wrong with you two? Emme, get off Kade! And Kade, keep your dick in your pants. No one wants to see that type of show!" I truly can't believe my eyes.

"You did last night. You sure weren't complaining when we were fucking in the bed next to yours." Emme declares as she gets off Kade and are both dying of laughter.

"What? You two fucked in front of me while I was asleep? Ewww!" Now, I'm just grossed out.

"We wanted to end the year right." Emme states. "I told you I was horny."

I give up. "You both are too much! Let's go. I'm drunk and need to rest."

"Sounds good." Emme and Kade say in unison with an insatiable desire protruding from them.

In the middle of the night, I have a dream. In it, Kade and Emme are having sex. Kade is behind Emme doing her doggy style. On Emme's right ass cheek, I notice it's a bright pink color and has the word SLUT imprinted on it. Later, Emme's riding Kade in the reverse cowgirl position and refers to him as "Master KD," clearly this is more of a sick nightmare. I try to wake up from my dream, but can't. I rub my eyes several times, but the attempt is useless. The scene is extremely vivid and I feel like some type of voyeur. Then, it hits me. *These assholes are fucking right in front of me again! I'm not dreaming!*

"I can't believe you guys are getting freaky right where I can see you! You're gross!" I feel dirty being in their presence and walk out. If it were another couple, I would gladly sit there and watch, but it's Kade and Emme...they're practically family. *Yuck!*

"Shoo...go away, Nina." I think I hear Emme say. *Did she just shoo me away?*

I still feel drunk and get the munchies. I grab a Snickers bar and gobble it up in seconds. Now, I'm wide awake and it's barely the middle of the night. I decide to go downstairs to the casino section of the hotel and walk around. When I reach the main level, I hear the beautiful melody of slot machines and coins clinking. I get a rush when a slot machine winks at me. Naturally, I wink back and make myself comfortable right in front of it. After losing sixty dollars within a ten minute timeframe to the one arm bandit, I decide to search for a loyal slot machine that will make me feel better and doesn't just wink at any random person like some loose tramp. As I'm walking around the casino searching for the perfect machine, I spot Josh at a poker table. I decide to remain in place behind a tall flower structure and observe him from a distance. *Oh, yeah...I'm in full blown stalker mode.*

Josh is wearing black, yet his broad shoulders, and lean build are easy to observe. His expression is somber, making his appearance mysterious and sexy. His hypnotic, hazel eyes compliment his lightly, tan skin and fine features perfectly. He has several stacks of poker chips in front of him. He's drinking hard liquor, cognac I assume since that's his drink of preference when gambling. As he places a bet, his expression is subdued. Once he wins the pot, his face remains impassive, but his posture alludes an air of confidence that's erotic as hell. He places a blind bet for the start of a new game, he takes a sip of his liquor, and discreetly licks his lower lip keeping part of it between his teeth as he focuses on the cards he was just dealt. *Oh, to be those lips. I reminisce on our own poker night that consisted of a carefree moment with uncontainable passion. How I've missed him. Instantly, I crave his kiss, his touch, his affection, his presence...*

A waitress wearing a black corset pulls me out of my reverie. She's a young, pretty blonde. She hands him another drink and bends down low enough for her chest to be near his face. *What the fuck is up with him and waitresses?*

He takes the drink without looking at her and hands her poker chips as a tip. She walks away with her eyes fixated on him. Yes, she wants him, but who wouldn't when it's clear he's dominating the table and exudes a raw sensuality that is difficult to resist.

I walk away and end my surveillance with comfort that he isn't on the prowl and is solely concentrating on his game. I know I shouldn't think that way, but I can't help it. He's still deeply penetrated in my heart. I decide to get my night's rest on Kade's bed since he's busy doing unimaginable things to Emme in my room.

Morning arrives and the sound of a buzzer wakes me up. I get up and find Kade, Emme, and Josh about to have breakfast at the nook table. I excuse myself and brush my teeth. I feel like crap. No more drinking for the next few days. *Yuck.*

"Morning. How'd you sleep last night?" Josh asks me. "We ordered almost everything on the menu, so help yourself."

"Thanks. I kept having these weird dreams last night." I glare at Emme and Kade. "By the way, I'm not drinking today; I have too much crap in my system."

"What were your dreams about?" Emme asks curiously.

"Ugh. They were about you and Kade in completely inappropriate positions." I get nauseous just thinking about their freaky shenanigans.

Immediately, Kade and Emme begin to giggle. Kade raises his hand and sings, "Guiiiiiiiiiiiilty." Now, everyone's laughing.

"Ewww! You guys are sick! I'm telling mom." I chuckle and accidentally snort. Now, we're all in hysterics.

We spend the remainder of the day alcohol free and in good spirits. We sight see and catch a Cirque du Soleil and burlesque show. Before we end the night, Josh asks to go on a non-date with me tomorrow. Emme and Kade made it clear earlier they wanted to relax tomorrow. I remind him of his promise and agree to go on the non-date with him.

The next day, I spend the morning relaxing in a cabana while Josh catches up on work. In the afternoon, he picks me up at my suite. We head to the valet section of the hotel and wait for Josh's rental. A sleek, metallic silver Bentley with tinted windows pulls up right in front of me. "You rented a Bentley?" I ask.

"Yeah. I thought you might like it. You said you like fast cars, this was all that was available on such short notice." He shrugs. "I hope it's okay." He opens the door for me.

"It's a bad ass car, but please remember this is a non-date and money doesn't impress me." I don't want him getting the wrong idea.

He gets in the driver's seat. "Don't over analyze things. I'm always working; I rarely get a chance to enjoy my money. I simply thought you would appreciate it. It's not part of a scheme to have you fall for me. I know where I stand. Trust me, you don't have to remind me. Now, can you agree to have some fun with me? I really hope you're more enthusiastic about our actual non-date. Loosen the fuck up, lady."

"Fine. So, where are we headed?" My curiosity quickly takes over.

"You'll see, Miss Impatient." He states, not giving me the slightest clue.

As Josh pulls up to the parking lot, my heart starts rapidly palpitating. *Is this what I think it is? No.* "An exotic car race track? Are you serious? Are we watching or driving?" I feel like a kid who's at Disneyland for the first time ever.

"We'll be driving thirteen different exotic cars each. Are you ready?" He asks, smiling at me warmly.

"Oh, my goodness! Hell yeah! Thank you! I didn't know this place existed." I'm beyond thrilled.

When we arrive, we enter the track's facility. Its décor is minimal consisting mostly of white, red, and black colors. We attend a thirty minute classroom briefing. Then, one of the instructors drives a discovery lap in a Porsche Cayenne GT with me as the passenger to get a feel for the track. I enthusiastically go through the list of cars I'll be driving, three Lamborghinis (Gallardo LP560, Supperleggera LP570, and Aventador LP700), three Ferraris (F430 F1, Scuderia, and 458

Italia), two Porsches (Cayman R and 997 Turbo S), an Ashton Martin V8, a Nissan GTR, a Mercedes SLS AMG, A McLaren MP4-12C, and an Audi R8. I'm in heaven. Without thinking, I jump on Josh, give him a big hug, and a kiss on the cheek right before we both get in our cars. It's finally time for me to drive with an instructor right by my side. I can't contain my eagerness.

Once I'm in the car, my instructor informs me there's a small camera located inside and cameras throughout the racetrack. He lets me know that Josh has already purchased the DVD of me racing to enjoy at a later time.

Awww...that's sweet.

Okay, I'm nervous, but I'm ready to do this.

The adrenaline rush I feel when putting the peddle to the floor and racing through the 1.2 mile track with seven turns and 1,800 feet of a straight path is off the charts. After my second lap, my instructor pushes me to achieve greater speed while still being safe. I drive the thirteen vehicles for the duration of five laps each, which total 65 laps around the track. The high performance cars race along smooth asphalt that provides an excellent ride with a superior grip. My instructor allows me to drive the cars as hard as I desire. So after a while, I drive them like I stole them. I'm able to see what these beasts are truly capable of achieving on the track. The enlarged entrance and exit in most of the turns allows for greater speed and less steering which provides a smoother drive from corner to corner. I revel in every minute of being on the track and racing, it's absolutely an amazing thrill. It's challenging, yet fun, and I'm able to see the powerful engines working. I race the Aventador last which turns out to be one of the most exhilarating experiences of my life...with my clothes on, that is.

It's twilight when we leave the track, I thank Josh once again. He hands me the DVD, I'm grateful for his thoughtfulness.

Although, I try not to look at Josh in a sexual manner, I can't help it. He walks to the Bentley with confidence. His tall structure and broad shoulders makes me want to wrap myself in his arms, but I don't even though he oozes an amatory vibe that drives me insane. As we're headed back to the hotel on the freeway, I still feel my adrenaline pumping and feel myself craving for Josh to be inside me. The sensation won't go away. I want his fat, long dick pounding me and making me spasm all over him. I want to feel his desire for me at my sex and travel throughout the rest of my body. I need him, I want him, I miss him, and I don't know how to resist him. The urge to have him in me only intensifies while he continues to drive. As I blatantly stare at his profile, I notice he's deep in thought. One moment, he's biting his lip, the next he's clenching his jaw. My focus then turns to the stubble along is jawline. Oh, my...I want him. BAD! *Calm down, Nina. Get your horny ass together. You cannot do this! You won't do this!*

Fuck it. I'm no longer thinking with my brain, but with my heart.

"Unbuckle your pants." I order him. "I'm about to pay back the poker debt I owe you." Josh stares at me with an incredulous look as he sees that I'm completely serious, yet he does as he's instructed. Immediately, I notice his erection and crave for his penetration.

"It's about fuckin' time." Josh simply states with a hungry and mischievous gaze.

"A debt is a debt. What better way to repay it than by doing it while driving a Bentley in Sin City? Now, push your seat as far back as possible, I'm going to get on top of you and do all the work. Your only job is to focus on the road ahead of you and keep us safe. Understand?" I ask with a business-like tone even though my inner flesh is on fire.

Josh's fiery gaze brings out a zealous expression in his features.

C. MICHELLE

He maintains his calm and responds by nodding, he's literally speechless, but ready for his fantasy to become a reality. I play the song, "Locked Out of Heaven" by Bruno Mars and put it on repeat. I quickly begin taking my clothes off until I'm left completely in the nude. At this time, I'm thankful for the tinted windows.

Josh clenches his jaw, slowly licks his full bottom lip, and tightly grips the steering wheel; his sexual manifestation is quickly making me lose my last bit of control. There's no time to waste, I place my hands on his shoulders for balance and slowly position my naked body on top of his solid frame as he's driving. Our close proximity has my heart accelerating and his clean, manly scent makes every inch of me yearn to have him in me. I don't need any assistance inserting his rock hard erection. I simply lower myself, savor his intense fullness, and allow all negative thoughts to escape me. I do away with foreplay and accept this as a simple fuck between us. Although my heart tells me different, I disregard the feeling, and focus my attention on my actions. I ride him hard by grinding my body onto him mercilessly. Our figures feel as one. I feel his passionate kisses and teeth graze my neck and shoulders. His moans drive me in a frenzy as I excitedly thrust my entrance upon his deliciously, fat and long dick. I can't contain myself any longer and allow the overwhelming pleasure to burst out of me. The orgasm is exhilarating (to say the least). I'm insatiable and continue to pound him with my sex for as long as I can. The feeling is too irresistible to let it end.

"Baby, I've missed you so much." Josh says in a deep, raspy voice. "You feel amazing, so tight, and wet. This is where I belong, inside of you." He whispers by my ear as he's stroking and firmly grasping my bare back with his right hand.

The sound of his voice, his words, and his touch send me over the edge again. *God, how I've missed him.*

180

This time, he joins me and we both finish together. The release is overpowering. I lean my head against his temple and attempt to catch my breath. Slowly, I try to remove myself from him, but he refuses to let me go.

"Stay like this." He commands as he tightens his grasp on me.

"No. I don't want us getting into an accident." Rationality finally hits me.

"Now, you're concerned with our safety?" He teases.

"Better late than never." I reply and carefully move to the passenger's seat. I get dressed and remain quiet for some time. Josh tries to hold my hand, but I remove it from his grip.

"How do you feel? What are you thinking? Tell me. Your silence is killing me." He admits.

"I'm starving. Can we get something to eat?" I ask hoping to buy time to gather my thoughts.

"Of course." He replies.

We end up having dinner at the Wynn's buffet. I'm ravenous by the time we get there and fill my plate with food. Both of us avoid discussing the incident that occurred in the Bentley.

"I've missed you." Josh quietly confesses. "You're my lady, I can't fuckin' lose you."

"Please, let's not do this now." I beg...even though I want to reply the same and throw myself at him once again. It was a moment of weakness in my part and I don't feel comfortable talking about it just yet. My spirit feels too weak and vulnerable.

When we're done eating, he informs me that he's going home tonight and is catching the last flight out. He indicates an issue arose at work that requires his full and immediate attention. We head back to the hotel in silence. We say goodbye as he walks me to my suite and agree to see each other once I return home. I thank him for our non-date and for the suite. I don't allow him to kiss or hug me, afraid that if he does I'll never let him go again.

Chapter 10 (Josh)

Celeste

I catch the last flight back to San Francisco just in time, heading home I only think of Nina. I can't believe how much I've missed and craved her. Feeling her, caressing her, and being inside of her made that car ride pure ecstasy. Today, she brought back the happiness I've been missing since she left me that dreadful day. Now, my only concern is that she's full of regrets. What will I do if she doesn't give me another chance? As we said goodbye earlier, she seemed distant.

Instead of dwelling on negativity, I choose to focus on having an optimistic perspective of my relationship with Nina. She'll be back tomorrow night and hopefully, she'll put my mind at ease.

The next day I wake up anxious, I want Nina to return. Leaving things unresolved between us makes me restless. The best solution for me is to dive into work and completely distract myself; otherwise I'll just go insane. I send her a quick text letting her know that I miss her. I don't get a response from her during the remainder of the day.

The following day, I don't hear from Nina again. I call her and leave a voicemail message. As soon as I wake up on Saturday morning, I check my phone to see if I have any missed calls or texts from her. Nothing. I recall her mentioning a photo shoot at Pier 39 early in the morning. Since we've already established that I have stalker tendencies, I take my ass over there.

I swear, I'm like gum stuck on her shoe...following her wherever she goes, but I don't give a FUCK! She's mine and I'll do whatever it takes to get her back.

I park my car as close to Fisherman's Warf as possible. I walk around searching for my lady. It doesn't matter that she dropped me like a bad habit, she's still mine. I'm not giving up on her that easily. As I approach the carousel found at the bay end of Pier 39, I see a vintage Harley-Davidson motorcycle, it's a turquoise color and has the most beautiful woman posing next to it. She's breathtaking. She's wearing a white, retro one piece swimsuit. For some reason, it reminds me of Marilyn Monroe. She has on red heels and a coordinating flower above her right ear. Her perfect wavy hair flows nicely down the left side of her face. Her swimsuit and light skin tone are a nice contrast against the turquoise bike. The photographer snaps several shots. Once he's finished and is in deep conversation with a woman who appears to be his assistant, I move towards Nina.

"Hey. So, what type of motorcycle is that exactly?" Is all that comes to mind.

"It's a 1949 Harley-Davidson FL Hydra-Glide. What are you doing here?" She asks with confusion set in her expression.

"I was worried about you. You haven't returned any of my calls or texts. Besides, I haven't stalked you lately; it's been almost a few days now." I joke with her.

We get interrupted by the photographer's assistant. The photo shoot has been relocated and Nina has to leave. She allows me to meet her at the cable car turntable where more pictures will be taken.

When I get there, the photographer is setting up his equipment. Nina is standing next to one of the trolleys. I approach her. "Why haven't you returned my calls?" I ask and get to the point.

"Josh, this isn't the best time or place to have this conversation." Nina looks away to avoid eye contact with me. *Don't look away, baby. I've missed your beautiful face.*

"Tell me the truth, do you regret what happened in Vegas? Because I don't. I haven't been able to get you off my mind." I admit. "I'm fuckin' going crazy here thinking about you!" It takes all my will power not to embrace her in my arms.

Nina lightly caresses the right side of my face. I delight in her delicate touch. "Josh, you and I can never be together again. I don't trust you. Without trust, there's nothing. Being with you in Vegas was amazing, but for those same reasons, I've returned even more heartbroken than when I left. My feelings for you are stronger than I ever could've expected, regardless I don't want to be with you anymore. Although I have already forgiven you, I will never forget or trust you with my heart. We can try to be friends, but that's it." Although, she looks exquisite, her expression is filled with sincere pain. I've never seen so much hurt behind her lovely chocolate eyes. It breaks my heart to know I'm the cause of her agony.

"I love you, Valentina. One day, I'll earn your trust. I swear it." I stare at her yearningly, willing her to believe the truth behind my words. She doesn't.

Just then, a girl who looks familiar interrupts our conversation as she approaches us. "Oh, my God, Josh! What are you doing here, hun? It's been so long since I've seen you! Damn, you still look mighty fine." She scans my body from head to toe with a blatant predatory look. She attempts to hug me once she's close enough. Immediately, I move away from her, not allowing her to touch me with evident disgust as my facial expression.

This bitch couldn't have picked a worse time to hang from my nuts. I close my eyes, clench my jaw on reflex, and run my hand through my hair trying my best not to lose the last bit of patience I have left. Too late. I notice Nina begin to walk away; I grab her arm and keep her in place while I give this skank in front of me a piece of my mind. "Check this out, girl. This is my lady, so before you approach me like you know me get your fuckin' facts straight. You look familiar, so I'm sure I fucked you once upon a time, but you can't come at me like we're folks and are still tight. Know your place, you were a one-time fuck and that was it. Don't portray a picture of us to my lady that isn't so."

The girl's shocked reaction is from humiliation, not from hurt. Clearly, her ego has never taken such a blow. "Calm down, I just came here to let Nina know that I'm ready to touch up her makeup." She rolls her eyes at me and walks away.

"You fucked my makeup artist? Seriously?" Nina's expression is full of disgust. "I can tell you fucked her a long time ago, but still...it stings."

Before I have a chance to discuss the incident with Nina, the photographer approaches us and informs Nina it's time for her to change into the next ensemble. She leaves without saying a word and enters a trailer that's being used as a dressing and makeup room. I sit down on some steps and patiently wait. For what? I don't know. I just know I can't leave.

Nina finally exits the trailer and is ready for her next photo shoot. She's wearing high waisted, hot pink capri pants with a black belt. The halter top she's wearing is black with white polka dots. She has on black, high heels that only have a strap on the front. With her hair in a high ponytail, she pulls off the retro look perfectly. To my surprise, I hear the photographer state he wants to get on the trolley and take pictures while it's in route.

Nina walks over to me. "I have to go. I'm sorry." And walks away.

I hit the gym hard to release my frustration, it doesn't help much. I head home and fall asleep in the afternoon. The last thing I want to think about is my shattered heart. I'm emotionally exhausted and need rest.

I wake up Sunday morning in a slump. I've never slept so much and still feel worse than when I fell asleep. I force myself to go to the office and focus on work. When I return, my mood has gone from melancholy to furious. I'm in a shitty mood and angry at the world. I conclude to give Nina her space and not bother her. I haven't given up on her, I'm simply allowing time to heal her wounds.

As I'm at work the next day, Nina calls. "Hey. Are you busy?" She asks.

"Not for you. What's up?" I wonder.

"Ummm...the photographer who took the photo shoot this weekend captured some pictures of you and me talking by the trolley. He really likes them and wants to know if you would be okay with him using them for his website." She says all in one breath. She sounds nervous.

"No." I simply state, but for some reason I sound like a dick.

"Why not? I've worked with him several times. He's a professional. What's the big deal?" I can sense Nina starting to get pissed.

"I can't really talk right now. Can I go over to your house this evening and explain? If we're going to try to be friends, I want to be honest with you and build a foundation of trust. So, is it okay if I stop by?" I ask with a mixture of hope and unsteady nerves.

"Fine. Stop by after work. I'll see you then." She hangs up.

As I approach Nina's house, I'm nervous. I never know what to expect from her. She always keeps me on my toes. I take a deep breath and knock on the door. She answers and has a surprised look on her face.

"Hey." I smile uncertainly.

"Hi! Oh, wow! Please come in. What a great surprise seeing you here, Celeste and Delia." Nina immediately gives my mom a hug.

"They're my back up. I like to roll with top flight security." I tease.

"Hey, sweetie. I hope it's okay we stopped by. I know you weren't expecting us, but I think it's time we have ourselves a little chat." My mom states as she returns Nina's hug.

"Oh, please...You're always welcomed in this house." Nina smiles warmly at my mom then turns her attention to Delia.

"Hola, Delia. I'm so glad you're here. Thank you for coming." She embraces Delia as well.

"Oh, is my pleasure. I bring you somesing, is tamales, quesadilla bread, and other goodies. I hope you enjoy." I just love Delia's accent. She's too cute.

"Oh, thank you. I definitely will." Nina genuinely looks thrilled with Delia's thoughtful gesture.

Nina leads us to her living room and offers us something to eat and drink. We all politely decline.

As we make ourselves comfortable in her living room, I decide to get to the point. "Nina, I know you're probably wondering why we're all gathered here today. I don't want to keep anything from you. I want you to one day trust me. You've confided in me and now, it's my turn to open up." I pause to gather my thoughts. "The reason I don't want that photographer to put pictures of me on his website is because

I'm in hiding." I notice the confusion clear across Nina's face.

"Nina, would you like to hear the story from the beginning?" My mom asks.

"Yes, please." Nina quietly responds.

My mom proceeds to tell her story. "My name is Kaitlyn O'Neill. I used to be an actress in the seventies and early eighties."

Nina interrupts. "Oh, my goodness! You're the actress who disappeared. I thought you looked familiar! When I was younger, my mom and I used to watch all your movies." Nina has a stunned look on her face. "So sorry. I won't interrupt again. Please continue." She apologizes.

"That's okay, dear." My mom lightly taps Nina's leg. "In 1984, during the shooting of a film in Houston, Texas, I met a man by the name of Damien Montiel. Right away, I was captivated by his presence. He emanated a strong essence of power and with his handsome good looks, he was definitely hard to resist. Although he was a mystery to me, I became enamored with him and his Spanish accent immediately. I hardly knew anything about him, yet I couldn't wait to see him every time we met. We always stayed in different elite hotels, which I assumed was his way of impressing me. I soon found out I was pregnant. When I told Damien of the news, he began to change. He became more controlling, possessive, jealous, and began demanding that I quit acting. One day, as I was sleeping in our hotel suite, I overheard a conversation Damien was having in Spanish with two men in the living area. I had taken Spanish with my private tutor growing up and my best friend spoke it fluently, so I understood the conversation pretty well. I heard Damien order the two men to kill an informant for treachery and to notify him when the next shipment of mota, which I knew stood for marijuana, would be ready along with the next coca trade, I was aware he was referring to cocaine.

At that moment, I felt all my breath leave my lungs, the room began to spin, and I held onto the wall for balance. As I composed myself, I ran to his suitcase and went through his belongings since he was still speaking to both men. I found paperwork and a picture ID with his picture and the name Mateo Blanco on all documents. At that moment, my heart literally stopped. Mateo Blanco was associated with one of the largest drug cartels in the world, Los Blancos Cartel. The only reason I knew this was because my father was a retired DEA (Drug Enforcement Administration) Chief of Operations and I used to overhear his name on several occasions. Blanco had a reputation of being absolutely ruthless. He was determined to quickly climb the hierarchy of his family's drug organization. With that in mind, I checked his other suitcase and found it filled with several hundred thousand dollars along with two handguns. I closed the suitcase and went back to bed before I was caught. I thought about my options of escape. Since the day I informed him of my pregnancy, he rarely left my side. I knew it would be impossible to leave him, but I didn't want to raise my baby in such a malicious and corrupt lifestyle. I was left with no alternative, but to escape regardless of the obstacles I'd face. When he entered my room minutes later, he found me asleep, so he thought. While he was in the shower, I changed and grabbed my purse. I checked my wallet that contained my ID and passport, both were gone. He had taken them. As I bent down to look for my shoes, I saw a blanket deep below the bed. I pulled it out, it was heavier than I expected, and noticed the blanket was covering up a stash of high-powered rifles. I knew I would have to hide and start a new life. I grabbed the suitcase full of money and left. I called my father and informed him of the situation. He got ahold of old contacts and urgently placed me in the witness protection program. By the time undercover agents arrived to the hotel room, it was empty. I began my new life with just the clothes on my back and a suitcase full of dirty money."

My mom takes a moment to reminisce on her past. "My life as Kaitlyn O'Neill ended and a new one as Deborah Stewart began. All my fame and glory were gone, but I didn't care. My priority was to protect my unborn baby. The witness protection program sent me to Brunswick, Missouri. After living my new life for five months, I received a call from my father informing me that Mateo Blanco's men were on their way to get me and that I needed to flee immediately. Apparently, Blanco had several law enforcement agents on his payroll who were able to provide him with my whereabouts. I gathered my money, left, and met my father who provided me with a manila envelope containing my new identity. This time, I was left in the hands of a law enforcement agency my father trusted to follow through on a new plan for me. Instead of staying in a small town like before, I was relocated to San Francisco as Celeste Ryan, it's been my home ever since."

My mom pauses and closes her eyes for a minute. We all remain silent. She continues. "One day, I drove down to Arizona and mailed my parents a letter without a return address informing them that I was okay. I was afraid of mailing it from home, terrified it would be traced back to me. Months later, I called one of my neighbors to check on my parents. I was informed they had been found tortured and slaughtered in their home a few months back." My mom wipes away her tears and I put my arm around her to console her.

She continues with her story and explanation. "I've been terrified of Mateo Blanco ever since. He knows I have his son, I may not know much about him, but I do know that he's full of malice and won't rest until he gets his revenge on me. As Josh grew older, he became the spitting image of his father, with a few exceptions. There's no way Mateo won't recognize Josh if the day were to come when he sees his son. Hopefully, now you understand why I didn't allow Josh to play professional baseball. For him to remain inconspicuous was not a reality if he were to be in the spotlight. It should also bring light to why pictures of him on the internet, simply drive this old woman in a panic. I'm sure I don't need to reiterate the severity of keeping my story confidential. If my son believes you to be such a friend that he wants to disclose our intimate secrets with you, then you have my trust and respect." My mom grabs Nina's hand and cups it between hers. She smiles at Nina lovingly.

"Thank you, Celeste for entrusting your private past with me, I won't speak of it to anyone. You have my word." Nina appears sincere. I believe her.

"Thank you, dear. Now, it's time for Delia and me to leave and allow you and my son to converse in private. We brought separate cars, so it shouldn't be a problem." My mom and Delia begin to gather their things.

"You don't have to leave, Celeste. Josh and I can talk later."

"I'm tired, sweetie. It's best I leave now." My mom gets up and gives Nina a hug.

"Nina, let me tell you somesing, you will have to visit me soon. I hope you enjoy the food." Delia smiles at Nina tenderly.

"Thank you both for coming and bringing me treats. I'll definitely enjoy devouring your delicious food, Delia." Nina states as she walks both ladies to the door.

Once they leave, Nina turns and faces me. "Thank you for trusting me." She says quietly and provides me with her undivided attention.

We head back to the living room. I prepare myself to tell her more about my father.

"I want to begin a true friendship with you. If you won't be in my life as my lady, then I'll do everything I can to keep you as my friend. I want you anyway I can have you. I know you don't trust me now, but I'm hoping that one day, you will. Would you like to hear more about Mateo Blanco?" I ask.

"Of course." She replies.

"Besides the murder of my grandparents, I believe my father was also responsible for the death of my mom's best friend. She was a reporter and wrote an article regarding my mother's disappearance. Somehow, she was able to post a picture of my mom and Blanco along with her article indicating my mom was last seen with the man in the picture. Days later, she was found murdered in her home. Articles regarding my mother's disappearance were never written again. After I gave up on my dream of going pro in high school, I chose not to immediately attend college. I became obsessed with finding out as much information regarding my father. If I was going to hate him, I was going to despise every detail about him. He made my revulsion towards him come with ease. He's behind countless murders, has engaged in kidnapping, ransom, and robberies. He's been linked to human trafficking for forced labor, prostitution, and rape. I found out his uncles, brothers, and cousins, all top members of his drug organization were either killed or arrested leaving him the leadership of Los Blancos Cartel. At one point, he was known as "the King of the Skies" for the massive airplane fleets he used in the transportation of cocaine from Columbia to Mexico. Blanco was arrested in 2009 and miraculously only did a year sentence in a Mexican prison. His right hand man, Diego Cruz used the organization to his benefit, took over one of the major trade routes in northeastern Mexico, and in the process started the Enemiga Cartel. Once Mateo Blanco was released from prison, he overtook his role in Los Blancos Cartel once again and formed an alliance with Diego Cruz to overrun other cartels for their trafficking routes. Their partnership proved to be a success and landed them in Forbes magazine's list of richest and most powerful men worldwide. Last month, their partnership came to an end over a dispute, now they're at war with each other. It makes me sick that my mother has lived in fear all these years due to my father. I feel helpless." I confess.

"It sounds as if that man and I say the term loosely, has his hands full. Hopefully, you and your mom don't cross his mind." Nina does her best to console me.

"You know, Blanco has twins, a son and a daughter. His son works for him and has a reputation of being just as ruthless. There hasn't been much documentation about the girl. She's in her early twenties. I'm assuming she uses an alias for protection." I state.

"Wow. That's crazy." Nina has a perplexed expression on her lovely features. She curiously asks, "Hey, quick question. So, is it safe to assume the initials K.O. on your tiger represent Kaitlyn O'Neill?"

For some reason, I laugh. "Yes. When I graduated high school, my mom felt horrible about not allowing me to fulfill my dreams. To ease her guilt and let her know that I loved her unconditionally, I got the tattoo of a tiger that represents my mom. The tiger's expression is fierce because that's how my mom is, she has done everything, and will do anything to protect me...I'm her cub." I shrug my shoulders.

"That's sweet, Josh. You're a good son. I've always wanted tattoos, but since I recently became comfortable in my own skin, I felt it would be best to wait. Besides, I haven't found anything that is meaningful and artistic. One day, I'll decorate my body when I find the right inspiration." Nina looks at me and bites the bottom of her lip, contemplating something. "Okay, to show you that I want to build on our trust foundation and really develop a friendship with you, I'll tell you the little I know about my grandfather and father."

I interject. "You don't have to. Don't get me wrong, I would love to hear it, but I don't want you to feel uncomfortable telling me."

"I want to. Now, don't interrupt. I'm afraid I'll lose my courage." She giggles clearly from being nervous. "When my mom was growing up, she was financially well off, she was surrounded by money and all the luxuries she could ever hope for. According to my mom, she met my father when she was twenty-one attending school at NYU. They met when she was on her way to school one day and formed a long distance relationship. He would occasionally stop by in New Jersey to see her when he was visiting his family in New York. He was handsome, but in a very rugged and mysterious sort of way. He was Mexican and she quickly grew to love his Spanish accent. He definitely stood out to her. He always bought her expensive perfume, high end clothing, and took her out to eat at elite restaurants. Sometimes, they would go a few months without seeing each other. Although, they didn't have an ideal relationship, my mom clung to the hope that he would take her away with him one day and choose to spend the rest of his life with her. He never mentioned love or gave her false hope. She knew it was only a matter of time for him to fall for her the way she had fallen in love with him. When my mom's family found out about her dating a 'dirty spic,' they gave her the ultimatum of leaving him or forgetting about them. My mom was well aware that her parents would never approve of her dating anyone who wasn't Italian. She felt trapped in her life. Since my mom refused to make a choice, her parents made the decision for her, and disowned her. In 1985, with the help of my father, my mom moved to San Francisco. She was heartbroken, but had heard so many wonderful things about this city, she embraced her new freedom with excitement. She continued with her education and held a part-time job at the bakery she now owns. After she obtained her Bachelor's degree in Business Management, my mom became pregnant with me. My dad told her he wasn't prepared to be a father and never returned to see her."

Nina sighs heavily with a crease on her forehead set as she carries on with her story. "Throughout the years, my mom has received packages full of money on a consistent basis. Even to this day, she still receives them. Growing up, she had heard her father was a 'wise guy' involved in the Italian Mafia; she just didn't want to believe it. She could only assume that now, he was sending her money as his way of showing her that he still cared. Even when he was committed to a five year prison sentence for racketeering and being in conspiracy to a Mob-controlled gambling operation, her father still managed to send her money. Despite that, my mom knew she couldn't return home and wouldn't be accepted since I was part 'spic,' according to her family. She could handle being rejected by her loved ones, but wouldn't tolerate anyone refusing me."

She pauses and looks sad for a slight moment then continues. "In the four years my mom dated my father, she realized she didn't know much about him. He was always mysterious about his life and job. My mom had fallen in love with the idea of him because she was a hopeless romantic. My father never told her he loved her, never said he would build a life with her, and when he said he would never return, she knew it was true because he never lied to her."

"What's his name? What does your mom do with the money her father sends her?" I ask curiously.

"I don't know my father's name. I have never wanted to know it. For what? He didn't want me, so there's no point in knowing anything about him. My mom raised me to value family, not money or materialistic things. I'm happy earning my own income and living within my means. If I could return the money just to see my mom's family accept us, I would. We don't want her father's money; we want her family's love and acceptance. They don't seem to understand that. There are some things money simply can't buy, so I cherish the people around me and love them for who they are. As for the money my mother receives, she invests the majority of the money on my behalf. I want nothing to do with it, but she's adamant that I have financial security. My monetary net worth is now over several millions."

"Wow. You said the majority of your money is invested, what about the rest?" I'm completely intrigued with her humble qualities.

"I give a substantial amount to charities involved with aiding victims of sexual abuse, children's research hospitals that provide free care when there's no insurance, and other miscellaneous organizations I feel have worthy causes in helping society." She replies.

"Valentina, you truly are a remarkable woman with a heart of gold." I look into her eyes lovingly and contain myself from reaching out to her.

"She sure is! My God! I can't believe how much drama you two just spit out!" Kade barges into the living room and interrupts our conversation. "I've been dying to get some tamales since I heard that lady say she brought some, I'm starving!"

Nina immediately looks at me with a worried expression on her face. "I'm so sorry. I completely forgot Kade was here, when I arrived home he was sleeping."

"That's okay. Don't worry about it." I ease her concern. "Kade, I need you to keep what you heard among our group. Don't mention it to anyone."

"Don't worry. As difficult as this may seem, I know when to keep my mouth shut. I'm not gonna lie though. I'm soooo glad I was here to listen! There's no way Cheesecake would've told me your family's secret. Once she gives her word, she's not breaking it for anything or anyone. Good thing I made myself comfortable on the floor by my door and listened to the whole conversation." Kade states nonchalantly, as if he didn't just violate our privacy.

"Kade! You're such a fuckin' nosey Nancy! What the fuck? You need to have more respect. It's one thing for you to listen to my conversations, it's something else when you eavesdrop on a private discussion involving guests. Not cool, Kade." Nina looks pissed.

"Okay. Sorry. I didn't know there was a protocol I was supposed to follow when guests come over. Hello? No one ever comes over! We're private people. You and I have always kept our acquaintances at a distance and never allowed them to enter our sanctuary. I really am sorry. Can we eat now?" Kade asks as he's helping himself to the food.

"Yeah, let's eat. Wow. Delia really outdid herself, she brought a lot of food. Wanna join us for dinner?" Nina asks smiling warmly at me. And for the first time in days, I feel as if we can truly begin building a friendship.

"Sure." We all enjoy our dinner with beers in a completely relaxed state while music plays from their surround sound.

Kade suggests we play dominoes and turns it into a drinking game, for every double tile played a double shot of tequila must be taken. "I have to go to work tomorrow, I can't get drunk." Valentina states.

"Relax...we'll only play one game. We already drank enough these past few days. Besides, I'm going to the gym with Em later tonight. I don't wanna get shit faced." Kade says as he shuffles the tiles.

Curiosity takes over me. "So, are you and Emme more than friends?" I ask.

Kade quickly responds. "No. There's nothing going on between us. Everyone knows I'm completely against being in relationships. I enjoy my freedom too much. I will never trust anyone besides Cheesecake and Mama V. Emme and I have always had a hostile friendship and now that we've included sex to the equation, we're simply going with the flow and having fun. There's no need to make things complicated."

As we're each getting our tiles, Nina reflects on Emme and Kade's friendship. "I think you two are having more than just fun. The chemistry between you guys has become intense lately." Nina looks at her dominoes and places a double-six tile in the center of the table. Kade ignores her comment and grabs three shot glasses along with a bottle of almond flavored tequila Emme gave them as a gift from Mexico. He also gets three beers for us to use as chasers. Since Nina played the heaviest tile, she's the first to pound her shot.

As the game progresses, Nina and I are the only ones who have played double tiles. The tequila is quickly starting to take effect with the combination of beers.

"Hey, Josh, have you ever heard Cheesecake sing?" Kade does his best to contain his laugh.

"Yes, he has and he thinks I'm amazing! Right, Josh?" Nina gives me an intense look willing me to agree.

"Of course, you have a beautiful voice." I say without skipping a beat.

Kade gives me a disbelieving glare. "Liar, liar, pants on freakin' fire. You know, if you want Cheesecake to trust you, you'll have to be honest with her. Right now, she can see through you and knows you're lying."

"When I heard her sing, the volume was cranked up to the song. She sounded good to me, besides I was distracted since she was dancing to the music." I defend myself.

Nina's beautiful browns are starting to look glassy. "I'll put an end to this now." She slightly slurs. "I'll sing along to whatever plays next."

The song, "Is this Love" by Bob Marley comes on. Nina begins giggling and gets up to dance around the table. Kade and I are amused with her behavior and anxiously await her talented vocals.

Nina begins to sing the reggae beat. *"I wanna love you and treat you right...I wanna love you every day and every night..."*

Awww...my baby's singing reminds me of a choking chicken, but it's the best sound I've ever heard.

She stops singing and starts talking to herself, but is looking straight at me. "Really, Bob? I think you're lying. I reeeeeeally think you're lying, Bob." Okay, so she's indirectly singing this song to me and she's no longer in good spirits. *Great.*

Nina continues to sing. *"Is this love...Is this love...Is this love...Is this love that I'm feelin'?"*

She stops singing and states, "No Mother Flower...it's not love. You're just horny, that's all." Now, Nina's expression has altered to a serious and hurt one.

Once again, she resumes with her singing. *"I wanna love you, I wanna love and treat...Love and treat you right."*

She pauses, looks straight at me, and says, "But, I can't...because you fucked up." Nina's stare is full of accusation. She walks around the table and approaches me, she grabs my beer and chugs it. That's my cue. I need to put this night behind us before we argue or before she says something she might regret tomorrow. Even worse, she might say an ugly truth about me I don't want to hear from her lips.

Once she's done with her beer, I grab her hand and lead Nina to her bedroom. She goes willingly. We kick off our shoes, pull the sheets, and climb into bed. She plays music from her small stereo next to her bed. Eric Benet's "You're the Only One," comes on. The lyrics to this song and Nina's presence bring a tightening to my chest that's unbearable. She turns to face her window, I hold her from behind, and inhale the scent of her hair. She smells sweet and clean, like strawberries. I slide my hand to her front side and gently caress her torso underneath her shirt. I've hurt Nina, she's trying to be friends, but there's no way she can let go of the past so easily. I have to continue earning her trust. In the meantime, I won't make any advances so she can understand that what I feel for her isn't just sexual, it's deeper than that, it's my vulnerable heart, respect, and commitment I'm giving her. Only time will prove the truth of my love. I fall asleep with Nina in my arms.

In the early morning, I wake up and realize I have an early meeting to attend. I feel Nina stirring, she turns, and lazily smiles at me.

"Hey." I brush the hair away from the side of her face.

"Hi." She responds.

"I have to go to work. I didn't mean to wake you. You still have an hour left to sleep, so rest up." I give her a kiss on her cheek.

"Friends?" She asks.

As much as it hurts me, "Friends." I confirm.

Chapter 11 (Nina)

Faces

Although it hurts to know that Josh and I will never be, being with him brings me an unconceivable amount of solace. Before I met him, I never imagined myself trusting anyone besides my mom and Kade. Slowly, I began to confide in Emme. To my surprise, I quickly believed in Josh. Even though he betrayed me, I'm willing to give our friendship a second chance. I've grown a lot. In the past, I would have cut him out of my life immediately, but something tells me he's worthy of another opportunity.

A few weeks have passed; Josh and I are getting along well. On a few occasions, we've hung out without the slightest attempt at anything else. At times, I have to maintain full control of my raging hormones and the feelings for him that I try so desperately to overcome. I miss our intimacy, I miss his comfort, and I miss waking up in his arms. Although these weeks have proved to be a challenge, we're taking baby steps on setting a strong foundation for our new friendship.

Monday after work, Kade and I head over to Celeste's gym as guests. Josh agrees to meet us there. I inform the group that my mom, Emme, and I will be participating in this year's "Walk for Life" march which will be held on Saturday.

"That's great, dear. May I ask why you're involved with this cause?" Celeste asks.

"I'm involved in this march to bring awareness to alternatives to abortion and to do it in remembrance of those babies who were not allowed a chance to live. It's not about being against a woman's right to choose or to judge anyone. It's simply to let women know their right to choose life or death not only changes the destiny of their unborn baby, it will forever change their life as well. I enjoy being active in my community." I shrug my shoulders and smile at Celeste.

Without hesitation, she asks if she can join us. Josh and Kade decide to partake in the march as well. I'm thrilled and give everyone all the details.

❧

Saturday morning, we all meet at my house. I introduce Celeste to Emme and my mom. Celeste and my mom instantly get along. "You look so familiar." I hear my mom tell Celeste.

I interrupt. We don't need to get into that topic today. "Dillon will be joining us in today's march. This evening, I have a meeting with him and a potential client. Dillon says this guy is loaded and is considering me to be the face of his new tequila line. Isn't that cool? Apparently, he saw pictures of me from the Bentley photo shoot. Does everyone want to meet up after my conference and have dinner together?"

Everyone agrees to meet at Dillon's studio after my meeting. From there, we'll head to Gary Danko's, a restaurant in the Russian Hill district. We're more than excited about to-day's events. With my friends and family by my side, I know nothing could possibly go wrong.

We arrive at the Civic Center to hear various speakers. Pro-Choice and Pro-Life protestors are at the rally. There's an estimated fifty thousand people in attendance. Belly dancers are to my right surrounded by a large crowd. As we begin the "Walk for Life" march down Market Street, I notice a man standing in front of a very large screen showing graphic pictures of aborted babies while he's lecturing about his beliefs. Really? Although, I see his point, there are small children walking amongst the crowd, there's no need for them to see that. I ignore him and keep walking. Something that also catches my attention is how Dillon and my mom haven't stopped talking and laughing with each other. They seem to have hit it off as friends. I'm glad.

Once we complete the march, we congregate outside a coffee shop before we go back home to get ready. As a lady is exiting, she accidentally bumps into my mom. Right away, the lady apologizes without looking at her. Once the lady directs her gaze towards my mom, she has a shocked expression on her face.

I know this woman, but from where?

The woman's skin is a pale tone. She has dirty blonde, shoulder length hair with several greys. Her deep blue eyes look tired and her face appears sucked in. She looks like someone whose drug of choice was meth some time in her past. The lady definitely looks familiar and the nagging feeling is only increasing.

"Oh, it's just you." The woman glares at my mom.

Just then, her face, her voice, and her evil stare register in my memory and I'm able to recall exactly who she is. Immediately, I turn my attention and concern towards Kade who has a disturbed look on his face.

Kade intervenes. "When you speak to Victoria Moretti, you do it with the upmost respect. Do you understand? I don't know who the fuck you think you are, but you definitely need to learn some manners among other things." Rage quickly overpowers Kade's expression.

"Hello, Kade. I see you're still with your disrespectful ways following the devil." The lady responds.

"Mother dearest, I see you're still a pretentious bitch putting up a façade for strangers." Kade replies to his mom.

"Cindy, you have a son?" One of the women with Kade's mom asks.

"Let's go, ladies. There's too much negativity and evil around here." Cindy ignores the question, turns her back to her son, and begins to walk away.

Kade stops her and the group she's with. "Not so fast. Ladies, you may not know this, but yes, I am this woman's son." Kade points at his mother. He directs his attention to the women Cindy is with. "I'm assuming you ladies are a part of her church group." The ladies surrounding Cindy all nod. Their expressions clearly demonstrate discomfort.

Although Kade has a smirk on his face, hurt is evident in his beautiful baby blues, but he continues to speak. "Well, let me tell you a few things about this woman. She is a piece of shit mom who beat me, starved me, and not once showed me the slightest bit of affection. When I was small, she used to bring several men over to the house and the rest of the time, she used to leave me alone to care for myself. There was never any food in our apartment, but she always had money to spend on herself and on alcohol. My neighbors felt sorry for me, took turns feeding me, and gave me the clothes their kids outgrew. One of the Mexican ladies, who was a field worker and hardly had anything for herself or her kids, regularly brought me a plate of food for dinner. One day, my mother was on her way out as the lady was dropping off my food, my mother became upset, and threw the food on the ground threatening to call immigration if she got near me again. I was only six years old and starving. When my mother left, I scraped the food from the floor and ate it. We rarely had electricity since it used to get turned off regularly. She never cleaned and had me living in filth. I spent as much time as I could in the streets as I grew older, any place was better than being in my home with drunken men who tried molesting me when my mom was left unconscious."

"That's enough!" Cindy exclaims with tears running down her face. She attempts to walk away again, but Kade grabs her arm, and doesn't let her go.

"Oh, I'm not done just yet." Kade looks at her with disgust and continues to release his tormented memories. "Once I became older and met Valentina, her mom, Ms. Moretti took me in as her son. She fed me, bought me brand new clothes, and made sure I was well taken care of. One day, after I had dropped off pastries from Ms. Moretti's bakery shop to my neighbors, my mom made me take her to Valentina's house. My mom demanded a thousand dollars from Ms. Moretti if she wanted to keep me." Kade pauses and wipes the tears from his eyes then points to his mother.

"This lady, my mother and I say the terms loosely, sold me for a mere thousand dollars. I never returned to her home again. Years later, I saw her as I was walking by a church with my first boyfriend, she was now a new woman completely involved with church, so she claimed. When I introduced her to my boyfriend, she said she would rather know I was dead than to know I was gay. So you see ladies, this woman who stands before you and preaches the word of God is a hypocritical, self-righteous, evil woman with absolutely no remorse for her actions. She stands in front of you crying out of humiliation, not from sorrow or regret." Kade looks sternly at each member of his mother's group. "I just thought you should know what type of evil you have amongst your group."

"I found God. He has forgiven all my sins." Cindy states in between sobs.

"News flash! God was never lost. He's not going to forgive you when you continue to be evil and judge others! If you're so changed and all about God, why haven't you looked for me? I'm the one you beat, starved, mistreated, neglected, and put at risk of being molested from the countless men you used to bring over! Let's not forget wishing death upon me for my sexual orientation. I'm supposed to forgive you too...not just God! Go ahead and continue acting self-righteous, you're not fooling anyone when your heart is full of hatred. You despise anyone who isn't white and curse gays. Do I need to remind you that Latinos and blacks fed your Irish little boy and gave me what little they had? It was a hell of a lot more than you ever gave me. Have some humility and accept your mistakes! I'm bisexual because I love people, I don't have a preference for men or women, I love them both. Race is irrelevant. If I go to hell for having nothing but love in my heart, so be it." Kade glares at Cindy with disgust.

"But, I can't see you going to heaven for simply preferring dick." Kade laces his last comment with venom.

Just then, my mom interrupts Kade's rant. "Thank you, Cindy, for giving me the best son a mother could wish for. You not wanting to be a part of his life isn't his loss. It's yours. Kade has grown to be a wonderful human being, with a vibrant personality, an intelligent mind, a beautiful soul, and a heart of gold. Although you weren't woman enough to raise him, love him, guide him, and support him, he has managed to be better off without you. The past several years, he has been surrounded by love every single day. So, I thank you for allowing me the privilege of raising Kade, my son."

"He's not your son." Cindy responds.

My mom looks at her with pity. "Do you think that because you gave birth to him that makes you his mother? Do I need to remind you that you were never there for him or even provided his necessities? Were you there when he was sick? Did you feed him? Provide him shelter? Clothe him? Most important...love him? Were you there helping him with his homework, taking him to his computer science conventions throughout the state, or even cheering him on while he played sports? No, you weren't because I was there every day caring for him, loving him, and ensuring him of his wonderful qualities. Any female can have kids, but it takes a real woman to raise them, love them, and make them a priority. We have all made mistakes, but you have never acknowledged your wrong doings, made any attempt at reestablishing a relationship with Kade, or even given him a simple apology. You're a pathetic excuse for a woman. Go back to your church and continue to preach the word of God that you don't even follow."

"Let's go." I intervene quietly. This woman isn't worth another second of our time. I grab Kade's arm and pull him away from the small crowd that has formed around us, he and my mom have said enough. Kade walks away with his head held high no longer shedding any tears. He looks at me and wraps his arm around my shoulder as we're leaving. "Why are you crying?" He asks with concern deep in his features.

"Because I hate to see you hurt." Is all I can say between my sobs.

After taking a few steps, my mother abruptly stops. "Come here, my son." She reaches out to Kade with open arms. "I'm so proud of you for standing up to her. Now, forget this situation happened and let go of any anger or resentment you have towards her. It's not healthy to hold onto hate and negative feelings."

"It's forgotten." Kade smiles lovingly at my mom and gives her a hug.

We walk back to the car in silence and I notice Emme and Kade holding hands. Elation consumes me knowing that Kade is surrounded by love and for the most part, has overcome the obstacles he was faced with as a child.

When we arrive to our vehicles, we agree to meet at Dillon's studio. I'll be taking a cab there, while Josh picks everyone else up. As I head home, exhaustion hits me. When I enter my house, I decide to watch a movie to relax, once it begins to play, I fall asleep.

I wake up in a panic. I'm sweaty and my breathing is accelerated, I simply recall the barrel of a gun pointed at me. I don't understand why I arouse in such a fright, maybe I shouldn't have fallen asleep while watching the movie, *Carlito's Way*. I realize I overslept. I quickly jump in the shower and begin to get ready.

This evening, I'm wearing a white, retro cap-sleeved dress that goes slightly above my knee with a woven lining and a sheer overlay. My bright lips coordinate with the hot pink stilettos I'm wearing and the matching colored flower above my styled side bun. When I put on my black coat, instantly, I recall being completely naked underneath it and surprising Josh. The way his eyes gazed hungrily at me that night makes me crave him desperately. Oh, how I miss his touch and having his face buried between my legs. *Nina! Snap out of it, girl! You need to focus on business right now! You're going to be late!*

I rush out of my room to find Josh, Celeste, Emme, Kade, and my mom all dressed up waiting for me in the living room. "Hey, you're early and you all look amazing." I observe.

I take a good look at Josh and notice he's wearing a three piece dark grey suit with a black shirt underneath along with a silk, grey tie. He has no stubble, just shaved and immediately,

I fantasize to run my lips along his jaw. He looks sophisticated and absolutely delicious. Right away, the song, "Suit and Tie" by J.T. comes to mind. A long sigh escapes me. I can't help it, Josh looks dreamy, definitely too good to be true.

"Yeah and you look hot as always, but you're late. We're taking separate vehicles, the moms will ride together in a different car per their request and the rest of us will go with Josh in his Range Rover. While you're in the meeting with Dillon, we'll be waiting for you across the street at the Japanese Steakhouse drinking sakes until Dillon can give us a tour of his studio." Kade sounds pleased with his agenda.

"You're finally taking out your date car?" I ask Josh teasingly.

"Yeah, it only collects dust in my garage. I decided to take it out for once and I'll have to admit, I prefer driving my truck." Josh shrugs as he declares his preference for his big truck with its roaring engine over his luxury SUV.

"Sounds good to me. Let's go." Before I leave the house, I pick up my clutch purse and portfolio. Just then, Josh grabs my arm.

"You look stunning." Josh tells me with admiration in his eyes. "Can I ask you for a favor?"

"Sure." I respond curiously.

"Will you please allow me to explain what happened with Nicole? I know you don't want me bringing it up, but it's been several weeks and I need to explain. I know this isn't the right time, but will you hear me out tonight after dinner?" He desperately pleads.

"I'm sorry, but that's behind me. I don't want to take steps backwards. I'm late; let's just drop that topic once and for all." I grab his hand and squeeze it, hoping he'll understand that no reason he gives me will justify his actions.

"Fine. I'll let it go for right now, but you will hear me out soon enough." He holds onto my hand and leads us out of my house.

We arrive at Dillon's studio, a three story red brick building. The outside sign reads, "Hampton – Fine Arts Gallery – American and International Paintings, Prints, and Sculptures." Josh drops me off. Everyone will be waiting for me at the Japanese Steakhouse to finish with my meeting and for Dillon to provide them with a personal tour of his gallery. I enter the building, at once, I'm astonished. Although I've worked with Dillon a few times, I've never been to his workshop. Inside is a high end galleria of art and here, I assumed it was just a typical print studio. As I enter, I observe the sculptures spread out in the middle of the first floor. Throughout the first two stories, I notice the walls are mounted with paintings in categories of Old and Modern Masters, Barbizon Painters, Impressionists, Artists of La Belle Époque and Contemporary. The salesman is locking up and informs me Dillon will be with me soon. I continue to browse.

Shortly after, I hear Dillon's voice behind me. "Nina, I apologize for the delay. Thank you so much for being here this evening. Our client is expecting us on the third floor, please follow me."

I give Dillon a small hug and allow him to lead the way. While I had been observing his gallery, I noticed a staircase towards the entrance and back of the gallery. We don't go towards either direction; instead, Dillon walks me to the elevator that is located in the center of the right wall. When we arrive to the third story, I realize it's specifically for his print collection. The photos of nature and the aftermath effects of natural disasters are breathtaking. Instantly, I wonder why he wastes his time taking pictures of me with cars when clearly he has such an artistic talent.

Dillon leads the way to his conference room. A man in a

suit is standing right by the door. When we enter, the client is sitting at the head of the table, two other men are standing on opposite ends of the room, all men remind me of the secret service for some reason. When the client sees us entering, he stands to greet me.

"Hello, Miss Moretti, a pleasure to finally meet such a stunning woman. Allow me to introduce myself, I am Daniel Martin." His accent is very alluring.

I provide him my hand expecting a handshake; instead, Mr. Martin turns it slightly and kisses the back of it. The client appears to be in his late fifties, early sixties. He's handsome with ebony colored hair, olive toned skin, and dark, mysterious eyes. His presence emanates power, wealth, and respect. Or is it fear? For some reason, I'm intimidated by him, something about this man is familiar, but not in a good way. Immediately, I disregard my anxiety and introduce myself. "Hello, Mr. Martin. The pleasure is all mine and thank you for wanting to meet with me today."

Dillon pulls out a chair, silently directing me to have a seat. As we all sit, Mr. Martin asks, "Miss Moretti, may I call you Nina?"

"Please do." I smile nervously at the client.

Mr. Martin gives me an amused look. "Nina, before we get down to business, tell me about the Bentley photo shoot. How do you know the owner of that vehicle?"

"Actually, I don't. I never met the client nor did I ask anything about him." I answer honestly.

Mr. Martin considers my response. "Well, he seems to be infatuated with you, Nina. He has several portraits of you, although none are sexual in nature. Don't get me wrong, you look exquisite in all of them, but he appears to have a special interest in you and holds you in high regards."

"This is news to me, Mr. Martin." I'm confused. What's his point?

Mr. Martin directs his attention to Dillon. "I understand you're the photographer of the Bentley photo shoot, how do you know the buyer of those pictures and how long have you been doing business with him?"

"My client list and the business I conduct with them are completely confidential. I apologize, Mr. Martin, but I cannot provide you with your requested information." Dillon diplomatically expresses his regret for not being able to answer his client's intrusive questions.

Mr. Martin smirks at Dillon. "Mr. Hampton, no need to apologize. Even though I appreciate your discretion, I will have to admit that I don't like rejection. With that in mind, let's continue with our meeting, shall we?"

We all agree. At that moment, I realize that in my hurry to arrive on time, I accidentally left my portfolio behind in Josh's Range Rover. "Mr. Martin, pardon me, but it seems I have forgotten my portfolio in the car. I can text someone to drop it off, if that's okay with you."

"Please do so, Nina. I would love to see more of your work." There's something about Mr. Martin that makes his look towards me feel sinister. He's behaving like a gentleman, so why is his presence making me feel so uncomfortable?

As I text both Kade and Josh requesting either one to drop off my portfolio, Dillon is on the phone with his sales associate directing him to leave the door unlocked. It's past closing and all of the gallery's employees will be off in a few minutes.

Mr. Martin begins to discuss his new tequila line along with his vision for his brand. He provides us with a shot of his tequila añejo which is considered to be premium. Mr. Martin indicates his tequila has been aged in oak for several years, not just the minimum year, therefore considering his brand to be the best and allowing for a hefty price for his superior quality.

Kade quietly interrupts our meeting when he drops off my

portfolio. I ask him to stay. At once, I sense Kade's unease, but he stays in the conference room with me and remains quiet while he plays with his phone.

I provide my portfolio to Mr. Martin. He appears to be impressed with my past work. We discuss the details of his contract. While he's making me one hell of an offer, I'm not convinced this is something I'd like to do. Being a pin-up model is my way of embracing my sexuality and simply doing it for fun. This tequila campaign would be a great opportunity for my career, if it weren't for Mr. Martin, I'd gladly accept. Unfortunately, something about him has me second guessing his proposal. Mr. Martin is adamant that I consider his offer of being the face of his tequila brand and join him in his new venture. The meeting is adjourned and we agree to meet tomorrow for dinner to discuss my decision.

As the meeting ends, the two security in the room leave before us. Dillion, Mr. Martin, Kade, and I head down stairs in the elevator with the guard who was outside the conference room earlier. I stand in the back of the elevator beside Mr. Martin. Dillion is in front of us and begins making recommendations of restaurants in the area as the elevator descends. When we arrive at the bottom floor, the elevator doors open, Kade and Dillon exit first. Once they've taken a few steps away from the elevator, they raise both hands and lower their bodies to the ground. Simultaneously, Mr. Martin puts me in a choke hold while his body completely wraps me from behind. Too soon, I feel the cool barrel of his gun against the temple of my head.

As the guard exits the elevator, he begins to shoot, there's gunfire from both directions for a brief moment. Suddenly, the guard's lifeless body drops to the ground covered in blood. Panic consumes me. I want to yell, and runaway, but I can't. At this time, an unfamiliar man steps in front of the elevator several feet away. I'm not able to focus on him because I'm trying desperately to loosen the arm that's cutting off my breathing circulation.

"Get out of my fucking way before I kill her!" Daniel Martin threatens the stranger. The man gestures to two men standing by the elevator to move and allows Daniel Martin to exit the elevator with me as his hostage.

All three men have their guns pointed at Daniel Martin, while he has his gun pointed at me and is standing at an angle near the wall right by the elevator.

Oh, dear God! I notice Josh on the ground unconscious to my immediate left. I don't see any blood. *Please, Lord don't let him be dead!* I plead. Just as I'm about to direct my attention to the stranger, I notice Celeste, my mom, and Emme are face down on the ground. My tears are uncontrollable. I'm living a nightmare and can't seem to wake up.

Just then, Mr. Martin speaks, "Why am I not surprised to see you, Diego? I knew you had it bad for this little cunt, but never would I have imagined that you would put so much at risk for her. What makes her so special? Why such a fascination with her? Why does she not know of you?" Mr. Martin's mind is running vigorously trying desperately to figure out the puzzle before him. "Drop your gun and answer my questions or I'll kill her. I'm a dead man either way; I might as well take down as many as I can with me." He threatens.

Diego? Who is this man? I've never met him in my life! Surely, I would remember him if I had, he's so tall and with such menacing features! What does he want with me? Why me? I urgently speculate.

At this time, my mom raises her head. "Noooooo! She's my daughter! Please, I beg you, don't hurt her!" She pleads.

I stare at my mom, willing her to calm down and ease her worry, but fail miserably.

Daniel Martin ignores my mom as she begs for my life and directs his attention to the stranger before us. "Drop your fucking gun and tell me what this whore means to you. I swear...she'll go down with me when I die if you don't tell me!"

The stranger drops his gun. "Mateo, Valentina is my daughter."

An array of confusion hits me with a striking force. *My father? What? How can that be? Who the fuck is Mateo?*

"You lied to me, you little cunt. You told me you didn't know the owner of the Bentley." His hold on me gets tighter around my neck for a few seconds, but then loosens it to hear my response.

Through excruciating pain, I reply, "I've never met my father. I don't know who he is. I don't even know his name. I don't know what's going on. I thought you were Daniel Martin, but that man is referring to you as Mateo. I have nothing to do with anything that's going on between you two. Please just let my family and friends go." I cry desperately.

"He calls me Mateo because my real name is Mateo Blanco. Maybe you've heard of me? Better yet, maybe you're one of my clients who purchases my fine drugs?" I can feel his hot breath against the side of my face as he speaks through his clenched teeth.

Mateo Blanco? Nooo...Josh's dad? Oh, dear God! Josh's dad is holding me hostage! What the fuck?

The stranger, my father, Diego speaks with a look of malevolence set in his features as he glares at Mateo Blanco. "When this is over, Mateo, you'll be wishing for death to take over from the slow and agonizing torture I have in mind for you."

Mateo ignores his threat. "You've been busy keeping secrets, I see. I knew it was worth taking this trip. Something told me Nina was the key to trapping you. Never in my wild-est dreams did I imagine you were hiding a daughter from me. All these years of working together and not once did I think you had a family. What else have you been hiding?"

The stranger, Diego remains quiet with abhorrence radiat-ing off him.

"If I die, I'll blow her brains out. Simple as that." Mateo lewdly licks the side of my face. My stomach turns and causes a vile sensation to rise up my throat.

"That's enough!" Celeste yells and raises her head with tears in her eyes.

Mateo tightens his hold on me without realizing it. "It can't be." I hear him whisper to himself. "Get up!" He commands Celeste. She does as she's directed. "Stand next to Diego." He instructs her. Again, Celeste complies. Now she's standing right in front of Mateo, just a few feet away from Diego.

"You conniving bitch! You stole from me and took away my child! What the fuck does this cunt mean to you?" He ges-tures towards me tightening his hold.

"She's become like a daughter to me. Please, I beg you...let her go, spare her life." Celeste weeps profusely.

"Get on your fucking knees and beg me like the dog you are!" Mateo orders with fury projecting from every cell in his body.

In her fragile state, Celeste lowers herself to her knees. "I beg you, let her go, Mateo." Her eyes are filled with tears of panic.

"What did you do with our child, Kaitlyn? I can call you Kaitlyn, right? Considering I don't know which name you're living under anymore!" Mateo yells with an uncontrollable fury.

At that moment, Celeste makes the mistake of directing her gaze to Josh who is lying on the ground to the left of me

218

unconscious. Immediately, she looks away. Unfortunately, that's all Mateo needed to realize his son was by his feet.

"You!" Mateo addresses Kade. Get up and turn this man over so that I can see his face." Kade gets up and slowly begins to walk towards Josh. "Now!" Mateo commands without the slightest bit of patience.

Kade turns the body over allowing Mateo to see Josh's face. "Get down on the fucking ground and face down!" Mateo directs Kade. Slowly, Kade follows his order.

Mateo turns to Diego. "You piece of shit! You knew Kaitlyn had my son and knew where they lived all these years! You kept them from me!" Mateo's rage is only escalating at this point.

"I haven't seen Diego throughout all these years—" Celeste gets interrupted by Mateo.

"Shut the fuck up, you worthless bitch!" Mateo shoots her without hesitation. Celeste instantly falls forward with blood spilling out beneath her.

"Noooo!" I yell, crying hysterically.

"Now, your precious little girl is next, mother fucker!" I can feel his rapid pulse vibrating. "You kept my child from me. I won't allow you to have yours." Mateo says his last statement slowly and with such calmness, it brings me chills and puts me in a greater panic.

"I'm not gonna ask you again, let my daughter go!" Diego's fury is pulsating through his skin. "Everyone working for me come to my side. Now!" Diego orders.

Three of Diego's men join his side along with one of Mateo's security. What catches me completely off guard is seeing Emme get up, walk towards Diego's direction, and stand by him.

At this time while Mateo has his attention focused on Diego, I feel a metal object being thrust onto my hand, I get a better grip and discreetly transfer it to my right hand. Urgently, I stab Mateo's thigh with all my force and twist the switch blade upwards. Mateo yells from agonizing pain as he loses his balance and begins to shoot without a specific target. As I'm ducking for cover, I see Josh stand and push me to the ground. As I'm collapsing, I feel a burning sensation by my shoulder and I feel Kade throw his body on me from a different direction. As Mateo's falling to the ground, I notice Josh rush him. Within seconds, I witness Josh shoot his father in the back of the head. Mateo somehow lands on his back and Josh seizes the opportunity to shoot him two more times on the chest and another time on his head to ensure he eliminates the threat that is his father.

Within seconds, a S.W.A.T. team enters the building just as Josh is dropping his gun. Once I manage to push Kade's heavy body off me, I realize he's been shot in the chest. His body is limp. He's unresponsive. And my heart is shattered.

"Noooo!" I scream while I'm frantically trying to wipe away his blood and nurse him back to life. "Someone, please help!" I beg in the middle of chaos.

I indistinctly hear more gunfire. Officers are in gun battle with one of Mateo's security who is on the second story. I pay it no mind and don't bother searching for cover. Kade's lifeless state is my only thought. Absentmindedly, I realize the shooting has seized. Diego and his men choose a different outcome and drop their guns. They raise their arms in defeat. Everyone in the room is directed to place their hands behind their heads. I'm unable to remain focused; my upper body is in excruciating pain. I'm vaguely able to comprehend that Josh is being escorted by police with handcuffs behind his back. It all goes black.

Chapter 12 (Nina)

Friends

I wake up to the sound of my mother's voice. She's reading something to me. I feel sore and thirsty. She looks up and smiles at me with tear filled eyes. She gets up to kiss my cheek. *Why is she crying? What happened?* I want to ask, but feel too dazed and exhausted to do so. Just then, I recall seeing Josh in handcuffs and even worse, remember the blood shed of Kade and Celeste.

With a burning sensation in my throat, I ask my mom about everyone's well-being.

"Celeste is in critical condition. She lost a lot of blood, but luckily no major organs were hit. Unfortunately, with her delicate state, it's more difficult for her body to recover." My mom says with deep sorrow. "I've been staying here since yesterday evening going back and forth from ICU to your room.

"How's Kade?" I ask, afraid of her response.

"He was shot in his lower left chest within the rib cage, but away from his mid-line. The bullet was removed yesterday in surgery without complications. If he continues to do well, he should be released from the hospital by the end of the week."

My mom smiles warmly at me with tears in her eyes.

Oh, thank God.

"What about Josh?" I ask nervously.

"Dillon is with him. I don't know anything else." My mom states.

As curious as I am about Emme and the man who claims to be my father, I decide not to ask about them. I feel emotionally spent and allow my exhaustion to take over. I fall asleep once again. The next morning, I'm allowed to leave the hospital since I only had a flesh wound on the outside of my shoulder. My mom left to gather some clothes for me to wear upon my release. As I'm waiting to be discharged, I ask the nurse about Celeste. She's doing slightly better, but is still in ICU. I question her about Kade.

"Why don't you ask me how I'm doing?" I hear Kade's voice nearby.

The nurse smiles and pushes both sets of curtains out of the way so that he and I can see each other. The nurse leaves allowing us some privacy.

Right away, I get up and rush to his bedside. I lightly plant a kiss on his forehead, afraid of hurting him if I give him a hug. "How many times will you go around saving me?" I ask jokingly.

"As many times as necessary, but let's try not to get ourselves involved in more shit. It hurts like a bitch!" He chuckles.

"I love you." At once, my waterworks start flowing from a mixture of feelings for my best friend and the thought of coming so close to losing him.

Kade's eyes become glossy; he does his best to contain his tears. "I love you too, Cheesecake. Now, stop it. I can't risk having my crocodile tears come out. There are too many cute nurses and a few fine interns to have me ugly crying. Don't ruin my game." He laughs and slightly flinches at the same time.

Since I see he's feeling better, I ask his version of yesterday's events.

Reluctantly, he begins to tell me his side. "I recognized him right away. Daniel Martin, I mean Mateo Blanco. His security also confirmed my suspicion. After I heard Celeste's story, I looked him up. Hello? I'm in front of a computer all day; of course, my curiosity was gonna take over. I wanted to see what he looked like and wanted to know more about him." Kade takes a sip of his water and continues. "I knew you didn't feel comfortable. Why else would you want your loud and obnoxious friend who has no filter with you in a business meeting? So, I sent Josh a text telling him that I 'thought' his dad was in the meeting with us. And you already know the rest."

"Who handed me the switch blade?" I'm nowhere near knowing all the rest.

"Oh, that would be me. After I turned Josh over, I ended up right next to the guard who was killed exiting the elevator; his leg was by my face. The guy had a gun holstered around his lower calf, but I knew if I attempted to grab it, I would draw attention to myself. Luckily, he had a switch blade inside his sock. I took it right when Celeste was shot. That's when Josh finally became conscious again. We both knew this was our only chance to get you out of Mateo's grasp. Unfortunately, we weren't in a good position to do much damage to him. Luckily, once you stabbed him and he released his hold, Josh quickly got up, grabbed a nearby gun, and pushed you to the ground. As your body fell, Josh was able to shoot his father perfectly from behind." Kade states lost in thought.

Just then, my mom enters our room. She's ecstatic to see Kade fully awake and me standing. Minutes later, the nurse provides me with my discharge papers and care instructions. I promise Kade I'll be here tomorrow after I stop by the police station first. My mom lets him know she'll be back once she gets me settled in.

The ride home is silent. So much has happened; I can't seem to wrap my mind around it all. We finally arrive at my house. After I shower, I'm anxious to question my mom now that we're in private. My mom hands me a cup of tea along with my medication as we make ourselves comfortable in the living room. She's prepared for the inquisition that's being directed at her. "First, let's start off with you being on the ground. What happened?" I ask.

My mom sighs heavily; clearly, she doesn't want to relive the experience. "Well, Josh ran out of the restaurant while he was in the middle of having a drink. He left abruptly without saying anything. We waited a few minutes for him to return, but he didn't. That's when Celeste paid the tab and we left. When we arrived at the gallery, we were able to see people inside to the right of the entrance, so we entered. That's when I saw him, your father. I knew he recognized me. I wasn't allowed to say anything. Without hesitation, his men pointed guns to our heads and signaled us to be quiet. They led us away from the entrance. When we approached the elevator, we saw Josh unconscious on the floor. We weren't allowed to get near him. Then, we were directed to lie on the ground face down. We had no choice but to comply with their instructions."

"Have you been in contact with Diego?" I ask.

"No. The last time I saw him was when I told him of my pregnancy." I see the hurt in my mom's eyes as she recalls that day.

"Did you know he was the leader of a drug cartel?" My question is irrelevant, but curiosity gets the best of me.

"No. To be honest, it explains a lot though. His life was a mystery to me. I never met any of his family or friends; he always traveled and always had large sums of money. I was too in love with him to care or question him. I was naïve and refused to accept the truth when my family brought it to my attention. I felt their hatred towards his ethnicity would make them say anything to discredit him." My mom answers truthfully.

My brain feels overwhelmed with revelations. I decide to call it a day and fall asleep early. Rest is imperative for tomorrow's long day ahead. I need to find out about Josh.

The next morning, I head to the police station for questioning. I answer their inquiries to the best of my ability omitting the minor detail of Josh shooting his father to death. I'm informed that Josh was not arrested; he was interrogated and has now been released. My heart skips a beat with excitement. Once we leave the station, I ask my mom to take me to the hospital. I know Josh will be there with his mother.

When we arrive, we're notified that Celeste is no longer in ICU. Relief washes over me. Before I search for Celeste and Josh, I check on Kade. He's recovering well and his spirit is up.

"Hey, Cheesecake. I'm so glad you're here. Did you hear about Celeste? She's my next door neighbor. How do you feel?" Kade asks with concern.

"I should be asking you that. I feel better. Do you need anything? Are you thirsty? Have you had any visitors?" He and I both know whom I'm referring to. His sterile room is filled with flowers and balloons wishing him to get well soon.

"I'm fine. Actually, I think I found my flavor of the week. She's a nurse here and has amazing tits with a voluptuous ass, she's incredible. Clearly, she's in the wrong profession. We're having fun. Every hour I press the nurse's button and she comes to my room. I tell her I need my pillows adjusted, so she fluffs them up for me. As she does that, she leans over me with her huge 'breasteses' practically smacking my face! And then, during the swing shift, there's an intern who I shit you not, looks like a combination of William Levy and Henry Cavill. And to think, I only thought Seattle Grace Hospital had all the eye candy within its grounds. I give this joint an A+ for customer service." Kade laughs as he holds on to his side. "I keep forgetting that I can't laugh yet. It hurts too fuckin' much." Kade pauses and repositions himself to be more comfortable. He looks sleepy. "Thanks, Cheesecake, but I don't need anything and yes, I have had visitors. A few friends stopped by earlier, apparently they heard about what happened to us on the news. Can you believe it? We're like a big deal around here. I wonder how much ass that will get me?" Okay, Kade is definitely feeling better if he's thinking of getting some. Since he is deliberately not mentioning Emme, I decide not to either.

As Kade's medication kicks in, I allow him privacy to sleep. I walk towards Celeste's room and find Josh speaking with the doctor. I go around them and enter the antiseptic room. My mom is sitting by her. Celeste looks pale and weak, but still manages to smile when she sees me. She appears more delicate than usual. I approach her and give her a kiss on the cheek, my tears land on her face. I wipe them and thank her. She faced her prime fear to spare my life. For that and for her love, I will be eternally grateful.

"I'm so glad you're safe, dear. I'm sorry you had to endure a taste of Mateo's wrath. But that's over with, I'm glad everyone survived and now we can continue to live in peace. Please, promise me that you'll stay by my son's side. I understand your relationship didn't work out and that's okay, but you're good for Josh. Remain in his life, even if it's just as friends. Since you came into his world, he has become a new man. He doesn't just live for the moment or treat women as objects. He's a good person, Nina. Let him prove that to you." Celeste pleads.

"Celeste, you and your son saved my life. I will love you both forever, but not just because of that, but because you have welcomed me and loved me unconditionally. The feeling is mutual." I kiss her on the cheek once again and decide to lighten the mood. "Now, you need to recover soon before Kade gets a sexual harassment lawsuit. He's having way too much fun with the nurses and interns next door." I giggle lightly.

"Yes, I noticed he's quite popular." She smiles lovingly at me.

As I'm heading out of Celeste's room, I run into Josh. There's so much I want to say to him and so many kisses I want to give him, but I don't say or do anything. I can't. I'm left speechless, too overwhelmed with feelings. He looks at me as if he were just seeing me for the very first time.

"Hey, lovely lady, how do you feel? I've been worried about you." He says with a sad, concerned expression, as his gorgeous hazel eyes examine every inch of my face. He approaches me. Instead of thanking him, I simply run into his arms and cry. His embrace feels heavenly as his strong arms enfold me and his re-freshing, clean scent awakens my senses. The tears I shed are from happiness that he was there to save me, joy knowing he is free and not incarcerated, and most important relief from see-ing him in front of me alive and well. We have so much to discuss, but now isn't the time nor the place to have such a con-versation. He agrees to talk at a later time. We both find ourselves locked in each other's arms unable to let go. I can re-main like this and hold him forever, but rationality strikes and makes me let go. He needs to be by his mother's side and I need to keep Kade company. Unwillingly, we separate.

I return to Kade's room and make myself as comfortable as possible on the chair beside his bed. I pull out my Kindle and wrap myself in a paranormal romance novel while Kade sleeps. A good love triangle involving a human, a vampire, and a werewolf is the perfect distraction. A few hours pass by, a nurse enters the room to check Kade's vital signs. I excuse myself to get something to eat downstairs at the cafeteria. I check Celeste's room to see if Josh or my mom is hungry. They're both starving. We decide to grab a quick bite for dinner at a taqueria across the street. As we're entering, I grab a daily paper from the newspaper stand. I notice our infamous, kingpin fathers made the headline news, one for his death and the other for his capture. Josh ignores the newspaper and my mom snatches it from me while leading me inside the restaurant.

When we return to the hospital, I'm looking forward to watching reruns of *Friends* with Kade. Even though he complains about the countless breakups between Ross and Rachel, I know he secretly loves the show. Right when I'm about to turn on the TV that's mounted on the upper left hand corner of the wall, Kade makes himself comfortable in an upright position on his bed. And then...Emme walks in.

Kade and I remain silent avoiding eye contact with her. She finally grabs a chair and sets it by the bed on the opposite end of me near Kade's feet, but doesn't say anything. Kade loses his patience. "Say something...shit." He glares at her. Clearly, I'm not the only one who feels betrayed.

Emme finally begins to speak. "I want to apologi—" Kade interrupts her. "Save your apology and start from the beginning. We want every fuckin' detail." Kade is livid and continues scowling at her.

Emme exhales deeply. As she's about to begin her explanation, she keeps her head down and eyes focused on her lap. "Fine. You both know I'm from Arizona. Well, my dad got into some financial trouble with Mr. Diego Cruz a while back. My dad was trafficking drugs for Los Blancos Cartel, but was stealing small portions to sell on the side. My dad became greedy and was desperate to climb the hierarchy of the cartel organization. His plan backfired on him. Mr. Cruz, who was Mr. Mateo Blanco's second in command at the time, found out. My dad had to pay for his mistake with his life and ours. Mr. Cruz sent lieutenants to bring my father to him along with our family. We were all brought to a warehouse to get killed. When Mr. Cruz noticed me, he became intrigued. He wanted to know everything about me. He made me an offer I simply couldn't refuse. In the drug business, second chances don't exist, but we were lucky. Mr. Cruz informed me that if I became his loyal informant regarding Nina, then he would spare my family's life. If I stopped following his orders, my family and I would die a slow and agonizing death. I accepted his offer. He moved us to San Francisco. He never indicated his relationship to you."

Emme finally makes eye contact with me. "His orders were specific, I had to tell him everything about you and intervene with your life whenever he deemed it necessary. He paid for my education at Berkeley and directed me to major in sociology just like you so that we could share classes and build a friendship. It's been four years since I accepted Mr. Cruz's offer and have been informing him of your whereabouts. During this time, he began running his own drug organization, making him a much more powerful and ruthless man than before." Emme gets quiet and looks away.

"Why do I feel there's something you're not telling us?" Kade questions her.

Emme takes a deep breath and exhales slowly. Now, she has her full attention directed at me. "Although I was grateful to Mr. Cruz for allowing us the opportunity to live, I quickly became resentful of everything and everyone. I gave up my dream to be an artist; I had just been accepted to attend the Art Institute of Chicago. Not attending that school crushed me. Soon, I began to envy and even hate you at times. You had everything at your reach and never took advantage of things. You chose to work for a living." Emmes expression changes to anger. "Hello? You're a millionaire! You don't need to fuckin' work! Guys drool all over you and you get bored with them after a day. You never allow anyone near you. In the beginning, I practically had to force my friendship on you. I made sure to keep my life private because I didn't want to share anything more than I had to with you."

Emme breaks her eye contact with me and focuses on her lap once again. "Josh didn't cheat on you with Nicole. I set it up to look as if he had. Nicole is my ex-girlfriend."

Emme pauses for a moment. I'm dying to say something, but decide against it and allow her to continue. "When we first met up with Josh and Dillon at the bar, I knew Nicole would be there. I sent her a text instructing her not to pay me any attention. Once I realized you had your eye on Josh. I sent Nicole another text asking her to flirt with him just to see what you would do. I asked her to apply at his job and planned for her to meet us by the Civic Center during the parade, at the Halloween Pub Crawl, at the dance club, and at his house. When we were at the club, I knew the only way of putting Josh in a compromising situation was by tricking him. So, she covered his eyes and kissed him. Josh returned her kiss assuming it was you. I lucked out when you didn't allow Josh the opportunity to explain what happened in his home. Since you told me you were going to his house after work, I asked Nicole to drop off his wallet that he accidentally left at the club the night you saw them kissing. When she dropped it off, she asked if she could come in and use his phone to call a cab. He agreed and left her by herself in the living room while he showered since he had just arrived from the gym. When you rang the doorbell, Nicole undid her shirt and tousled her hair to make it seem like they had just fucked. The hickeys you saw on her chest were from me. Sometimes, we still mess around. The icing on the cake was that you saw him right after he had gotten out of the shower. He never purposely touched her. Nicole and I just made it appear as if he had. She loves stirring up drama and was more than willing to go along with each of my plans to break you two up. Initially, I did it to mess with you, then when I informed Mr. Cruz you were seeing someone, he asked me about Josh. I told him he had the reputation of a player and had admitted he never wanted to get serious with anyone. Immediately, Mr. Cruz directed me to keep him informed regarding your relationship. He didn't want me to intervene just yet, since he was aware you didn't care for commitments either, but I decided to get involved anyway." She remains quiet once again.

"Is that it? Are you done?" I ask.

"Yes." Emme answers sheepishly.

Kade speaks up. "You fuckin' scandalous bitch! All my Cheesecake ever did was welcome you into her life, love you, care for you, and worry about you. She was a true friend and this is how you repay her? By betraying her and ruining her relationship? How many times didn't you see her depressed because of Josh? How many times didn't you witness tears escape her eyes? She didn't pry into your life out of respect for you! You resented her? Bitch, please! You should have been resenting your greedy, selfish ass father for wanting that quick money and as a result put himself and your family at risk of being murdered! That's who you should have been angry with, not my Cheesecake! It's not her fault your dad and her dad put you through that. I could have easily understood being Nina's dad's informant, anyone in your place would have taken his offer, but for you to purposely hurt my Cheesecake...no, nothing justifies your actions. Any serious feelings that may have started to develop between us are gone. I'm done with you."

Emme raises her head. She has too much pride to continue showing weakness by looking down. "I truly am sorry for the hurt I caused. I really do love you both; I simply allowed my jealousy and resentment to get the best of me." Her eyes have now become glossy and she's trying desperately not to shed a tear. *Too little, too late.*

I know I should conduct myself like a lady and show some empathy, but I don't give a fuck at this moment. I simply want this bitch gone and out of my life for good. She gets no pity from me. "I should tell you to kiss my ass and lick it too, but I'd rather you leave and take your sorry ass apology with you. I don't wanna see you again. I loved you like a sister and you basically stomped on my heart and spit in my face. You and that whore, Nicole can both kick rocks. Deuces, bitch!" I salute her with the peace sign. "Don't let the door hit your conniving ass on your way out." I glare at her, willing her to say something. She doesn't. Emme slowly leaves the room and doesn't look back.

Kade squeezes my hand. "What a bitch. Bitch, bitch, bitch, bitch...AND...some more bitch. I can't believe I fucked her and let her refer to me as Master KD. Why didn't you stop me?" He laughs. Although he's joking, I can still see the hurt behind his eyes.

"Forget her! Where's that boobilicious and bootylicious nurse when you need her?" I giggle trying to cover up my pain as well.

"You know what you have to do now, don't you?" Kade asks.

"No. What?" I'm confused.

Kade gives me a disbelieving look. "Hello? You need to go searchin' for your man, boo! And ride him long and fierce. Since I'm stuck in this place and can't get any, you need to get some for the both of us. And don't you worry, I won't even think about telling you that I told you so regarding Josh. It would be in poor character to remind you that I felt as if something just didn't make sense about him cheating. And I definitely wouldn't dream of bringing up that I told you several times to allow him the opportunity to explain. Lucky for you, I don't need to always be right even though I usually am. I'm just sayin'."

"Gee...Thanks for not rubbing it in." I roll my eyes at Kade. "I feel terrible. What should I say, what should I do, what if he doesn't forgive me? What if he rejects me?" Instantly, I begin to get nervous. "I don't think now is a good time to have a talk with Josh. His mom is still in a delicate state next door. I'll wait until she gets better and continue being there for him as a friend." I'm determined to wait. The last thing he needs is to discuss Emme's provoked drama. He has enough on his plate. I'll apologize for jumping to conclusions and not allowing him a chance to explain at a later time.

Chapter 13 (Nina)

Visitor

A week has passed since that dreadful evening. Today, Kade is finally getting discharged from the hospital. I pull up to the front of the building as a nurse is pushing Kade in a wheelchair past the automatic doors. He and the nurse have wicked smirks planted on their faces as they approach my vehicle. I decide it's best not to ask what the looks are all about. I help Kade get inside my car.

"Oh, Betty, how I've missed you." Kade whispers as he's getting inside the car. He makes a poor attempt to control his enthusiasm about going home. The nurse waves at him as she walks away pushing the empty wheelchair.

"Mom is at our house baking your favorite desserts. I just finished making a special lunch." I raise my eyebrows twice at Kade as I start the engine and drive away.

He smiles. "By the time I'm completely recovered, I'm gonna be horizontally challenged again. It's okay. I'll hit the gym hard and get back to my healthy regimen, but for now, I'm gonna enjoy Mama V's pastries and your cooking. I can't wait to be home!" He's thrilled to finally be able to rest in the comfort of his own bed.

"Once you get settled, I'll be going back to the hospital to be with Celeste. I'm so glad her recovery is progressing well. Josh rarely leaves her side, I'll make sure to kick him out so that he can get some rest." I pause for a few seconds, contemplating on the favor I'm about to ask Kade. I bite my bottom lip; my nerves are getting the best of me. *Screw it. Just ask him, Nina!*

"Hey, Kade...you know how I think you're like the bestest, most attractive friend in the whole wide world, right? Well—" Kade interrupts me.

"Spill it, Cheesecake. What do you want? This ought to be good if you're resorting to lame flattery." Kade smirks at me, highly amused.

"I need a favor. I'm hoping you can help me, but I don't want you to tell anyone." I say nervously. As I'm driving home, I have his full attention so I ask him my favor and tell him my plan. Right away, Kade shares my anxiety, but agrees to help me out whatever way he can.

It's Wednesday, a few days have passed since I asked Kade for his assistance with my preposterous scheme. After several phone calls, he was able to come through for me, as always. Now, I'm headed to bring the truth to light, hopefully, the reality won't be too difficult to endure.

I arrive at the Federal Detention Facility Diego Cruz was transferred to a few days ago after being held at county jail. As I pull up to the parking lot, apprehension stops me in my tracks. I can't move, my hands feel sweaty, and I feel my stomach twisting. I can't do this. The tightness in my chest is becoming unbearable. What am I doing here? What was I thinking? This is a bad idea. I shouldn't be here. *Relax, Nina. Take deep breaths, you can and will do this.*

The grey structure surrounded by a chain-link fence with barbed wire looks absolutely dreary. I don't want to go in, but I force myself to exit my car and head to the entrance of the visiting section even though it's not during administration hours. With just my driver's license and keys in hand, I enter the ashen building. My nerves feel as if they're about to combust. As I enter, I don't make eye contact with the correctional officer. I hand him my ID and inform him I've been granted permission by the warden to meet with inmate Diego Cruz. I'm instructed to sign the visiting list while he verifies my early and unheard of appointment. Once he gets confirmation, he directs me to remove all items from my pockets; he instructs me to walk through a metal detector and has a female officer do a pat search of my body. The guard then guides me through the building, to the right is a large sign that reads VISITING along with the rules and hours, but we don't head in that direction. We take a left that leads us to another hallway. We enter a small empty room with another door on the opposite end. There's a camera at the top corner looking down upon us that catches my attention. The door immediately locks behind us and then the sound of a buzzer allows us to enter the next hallway that indicates it is for parole agents and attorneys. The officer leads me to a tiny office that is so small it is more like a booth, it has a chair and a small metal table attached to the wall, the upper part of the wall is a thick glass window. The officer informs me I have been allowed an hour visit and leaves. Ten minutes later, Diego Cruz stands before me and has a seat on the opposite end of the window. Shock doesn't begin to describe his expression. I'm thankful for the element of surprise, the lack of prior notice of my visit. Once again, I'm grateful to Kade for coming through for me with this favor.

He reaches the phone propped against the wall facing him; I do the same on my side. I take a moment to closely observe him. He's a handsome man, but appears tired and completely defeated. Almost as if he's given up on himself. He has olive toned skin, dark hair in a tight fade, and deep brown eyes. He has a long mustache that connects to his goatee. Even though he sits before me humbly, his presence is still intimidating. "Hija...What are you doing here? I'm supposed to place people on a visiting list. How did you manage to get an exception?" It feels strange hearing his voice along with his accent; we're so close, yet completely out of each other's reach.

"Please don't refer to me as your daughter. I came here for clarification on things that have me perplexed. Our time is limited, if it's okay with you, I'd like to know as much information regarding you, my mom, and Mateo Blanco." This encounter isn't about reuniting with my long, lost father; it's about getting answers, nothing more.

He hesitates and pinches the bridge of his nose with his eyes closed. "Fine. You deserve to know my side." With somber articulation, Diego Cruz begins to tell me his story. "I grew up in unimaginable poverty. I lived with my mother and youngest sister. I stole regularly and did whatever it took to put food on the table. As I grew older, I became more relentless. I was determined to get money fast and through any means. I always made sure to provide for my family. Even after my sister began a family of her own, I still provided for everyone. In my early twenties, I was introduced to trafficking drugs by my best friend, Mateo Blanco. The fast money quickly became addicting. I was willing to eliminate anyone that stood in my way of getting rich. By the early eighties, Mateo's family soon considered me part of their organization. In time, they became incarcerated or killed. Mateo eventually became leader and I, his second in command. I traveled a lot to the U.S. conducting business. During one of my trips visiting some Columbians and New York mobsters on behalf of Mateo, I met your mother while she was attending school. I liked her, but I wasn't serious about her. Unfortunately, our relationship caused her to get disowned by her family. Her dad knew about my part in the drug business. He was in the mafia and looked down upon my lifestyle. Gambling and racketeering, that was okay with him, but not drugs, that was beneath him." He pauses and chuckles sarcastically.

"Your mom decided it was best for her to start a new life away from her controlling family. So, I helped her move across the country to San Francisco where she could begin a new life independently. I would see her on occasion, never telling her when we would meet next. Despite allowing a long time passing from each visit, I always found her happy to see me.

During this time, Mateo began dating an actress, an actress who I used to fantasize about many times. When I finally met her, I realized she was more beautiful in person than in her movies. I couldn't get her out of my mind. One day after a meeting with Mateo, he called me shortly after and ordered a search for Kaitlyn, the actress. Apparently, she had fled with her and Mateo's unborn baby and a large sum of his money. I was ordered to find her before she ran to the police. I had to threaten and force several cops to provide all pertinent information regarding the protection of Kaitlyn. It took a few months to find her, but I did it. Before I gave the information to Mateo, I called her father. One of the cops told me her dad used to be with DEA. I left an anonymous message stating Mateo was aware of Kaitlyn's new identity along with her whereabouts and needed to leave now in order to remain safe. By the time I reached Missouri with lieutenants from the cartel, she was gone. My plan to keep her safe worked. Almost immediately, I was able to coerce the new agents handling Kaitlyn's protection to relocate her to San Francisco. I knew that once Kaitlyn had her baby and was found by Mateo, he would kill her. I couldn't have her death on my conscience. I loved her. I wanted her safe and was determined to keep an eye on her from a distance.

Despite my love for another woman, I continued seeing your mother. A year later, she informed me that she was pregnant. Immediately, I ended the relationship. I was well aware of what my lifestyle entailed and having a family wasn't one of them. I loved money and power, but it all came at a high price. I knew that if I ever made a mistake, my mother, sister, and I would pay the price with our lives. I didn't want to put you or your mother through such a risk. Although I kept my distance, I regularly provided you both with large sums of money. It was the least I could do." He looks down at his hands with shame. "Throughout these years, I saw you grow up, but never allowed myself to get near you. I knew you were in the best hands."

I take a moment to allow this new found information to register. "You provided us with money? This whole time, I thought it was my mom's father."

"No, he pissed me off for treating your mom the way he did. I had him set up. That's why he ended up in prison." Diego admits.

"Oh." A question comes to mind right away, I fear the answer. I push my concern aside and ask it anyway. "Were you involved in the murders of Celeste's parents and best friend?"

His look is subdued, he closes his eyes slowly and once he opens them again, he maintains eye contact with me. I notice the color of his eyes is the same shade of brown as mine. I also realize anything he says may incriminate him further. Regardless, he responds, "Yes." I feel my heart shatter. "I did it on behalf of Mateo's orders, but I was responsible for the execution. You can ask me whatever you want, I have nothing to hide. I'll be getting served with a life sentence, if I'm lucky. I've accepted my fate. It's the least of what I deserve for all my malicious actions."

I swallow past the lump in my throat and decide to take advantage of the situation. I want to know as much as possible. "What made you use Emme as an informant?" Saying her name still brings me pain.

"You were in your second year at Berkeley, you began dating, going out, dressing differently, it was a pretty drastic change on your part. I became concerned. She was your age and was in a bad position; I seized the opportunity to find out more about you on a personal level. I was worried." Diego confesses.

His reasoning comes across as very fatherly. I push the thought aside and continue listening to him. "I became very anxious regarding you once you became a teenager. During one of my visits to San Francisco, I realized you had changed middle schools. Something didn't seem right. I contacted the counselor at your new school to find out how you were doing. She informed me that you didn't speak, that you had been in school for about a month and didn't talk in class or to anyone." Diego's eyes become red and swell up with tears that he refuses to shed. I look down on my hands, concentrating on his words.

"I went to your old school and asked the kids around if they knew you. I made sure to ask only individuals. I paid them to tell me everything they knew, most of the information was useless, until I found some piece of shit little bastard who was high. He said you had the reputation of being easy. He mentioned you gave it up to him and his friends at the same time. He also stated the whole school knew and that's why you were transferred elsewhere." His words bring a blow to my chest; I look up and see Diego's tears running down his face.

"I made him tell me the names of the other boys. He did. I knocked him out and dragged him into the car I was driving; I brought him to a closed location and beat the truth out of him. He admitted that he and two of his friends forced themselves on you." Diego becomes silent and after a few moments, he continues. "That day, I got rid of him and the next day, I did away with the other two boys." Diego declares in a dignified manner.

Shock overcomes me. I vaguely recall hearing about one of the boys being a runaway or being missing years ago, but remember getting nauseous at the sound of his name. I quickly drew him out of my mind, not giving him a second thought. I always wondered what I would do if I ran into those three boys again, but that moment never came. Now I know why, my father killed them to avenge me. His truth sits heavy in my heart. I remain quiet, not sure what to say to his revelations.

Diego studies me carefully, unsure of continuing to shed light to his actions. He works past his hesitation and proceeds to speak. "I remained by Mateo's side for several years. Killing him wasn't an option for me, although it would have been easy to do. The repercussions would have been too immense. His extensive family would have put an immediate hit on my head. I've never feared death, but until you came into my life, I was frightened of not being there to protect you. I couldn't get rid of Mateo, I felt that would also leave Kaitlyn in a vulnerable state since his youngest son has been raised to hate and retaliate against her. Keeping Mateo alive meant I was able to be informed of his plans and whereabouts. Once he was incarcerated, I took the opportunity and became the leader of my own drug organization. Upon Mateo's release from prison, we became allies to overturn other cartels and their areas. Our alliance provided us a major fortune. Business was fine between us until he saw portraits of you. He inquired a lot about you. He wanted to know where I had found you since I have large pictures of you that were turned into art throughout my homes and offices. I downplayed you by indicating you were just some model and that I didn't know much about you. Since Mateo has a thing for trophy girlfriends, you quickly became an interest to him. We argued about you and ended our alliance." An evil glare overpowers Diego's eyes as he reminisces about that quarrel with Mateo.

"Somehow, Mateo found out that Dillon was the photographer of every portrait I have of you. Mateo coveted you because he wanted to take what was mine. He assumed I loved you in a romantic way, never did he imagine it was in a fatherly manner. One of my informants was security for Mateo. He notified me that Mateo was meeting with Dillon and a model for one of his businesses. Instantly, I knew he had found you. I rushed here as fast as I could under one of my aliases. The rest, you're aware of." Diego exhales deeply, finally feeling relief for admitting his truth to me.

I'm left in an emotional state of shambles, my head is spinning, and my heart is racing. All this new information has me feeling distraught, yet slightly in awe with the man in front of me. Diego Cruz is a ruthless man, a murderer, drug trafficker, the leader of a cartel, and...my father. Most of his actions are merciless and despicable, but a few were caused out of love for Celeste and me. How can I respect him or tolerate him when his hands are full of innocent blood shed? Do some of his reasons justify his actions and make him less of a monster?

As my mind is in turmoil, Diego interrupts my thoughts. "I know I've done malicious things in this world, things that I am not proud of. I'm ashamed of the example I've set as a father. I

know I don't deserve your forgiveness, but know that I am truly sorry for abandoning you, not protecting you enough,
putting you in danger, and most important, for never giving
you my love. Despite being an evil man, you have always been
in my heart. I love you, hija and hope that one day you'll be
able to grant me the forgiveness that I know I don't deserve.
Your mother is wonderful woman who did an amazing job raising you. You're the pride in my eyes, the only thing in this
world I did right. I don't have the entitlement to take claim on
you, but I want you to know how much I admire the woman
you have become, you're strong, determined, intelligent, absolutely beautiful, and a fighter. Staying away from you was the
only way of ensuring your safety. I hope that one day, you can
understand that." Now, Diego's tears are flowing freely. Just
then, the guard walks in and informs me our visit is over.
Where did the time go? It feels as if I just got here. I barely said
a few words.

"I'll put your name on the visiting list, just in case you have
any more questions for me." Diego says hopefully. "It was really nice seeing you. Thank you for coming. Drive safely. I
love you, hija." I can easily see he doesn't want me to leave. I
nod and give him a half smile as I hang up the phone and
stand to depart. There's so much I would like to say and ask,
but I can't seem to speak past the lump in my throat. I wave at
him slightly as a traitorous tear escapes my eye. I walk out of
the room leaving my father behind.

I return to my car feeling distraught. I sit in the parking lot
of the dreary building gathering my thoughts. For some reason, the chain with the dog tags of both Bettys catches my
attention. I remove the chain from the rear view mirror and
notice the back of one of the dog tags reads, "The cost of forgiveness is nothing, yet its value is priceless." My chest
tightens. Josh and Diego come to mind. The other dog tag has

engraved, "I love you. You're always in my thoughts. – Josh" It's strange how I am just now noticing his words that have been with me since the day I received his gift.

As I'm driving home, I do my best not to think of the disturbing conversation I had with Diego. I'll be reliving the emotions from that discussion once I retell it to everyone who is directly affected by my father's actions. Right away, I think of Josh. In a way, my father saved him and his mom from Mateo, but on the other hand, Diego murdered his grandparents. I have to tell him, he deserves to have closure in his life regarding his family. How will he feel? Whatever he experiences, I'll be there to support him. I decide to push all my thoughts aside and simply enjoy the drive with Betty. I turn on some music, the song, "Heavy Cross" by the Gossip begins to play, I crank up the volume and lower the rag top of my car. The loud lyrics vibrating through my soul and the long drive put my nerves at ease.

I head to the hospital. I can't wait to see Josh and finally let him know that I'm aware he didn't cheat. I don't want another minute to pass without the truth being exposed. His mom is feeling much better and I simply can't hold back on loving him any longer. Later, we can discuss the conversation I had with Diego, but as of now, I need to be in his arms.

I walk into Celeste's room and I'm caught completely by surprise. To my left is a stranger, a man I've never met. He's an older, distinguished gentleman dressed in a refined suit. He's handsome with silver hair; his tan face looks at Celeste with absolute adoration.

"Nina, my dear, I'm so glad to see you. Please, let me introduce you to my friend, Michael." Celeste is beaming. She's definitely feeling a lot better. "He's the friend I told you about who lives in my building." She adds.

Oh, her male friend. Of course, I remember hearing about him. Josh jokingly referred to him as a gigolo. "Hello, Michael.

It's nice to finally meet you." I'm thrilled to meet him, knowing that Celeste has a friend who is concerned for her, puts my mind at ease. They both seem to be happy in each other's company.

"The pleasure is all mine, Nina. I would have been here sooner, but I just found out today that my Celeste was in the hospital. I've been a mess. It's been nearly two weeks since I last heard from her. The worst thoughts crossed my mind. I'm just relieved she's feeling better and may even be released this weekend if she continues to do well. I'm so glad I thought of asking the concierge of her whereabouts. He told me her son, Josh informed him of Celeste's hospitalization when he stopped by to pick up some of her personal things. I came as soon as I found out." Michael's rambling is endearing. At once, I like him.

"Well, I'm glad you're here and keeping her good company." I can't help but smile warmly at the two of them.

"Me too." Michael says with a sigh of relief.

I turn my attention to my right side. Sitting beside Celeste is none other than my mom and next to her, holding her hand is Dillon. As an automatic reflex to my shock, my jaw drops. Well, well, well look who became extra friendly. "Hello, mother. Hi, Dillon. How are you guys? Anything new happen lately? Anything you care to discuss?" I ask with extreme curiosity seeping from my questions.

My mom looks at Dillon with a radiant smile and says, "Nope." Dillon smiles shyly and runs his free hand through his hair. My mom then directs her focus on me and gives me a wink along with a devilish smirk. *Oh. My. God. My mom's a cougar! Way to go, mom!* She's slightly over a decade older than Dillon. I couldn't be happier for them.

After seeing both ladies happy and moving on with their lives, I decide it's best to hold onto the conversation I had with Diego. Why rain on their parade? We've all been through a lot lately; happiness on all ends is well deserved. Once Celeste is fully recovered and I'm able to speak with her and my mom in private, I'll notify them of my discussion with Diego and my new found information. After all, they deserve to have closure as well. For now, they need to just focus on their relationships and living a peaceful, happy life.

"Celeste, where's Josh?" I ask.

"He left a short while ago; he had to take care of some work issues." She replies.

Damn! I missed him. I guess I'm going to have to go hunting for my man. "Okay, well I'll let you crazy kids continue to get acquainted. Call me if you need anything, otherwise, I'll be here tomorrow for a nice, LONG visit." I emphasize the word long, it's important they know I want all the juicy details about them going steady with these boys. I grin at Celeste and my mom while raising my eyebrows twice at them. They both laugh. They're so cute.

I look at the time and realize that Josh is probably at his office. Since he's usually the stalker, I decide to reverse the rolls. I ask Siri on my iPhone the location of E-Con Solutions.

Siri responds in her automated voice with, "I found fifteen places matching 'Econ' a little ways from you."

I scroll through the list she provides and realize none of those companies belong to Josh. I reply to her response. "Siri, you're pissing me off. You gave me all the wrong businesses."

"You know what they say about blaming the messenger, Nina." Siri has the audacity to be a smart ass and give me an attitude. I'm so not in the mood for her. I need to find my man. Why haven't I ever been to his job?

"Ugh! I'm pissed, Siri!" I yell into my phone.

"Not at me, I hope." Siri replies.

"You're not doing your fuckin' job and giving me the info I need!" Now, this bitch is really crawling under my skin.

"I think that's subject to opinion, Nina." Siri informs me in her robotic voice.

Screw this bitch, I'm done with her. She's testing my non-existent patience. I get on the internet using my phone. Leave it to Google to come through for me. I'm a happy camper once I get the address to Josh's company. *Wait a second; did I just get into a fight with my phone?*

I finally arrive to Josh's work. Instantly, I'm astonished with the sky rise structure and its grandeur, it's located in the heart of the Financial district. The skyscraper has a tall base that is glass enclosed; the shape of the building is cylindrical with granite and glass edges. Right away, I recognize this place; it envelops a public plaza that is used in the summer-time for concerts. I used to come by during lunch all the time and listen to the various genres of music. What a small world. As I enter, I ask the information attendant which floor E-Con Solutions is found. He directs me to take the elevator and head to the fortieth floor.

When I finally reach that level and the elevator doors open, I step into the lobby of Josh's office. The bamboo floors catch my attention for some reason. The large receptionist's area is covered with colored glass that has such an intricate pattern it looks like a beautiful piece of art. That's about the only color I see. Everything else is a neutral tone with polished steel. The style is modern, minimal, and luxurious. If I know Josh, I'm sure he insisted on everything in his floor being eco-friendly.

I ask the young and pretty receptionist if I can see Mr. Ryan. She inquires if I have an appointment with him. Embarrassed, I tell her no. It was very presumptuous of me to assume Josh would drop what he was doing just to see me. The receptionist informs me he's gone for the day. She believes he may be at the company's warehouse. I ask her if she can call to see if he's there, so that I don't have to make another pointless trip. I don't want to call Josh myself; I want to completely catch him off guard. I know it sounds silly, but it's what I want to do.

The receptionist informs me that he did stop by the warehouse and left a few minutes ago. I thank her for her time and rush to the elevator. It seems to take forever to arrive. I finally leave and head out to get my man. I continue with my stalker tendencies and drive to his house. When I get there, I ring the doorbell several times. No answer. Screw it. If I'm going to play the role, I might as well do it right. I grab the key that's located above the light sconce near his door. I enter Josh's house and make myself comfortable in his living room while I wait for him. Luckily, one of my favorite movies is on TV. Eventually, I fall asleep on his couch watching the movie, *Troop Beverly Hills*...don't judge me.

I wake up slightly past dawn. I realize Josh didn't spend the night in his house. Instantly, my spirit is broken. I turn everything off and leave his house. As I'm driving home, my imagination begins to speculate thoughts of Josh moving on. Did I lose him? I wonder. My mood is past melancholy, I feel full blown depression hit me. By the time I arrive home, I'm ready to let sleep overtake me and help me forget about Josh not being at his house. I know he wasn't in the hospital with his mom because visiting ends in the late evening. I need to shut him off from my mind, so I fall asleep.

CHAPTER 14 (NINA)

OKAY

I wake up to the sound of my phone ringing. I look at the screen and notice Josh has called me three times and left voicemail messages. I listen to his recorded voice where he's asking me to get in contact with him soon. I feel flustered and contemplate on calling him. *Don't be such a drama queen, Nina! Call his ass! Enough with the damn pity party already!*

I don't feel like mentally fighting with myself so I cave and give Josh a call.

"Hey." He answers with his deep voice. "Is everything okay? I was told you stopped by the office yesterday. Why didn't you call me?" Mmmm...I forgot how sexy his voice sounds, it's been a long time since we last spoke on the phone. Usually, we just send each other brief text messages. Oh, how I miss him. I sigh.

"Nina?" He asks with concern in his voice. I don't want him to worry, that wasn't my intention. He has a lot on his mind as is, no need for me to make him think something bad has occurred.

"Everything is fine. I just wanted to talk to you, that's all. No biggie." I respond, but omit being at his house. Inside, I'm dying to know where the hell he was last night. I don't ask though, I don't have the right to interrogate him.

"I wish you would've called me. After I left work, I went to the airport. I just got out of a meeting in Arkansas. I was at the headquarters of a large retailer that has decided to convert to solar power instead of using power grids. We got the account and now, the first phase of the contract will consist of adding solar panels to every store for this retailer within the west coast and mid-west states. In the second phase, we'll work on the east coast. Eventually, we'll convert each store to solar power nationwide with the potential of doing its international locations as well. I'm really excited." I can feel his enthusiasm.

"I'm so happy for you! Congrats!" Although I truly am happy for him and relieved that he wasn't home due to work related reasons, I can't help but feel down, I want to be by his side celebrating. *Damn, Nina! Since when did you get so needy and whiny?*

"Thanks. Well, I have to go. I have a lot of work to do. I'll see you next week when I fly back home. Okay?"

"Okay." I sadly respond.

"Nina, can you please take care of my mom and call me if anything arises?" He asks.

"Sure thing. Don't worry about anything. Focus on your work. I'll see you when you get back. Bye." I reluctantly hang up the phone. Next week? Ugh! That's what I get for not allowing him the chance to explain himself. Now, I have to suffer and wait. Nothing sucks more than waiting.

I get up and find Kade in the kitchen making a chicken stir fry on the wok. "Sup, Cheesecake? Why so blue?" He questions.

I look at the time and realize it's the early afternoon. Wow. I slept a lot. And now, I'm famished. "I'm stupid. Nothing new. Please tell me you're making enough for both of us. I'm starving!"

"Don't even trip, I got you boo. I knew you'd be hungry once you woke up. You've been sleeping all day. Is it the pain medication you're taking or what?" Kade asks as he continues to cook our late lunch.

I sigh deeply. "The visit with Diego took a toll on me and then I went on a stalker venture searching for Josh. I can't be without him anymore. I want to tell him how I feel and that I know he didn't cheat. He's in Arkansas on a business trip and won't return until next week. I'm just bummed, that's all. By the way, I'm a shitty friend. I should be cooking. You're still recovering from your wound. Here, let me take over."

"Actually, I feel great. So, sit your butt back down. I hate being a lush on the couch and not doing anything. I can't wait to start working out again. Next week will be here before you know it. Now, tell me what happened during the visit with Diego." Kade requests cautiously.

I begin to retell every detail of my conversation with Diego during our meal. Even though a few gasps escape him, Kade listens attentively without interrupting. I'm glad he doesn't ask any questions because I'm still not sure how I feel about the situation.

"Please tell your friend that I'm truly thankful he was able to ask his dad to pull that favor for me." I tell Kade.

"I already told him the first hundred times you mentioned it, I guess having a warden as a father comes in handy sometimes. He said that when he asked his dad, his father immediately made the arrangements for your visit."

"That was nice of him. Hey, do you wanna have a movie marathon tonight?" I ask. "I can sleep in tomorrow since I don't go back to work until next week, per the doctor's orders." I add.

"Sorry, I can't. I'm going out. I have a date." He grins at me.

"What? With who?" I ask intrusively.

"With one of the surgical interns I met at the hospital. He has dark caramel skin with grey eyes, he looks absolutely yummy. I met him on my first conscious day there, I gave him my number and he's been calling me every day. Once I told him I was feeling better, he asked me out on a date. He seems like a genuinely nice person. We'll see what happens." He states shyly.

With great concern, I get up and feel his forehead. "Kade are you feeling okay? Not once did you say anything inappropriate or perverted about your date."

"I know. Weird, isn't it? Well, I guess I'm open to being in a relationship. I know I never cared to before, but—" Kade hesitates for a minute then continues. "But being with Em made me realize I actually enjoy intimacy, not just fucking. Em was definitely the wrong person for me, but I'm glad I learned something from being with her. Now, I won't have such a closed mind when it comes to relationships. I'll go with the flow assuming I feel comfortable with that person. Now don't get me wrong, I'll still have my occasional 'wam bam thank you mam' but not if I find someone I truly like." He smiles warmly at me.

"I'm so happy for you. You're growing up. You've become a fine young man who I'm absolutely proud of. I can't believe it took getting shot to knock some sense into you!" We both laugh.

"Oh, my goodness! I can't believe I forgot to tell you! My mom and Dillon are dating!" I yell with too much enthusiasm.

"What? Mama V's a cougar?" Kade asks with shock written all over his face.

"My thoughts exactly." I respond giggling.

"Good for her! She deserves to have some prime meat. It's about time she puts all our Christmas presents to use." He ponders on the fact that our mom is finally dating again. His joking tone changes. "Dillon is a good guy. I really think they'll be happy together."

"I think so too." We both look at each other with cheesy smiles planted on our faces.

Once I've picked up around the house, I decide to get on Lucifer for a bit. I still can't run, but decide to go for a nice paced walk on my treadmill while listening to some Freestyle music. After I'm done, I take a long hot shower. When I return to the living room, Kade is on his way out.

"Cheesecake, I'm stopping by the hospital to check on Celeste, from there I'll be going on my date. Don't wait up." He gives me a devilish grin.

"Okay. Have fun. Please let Celeste know I'll be there tomorrow morning to visit. Drive safely. Love you!" I smile at my bestie.

"Love you back." Kade responds as he walks out grinning.

Now, back to another important issue, which movie should I watch, *The Notebook* or *Interview with a Vampire*? I've only seen each movie about a million times and it's been over a month since I last saw either one. Eventually, I opt for Brad Pitt as a vampire. I feel he'll be a better cure for my melancholy mood. I dim the lights and grab a beer. Once I'm nice and cozy with my *Twilight* fleece blanket on the couch, I press play, and begin to watch the movie. Just then, I hear the door open and shut.

"Kade, what did you forget? You're not getting cold feet about your date, are you?" I ask teasingly.

"No. Not at all." A familiar deep voice responds. I look up and see Josh's glorious body standing right by my feet. He takes a slight step back and leans his back against the wall. He seems tense. His stubble is the thickest it's ever been. He's clenching his jaw with a determined expression. He puts his hands in his pockets and maintains stern eye contact with me. His gaze alone makes me melt.

"Josh? What are you doing here?" I ask completely baffled.

He looks down upon me with a serious countenance. "Quiet." He commands with grand authority.

"I'll be doing the talking." Josh pauses for a slight moment while his eyes scan every inch of my body.

"I didn't cheat on you. I love you. There's no other woman who can come close to you and what you mean to me. Knowing you were near my father in danger drove me insane. Every second that passed before I was able to reach you felt like a nightmare. You're imprinted in my heart and living my life without you is not an option. We belong together. You're my lady and I refuse to let you go." He clenches his jaw and gazes at me intensely. His determination to be heard and raw power doesn't allow me to think. I force myself to speak, but only one feeble word escapes my lips.

"Okay." I say in a raspy voice. I stare into the depth of his beautiful hazel eyes that are now fiercely devouring me with his stare. The visual manifestation of his sexual hunger for me gives me the strength I need to make my move. I stand and walk over to him. I grab the back of his hand and caress it against my cheek, I turn slightly, and begin to lightly plant kisses on it.

"I'm sorry for not trusting you, for not allowing you to explain yourself, and for hurting you." I raise my head and shyly peek at his striking face.

"I was wrong. I don't want to live without you either. You make my heart complete. I love you and—" His sudden move interrupts my thought. Immediately, he stands upright and then lowers his upper body to engulf me in his arms. Although he ravenously approaches me with his mouth, his lips feel soft against mine. I enthusiastically welcome his tongue as it slowly eases its way in. He moves his strong hands so that one can rest on the nape of my neck and the other can caress my cheek with his thumb. His kisses feel divine and I finally feel like I'm right where I belong...in his arms.

A quite moan escapes me as Josh tightens his embrace with his arms of steel. Right away, I sense the hardness of his erection and feel my entrance become slick with anticipation. Oh, how I've missed this man. I lower my hand between us to feel his thickness, instantly, I crave to have him in me.

The pressure of our kisses becomes more aggressive along with our breathing. "I've missed you so much, baby. Don't ever...leave me...again." He manages to say in between kisses.

"Never. I'm yours. Today, tomorrow, for as long as you'll have me. I'm not going anywhere if you're not by my side." I say in one quick breath. Just then, Josh's look becomes lustful, without a second thought, he lifts me up. I wrap my legs around his waist while he turns and pins me up against the wall.

I quickly take off my shirt, Josh's eyes focus on my bare breasts with admiration. He gives me a devilish smirk then continues to kiss me, working his way past my neck, and down to my chest. He grabs one nipple with his mouth while he pinches the other with his free hand. The sensation has me longing to go over the edge. I allow my pinned up sexual frustration to let loose. "Babe! I need your fat dick inside me. I need you pounding me and showing me how much you really missed me. Fuck me, daddy, please!" I beg my man shamelessly as my entrance eagerly awaits him.

Josh steps away from the wall while I'm still clinging onto him with my legs wrapped around his waist. His swollen length is desperate to salute me as it grinds against me. He throws me on the couch and quickly takes his shirt off. Although that move completely caught my shoulder off guard, I know I should be screaming from the pain, but I push the thought aside. The adrenaline I'm experiencing has me feeling numb to my aching wound. In record time, I take my shorts and panties off. I look up and admiringly gaze at his beautifully sculpted chest, nicely defined arms, and his perfectly shaped washboard abs.

"I need to be in you. I wanna feel your tight pussy throbbing against my dick. But first, I need to savor you and have your juice all over my mouth." Josh says lasciviously as he lowers his body and rests his face between my sex. Instantly, I feel his tongue mercilessly stroking my most sensitive area back and forth. "Damn, baby...you taste so fuckin' delicious, I could eat you all night." Just then, he grabs my clit between his lips and begins to suck as he places two fingers inside me. With the sucking of my swollen tissue and his fingers penetrating my opening, I feel my body tighten as my orgasm ripples through every inch of my body. After such an overpowering climax, I'm left gasping for air.

As Josh begins to climb up my body, he unbuckles his belt, and unzips his pants. Swiftly, he takes off the remainder of his clothes and towers over me. With raw passion, Josh stares into the profoundness of my eyes. "I love you, Valentina. You're the only woman for me. Don't ever forget that. Make love to me, baby." And with those words, he thrusts himself inside of me, not allowing me the chance to declare my adoration for him. His fullness overwhelms me and leaves me speechless. His clean, manly scent, his delightful taste, and sensuous touch feel exquisite against my senses. His insertions change from penetrating me deep, with a fast pace, to almost pulling out and pounding me with a slow, strong force. After repetitive movements, both sensations send me over the edge and have my entrance convulsing once again.

While I'm at my peak, I tell him how I feel. I'm done holding back. "Oh babe, this is where you belong. Inside of me.

You feel so fuckin' good. I love you." I say my words with a soft, hoarse voice due to all my heavy panting. Within seconds, I feel Josh's body tighten. I notice every definition on his arms become even more prominent. He hovers over me for a long moment, not wanting to separate. I don't blame him; I feel perfect having him in me.

Eventually, we separate. I'm dying of thirst, my lips feel extremely parched. Thank goodness my beer is nearby. Josh grabs his duffel bag; he changes into some grey shorts and a black tank top. I put on the clothes I was wearing before my man and I reunited. I love the sound of that...my man.

"Want something to drink?" I ask Josh.

"Yeah, I'll have a beer. You make it look so refreshing." He gives me his boyish grin that I love so much while he runs his hand through his tousled hair.

I grab a beer for him and head back to the living room. I twist the cap and hand the ice cold beer to Josh. He's sitting on the couch in an upright position. I straddle him as I take a swig of my drink. He smiles at me lovingly and I return the look back to him.

"You know we need to talk, right?" I ask him cautiously.

"I know." He responds with a look of admiration for me.

I decide to treat this conversation like a band aid. For me, it's best to yank it quickly, instead of peeling it off slowly. First, I inform him of the situation with Emme and Nicole.

He's disgusted with both girls and never wants to run into them again. "Damn. Who needs enemies when you have friends like that? I guess stirring up drama is the only thing simple minds are good at. Don't waste your time giving either one a second thought; they're petty, mean spirited girls who have nothing better to do with their time. They're pathetic, let them be. I'm just glad that's behind us now and that nothing will ever come between us again. I refuse to lose you. I can guarantee I'll mess up, but I will never intentionally hurt you. I don't know the slightest thing about being with someone, but I do have the common sense to know that fidelity, trust, and respect are major components to a strong foundation of any relationship. Have patience with me and don't hold my past against me, I was a different person back then. I know I can be the man you deserve now." Josh says solemnly as he gazes into my eyes willing me to believe the truth behind his words.

"I trust you. I know you won't hurt me on purpose. I have a lot of work to do myself. I'm quick to shut someone out if I feel hurt. Not allowing you the opportunity to explain was wrong. I guess we'll be learning and growing together. That makes me happy." I smile lovingly at my man. I caress his face and feel the scar right on his hairline, a reminder of my violent behavior and mistake. "Babe, I really am sorry for hitting you with my shoe. I was just really pissed at the time. I couldn't think straight, regardless there's no excuse. I should've walked away and not resorted to violence." Learning from my mistakes makes me wiser, but ignoring them would make me a fool.

Josh gives me a peck on the nose. "I understand. I don't condone it, but I can comprehend the combination of your hurt and rage. I'm surprised I'm not six feet under, with you being half mafia and half kingpin." He chuckles. I laugh, the comparison to *The Godfather* and *Scarface* is amusing. I can't change where I come from, so I might as well embrace it. That doesn't mean my origins define me.

For the second part of our discussion, I decide to grab two more beers. I need all the liquid courage I can conjure up. Once I return with the drinks, I sit beside him. Slowly, I begin by telling him of the purpose of my visit with Diego. I then proceed with informing him of Diego's love for Celeste, how he protected her and had her relocated to San Francisco. I also mention that he was responsible for the money I received regularly throughout my life. Josh listens intently without interrupting me. I sigh deeply and take a quick moment to gather my thoughts. Nervously, I proceed to inform him that Diego was responsible for the death of his grandparents along with the murder of Celeste's best friend. Repeating those words to Josh breaks my heart. My emotions are in a state of chaos. Part of me understands why Diego committed those heinous crimes; the other part is ashamed that he has blood shed of innocent people on his hands. I look down and stare at the beer resting in between my inner thighs.

Josh remains quite for some time and then notices that I've completely shut down. "What's wrong, lovely lady?" Josh asks cautiously. "Why so sad?"

My eyes swell up with unwelcomed tears. Before I can stop myself, I tell Josh the truth. "I know my dad is a horrible person who did malicious things in his life, but I wanna get to know him." I sob quietly. "I know I should hate him and I should stay away, but I don't want to. I never craved for the love of my father. I always accepted that he didn't want me, but now that I know why he left me and the things he's done to be near me, have me confused. He's in prison now. He'll be committed there for life; I don't want to leave him alone when he needs me the most. In his own way, he loved and protected me. I feel horrible for not wanting to turn my back against him. Your father was just as bad and you're not allowing him or his death to manipulate your feelings. I feel so weak compared to you." I confess and begin crying uncontrollably.

Josh places his arm around my shoulder and kisses my cheek in an attempt to comfort me. "Baby, you can't compare your father to Mateo, they're two completely different men with the only similarity being the drug business. Mateo was a ruthless man who used his power to have my grandparents killed, he was after my mom to avenge her betrayal, and he wanted me because he saw me as his property. If he loved me like a father, he wouldn't have hurt my mom. His revenge was more important to him, not my feelings. Things aren't always black and white. I've been waiting for the guilt to consume me after killing him, yet it hasn't. Instead, I feel relief. Although I don't have the right to take anyone's life, I was left with no alternative. I'm content with finally having closure for that chapter of my life and having peace." Josh stops and lifts my chin with his index finger to ensure he has my undivided attention.

"Your dad loves you. He came to San Francisco the minute he heard Mateo was after you. He had the heart and courage to keep my mom and me safe, despite the orders he was given to follow all those years ago. Your dad also made sure you were financially taken care of, although money doesn't buy you everything, it was his way of showing you he cared since he couldn't allow himself near you. He did his best to protect you by staying away from you. He also made the boys who raped you, pay with their lives. I don't know any parent who wouldn't have done the same. Was it wrong? Yes. Was it justified? That's debatable. What isn't in question is the reason behind your father's actions. He did it out of love. His feelings for you are so strong that he became filled with rage at the thought of his little girl being violated and treated so inhumanely. You can't compare your dad with Mateo. He loves you. What he did to my grandparents hurts me because I know the truth will devastate my mom, but she's a woman who understands reason. He wasn't able to save everyone. He made a choice and opted to keep my mom safe. Although I resent him, I also have reasons to be grateful to him. If you want to get to know your dad and build a relationship with him...then do it. Don't let guilt stop you. I'll support you with whatever decision you make." Josh embraces me to provide the comfort I desperately need from him.

"Thank you." I wipe my tears away, gather my hair, and put it in a bun. "I'll start by writing him letters. Baby steps." I smile past my waterworks.

The rest of the night we discuss the shootings, his time in jail, and the interrogation he went through with the Feds. "They didn't have proof I shot Mateo, so they let me go. They weren't interested in me at all. They had the leader of Los Blancos Cartel dead and the head of the Enemiga Cartel in custody along with some of his lieutenants; I was the least of their concerns." Josh says matter-of-factly.

"What happened to the gun?" I asked confused.

"Your mom took it." He shrugs his shoulders and responds nonchalantly.

"What? How do you know? What did she do with it?" Shock doesn't begin to explain how I feel.

"Kade told me when I was visiting him in the hospital. Later, I thanked your mom. She told me she got rid of it and that I didn't have anything to worry about. I love how you guys are down for anyone within your circle. I feel pretty special." He gives me a lazy boyish smirk that instantly makes my heart melt.

"Well, you are special. And my mom is pretty bad ass, now that she's a cougar and dating Dillon, she's living on the wild side." I giggle and accidentally snort. That only makes me laugh harder; too soon my man joins me with his own hysterics.

Then, it hits me. "Hey! Aren't you supposed to be in Arkansas at some meeting?"

"Yeah, but after I spoke with you, I needed to rush over here. It's not like you to go chasing after me at work just to talk. I took a chance and decided to confront you with the truth along with my feelings. I'll do anything for you, baby." He admits.

"Yes, I can see that. I do have a confession though. I was on full blown stalker mode yesterday. I even went to your house and stayed there waiting for you. I couldn't wait to be in your arms." I pout.

"Awww...you stalked me? That's so fuckin' sweet, baby. Sometimes you can be so romantic." He grins at me. "Okay, since we're confessing here, then let me get this out of my chest. When we went on our first non-date, I rented out the whole shooting range. I wanted you to myself and didn't want anyone cock blocking, in case I got lucky." Josh gives a low chuckle.

"I can't believe you! You planned on getting a taste of my cookie that night? So much for our non-date and you being a gentleman!" I fake an appalled expression.

"Baby, do I need to remind you that you jumped my bones that night? You saw this piece of filet mignon and wanted a bite all for yourself. It's not my fault you find me so irresistible you just had to rape me in the car. I distinctly recall being at your mercy and loving your warm cookie." Josh raises his right eyebrow and gives me a devilish smirk.

"I didn't rape you, rape you...I only raped you. There's a difference. Besides, not once did I hear you complaining. Hmph..." I look away with my arms crossed.

"Complain? That was the best cookie I've ever had!" He laughs.

The remainder of the evening Josh and I cuddle on the couch watching comedy shows I have recorded on my DVR. I feel at peace and after revealing the truth to Josh, I feel as if a tremendous weight has been lifted off my shoulders.

We continue to drink the night away, neither one of us wanting it to end. A bit after dawn Kade walks in, finds Josh and I pretty buzzed and all over each other.

"Well, well, well, look at what we have here. If it isn't the two love birds finally reunited." Kade smirks. "So did you guys fuck and make up? Are we all a big happy family once again? Because I swear, hearing my Cheesecake sing due to depression is a spine-chilling sound. No one should have to endure such torcher." Kade jokes as his happy mood emanates throughout his face.

My jaw drops. "You're lucky I just got some, otherwise I'd give you a piece of my mind for making fun of my talented vocal skills. Don't hate." I slightly slur. Oh, yeah. The beer is definitely taking a toll.

"There you go, always choppin' your gums about your dreadful singing. You should concentrate more on your hair. You have a turd on your head for crying out loud! You're killing me Cheesecake, you're really killing me." He laughs out loud.

"Whatever. How did your date go?" I ask curiously.

"It was pretty bad ass! He's genuinely a nice person and I can tell he's an undercover freak. I'm seeing him again this weekend. I definitely see potential in him." He winks at me. "Okay, kids. I'm gonna crash. I'm exhausted. Don't wake me with all the fucking you'll be doing." Kade stops by the hallway before he goes inside his room. "Seriously, I'm glad you guys are back together. I know you'll be happy, you two were meant for one another...you're both crazy as shit! That's for sure." And with that, my best friend walks away smiling at us.

"Do you think we're meant for each other?" I turn to Josh and ask him as I analyze his beautiful, honey colored eyes with specks of green and incredibly long lashes.

"Of course! We've already established that we both have stalker tendencies and refuse to live without the other. You're my lady, I'm your fuckin' man, and that's how it will always be. Forever. I love you, baby. I'm the gum stuck on your shoe.

You're not getting rid of me that easily ever again. You're perfect for me and I wanna be the same for you. So, let's make our relationship beautiful and live a happy life together." He declares with deep affection in his eyes.

"Good. Because I love you too and never want to leave your side." I answer simply. Knowing that my man adores me and that our families are safe and happy with their lives, brings me incredible joy; allowing myself to forgive my father, gives me peace of mind. With such positivity in my life, I can now put my demons to rest and live a blissful life with the man I love.

Author's Biography

C. Michelle loves a good laugh...you know, the type that accidentally makes you snort. Yeah, that kind. Her love of all things funny, romantic, and bad ass led to the writing of her debut novel, *Pinned Up*. C. Michelle resides in northern California with her husband and three children. She is currently working on the completion of the *Pinned Up* trilogy. Initially, *Pinned Up* was written as a stand-alone novel, but since the characters continue to harass her during the middle of the night, while she's driving, when she's eating, and while she's running against her will...she decided to continue with their stories.

C. Michelle earned a Bachelor of Science in Business Management and a Master of Business Administration degree while working as a probation officer and probation counselor. She also served her community as a Victim Awareness Program instructor and an Aggression Replacement Training facilitator.

Visit her blog – cmichelle.com

Follow her on Twitter – twitter.com/cmichellewrite

Like her on Facebook – www.facebook.com/cmichelle.write

Follow her on Goodreads – www.goodreads.com/author/show/7064906.C_Michelle

COMING SPRING 2014

PINNED DOWN

BOOK 2 IN THE PINNED UP TRILOGY